DEATH IN RHEIMS

Tom Walsingham Mysteries
Book Three

C. P. Giuliani

SAPERE
BOOKS

DEATH IN
RHEIMS

Published by Sapere Books.

24 Trafalgar Road, Ilkley, LS29 8HH,
United Kingdom

saperebooks.com

ISBN: 978-0-85495-013-3

To my father.
I wish you were here to see it all.

ACKNOWLEDGEMENTS

One of the many things I love about writing historical mysteries is research. One of the many things I love about research is the way one, when in doubt or at a loss, can ask for help and receive kind and knowledgeable answers.

This time, my biggest troubles concerned the exact location of the English College in Rheims — something that is actually no longer known with any certainty. So it became a matter of plausible guesswork, and I must thank Monsieur Francis Leroy, Président-archiviste de la SAVR (Société des Amis du Vieux Reims), for providing me with a wealth of very useful information on the subject.

Father Oliver Holt at Douai Abbey was also very kind.

And this has nothing to do with the location of the college — but is no less important: thank you, Rosie, for getting Nick Skeres to Rheims.

PROLOGUE

He was dreaming of home.

He knew it was a dream, the sort a fever will give you, all colours and roaring in your ears.

The brook by the old mill — if only he could reach it and splash a handful of water on his burning face — all a-gurgle with spring, and the magpies, a field full of them, black and white on the green grass, and running feet, and whispers, and the bells of Chelsfield singing across the water.

They were back, just as he'd promised.

A promise kept is a blessing, his grandmother used to say... And all the magpies cawed of promises and called: *Hugh! Hugh! Hugh!*

He laughed then, and ran, catching a hand as he went. He splashed in the chill water, and the birds flew all about him, *parce mihi, Domine*, and the bells rang. Black and white feathers were closing in, no matter how he batted them away.

No, cried the magpies all at once, a hundred throats raw and hoarse.

No — and the harder they ran, the less air they had to breathe...

No — and the mill's bridge creaked and gave under the magpies' feet, and the water was deep and hard-handed, and black and white, and merciless, and full of pain — and then of nothing.

CHAPTER 1

21st of May 1585, on the road to Rheims, in the French region of Champagne

"Roland," Tom Walsingham repeated — for what had to be the dozenth time in an hour. "My name is Thomas Roland, and I travel to Rheims on a matter of business." He pronounced the name French-wise, voice quite level, and never took his eyes from the soldier's narrow gaze — as though it made a difference.

The man, an arquebusier in breastplate and drenched felt hat, sucked his teeth, and grunted. "And you've come from England," he said.

"Yes."

"And this man's your lawyer."

"Yes." This, too, had been stated many times.

Over the saddle of Tom's horse, the soldier spared a glance for the long, lanky figure of Thomas Watson, who waited in turn.

"Your lawyer, eh?" The Frenchman said *lawyer* the way another might say *cockroach*. "And you have business in Rheims."

Oh Lord give me patience…! Tom counted to ten — in Latin — and took a deep breath of the damp air that smelt of rain and wet horse. He caught Watson's warning look — as though he might go and pick quarrels with the French soldiery. But it had been a long day on the muddy roads of Champagne, where spring was supposed to be sweet and wasn't, with the King's soldiers — and sometimes those of the King's rival, the Duke of Guise — stopping travellers at every step.

Now at last Rheims was well in view, no more than half a mile away down the hill, walls stout and black spires countless, like a bristly beast with the grey tail of the Vesle coiled around its flanks. There it sat, and this dunce of an arquebusier played at the greatest obtuseness, as though Tom hadn't just bribed his corporal.

"If you go in there ... who knows!" the soldier warned. "They are all for the Guise, in there. Not that we like heretics — or the English — but those ones...!"

"Ay, well," said Tom, taking his best air of sour virtue. Wasn't he supposed to be of Huguenot blood, after all? "As a good Christian, I trust I'll offend no one and no one will offend me."

A horse-width away, Watson could be heard shifting his weight, and the arquebusier pushed back his hat, patently convinced he had to do with a half-wit.

"And what business is it?" he asked. "You have business in Rheims, you said." And there it went again, the taste of the French for picking fault with the honesty of all Englishmen.

"My father's cousin died," Tom said. More than half the truth, for Guillaume Thibaud, merchant of wool, and intelligencer for the English *had* died in Rheims, and he *was* kin to a real Thomas Roland in London. "And I'm here to see to his will." Less than the truth — but plausible enough.

The soldier hummed and glanced at the supposed lawyer. "Making a row, are they?" he asked.

"Last testaments!" Watson, half a lawyer in truth, pulled a mournful face. "Stretch them across two kingdoms and two branches of a family — and what have you? A maze!"

And look at the arquebusier, look how he hummed again, and nodded.

"Ay, well..." Tom fished in his purse for yet another silver coin, and pushed it into the soldier's gloved palm. "'Tis a sad state of things, when all comes down to gold and silver," he groused. "Still, business must be sorted, mustn't it?"

It wasn't true that all soldiers were governed by the oldest instincts, but this one apparently belonged to the simpler sort. He beamed at the bribe, such a contented smile as would have graced a cherub. It made him look young of a sudden, as he half-bowed out of the way — devil pinch him!

"If it must," he said, with a shrug. "Just mind they don't shoot at you as you cross."

"Shoot at us!" Tom paused in the act of regaining the saddle. "Haven't your King and the Guise a truce?"

The man snorted and spat in the mud — to show just what he thought of making truces with the Duke of Guise — before calling over his shoulder to a couple of his fellows, to let the two travellers by. And when he wished them *bonne chance*, it sounded more like a jeer than anything else.

Tom and Watson traversed the village huddled by the road on the hill's shallow hump — no more than a handful of cottages, all grey in the afternoon rain. Only the soldiers were to be seen about, loitering in lazy, buff-cloaked knots, playing dice or talking. No villagers showed — but then all who could had chosen discretion and left.

On they cantered under the thickening rain, between expanses of wet orchards and wetter fields, dotted with cottages in twos and threes. And all — cottages, fields, and road — all was empty and deserted. Be it the rain or the threat of war, the road had scant traffic at a time when the people of Rheims should have been going about their business. They overtook one slow horse-drawn cart as they entered another village — a *faubourg* this side of the Vesle, all spread in a row along the road, with a turreted church and what looked like an outer gate.

"And now for the *Milice*," Tom muttered under his breath. "Greedy knaves too, I'll wager."

And, as Tom had been waiting for him to do for some time, Watson tutted, "Yes, Tityrus — I hardly know you anymore! Letting that lout irk you out of yet another perfectly good demi-teston!"

Tom tugged his hat low on his brow and said nothing, trotting along without much hope that the subject would be dropped.

But then, Watson drop a subject that amused him? And indeed Watson, swarthy face twisted in laughter, teased on. "It wants fine judgment, my lad: too little, and you'll buy yourself trouble; too much, and they'll take you for a loaf of sugar…"

Had Watson always been like this? It had been some time since they'd shared a roof in Paris, as fellow intelligencers and good friends. Had the man grown sour in his barbs, or was it just that Tom resented them more? Now, given the choice between sulking in stoic silence, or letting himself be baited, Tom went for the easier course.

"I've been bribing my way around France for half my life, you know," he said, earning himself a laugh and more tutting.

"A trifling exaggerated, but not much — and that's what makes it all the sadder, Tityrus: not two years back in England, and you've lost the art. Whatever would Sir Francis say?"

Yes — Sir Francis indeed. Sir Francis Walsingham, Tom's own kinsman, Secretary of State and spymaster to Her Highness the Queen of England — although that was only whispered. Sir Francis, who had sent Tom all the way through simmering France to look into the death of an agent, the reappearance of another, and the circumstances of a dangerous enemy — and as for what he'd have to say… "Nothing good," Tom muttered, reining in his horse. "Nothing good at all, if we get ourselves arrested before we even enter Rheims."

Watson followed suit and, at the most unthreatening pace, they approached the gatehouse, where a morion-covered head leant out of the gate with an air of wary ferociousness and a call to halt.

Tom and Watson obeyed, stopping in the shadow of the steep-roofed gatehouse that straddled the road with its squat buttressed walls and cross-shaped arrow-slits. It gleamed black against the wet sky, soaked with all the water of a rainy spring, and it boasted a drawbridge over a smaller branch of the river.

"*Arrêtez!*" the soldier called again, a fiercely bearded fellow in corselet and morion, who carried his half-pike the way he'd hold a broomstick. It was a most useless order, since they were already dismounting — but it was interesting in itself, unqualified as it was.

It had been given neither in the King's name, nor that of the Duc de Guise, nor his nephew, the young Cardinal who was the city's archbishop and duke — and who, by all accounts, had visited Rheims lately in grand pomp.

Up against the drizzle, Tom squinted at the small turret that topped the gatehouse's roof. Whatever colours were up there hung limp and sodden, a few brighter patches against a darker field. It could have been the Guise red, blue and yellow or the royal lilies in gold on blue — or perhaps the city's colours.

All the time, the soldier watched not just the two travellers, but beyond them, up along the road — and whether having been let through by the King's men was a commendation or a grave sin, still remained to be seen.

A second man approached — younger and better groomed. An officer perhaps, wearing a large if drenched plume in his hat, and a very big sword. He took charge, asking the usual questions of the two newcomers' names and business.

The answers he took with a hard look. "Do you English not know to stay away from other folks' wars?"

"I was told of the suspension of arms," Tom explained again. This time, it earned a bark of laughter.

"The truce, ay. Not worth the paper they used to write it down! But then, you English like that. You hope that Leaguers, King's men, Huguenots, we'll all cut each other's throats, and in the end you'll only have to step across la Manche, and grab what's left, eh? Now that your Queen can't wed the King's brother anymore…"

Oh, *that* again! Tom scoffed. "I care little who cuts whose throat. All I want is to be in Rheims before curfew, do my business, and be off to London."

"Wish you all were off," the officer groused. "Lousy with the English, Rheims is. Can't throw a stone but you hit one of them! And thank *le Bon Dieu* we didn't get an English Queen, too!" And as he closed this tirade, he turned to raise his chin in question at his bearded man, who had been watching the road. The *Milice* of Rheims had an air of waiting for no good from the direction of the royal camp.

Another sideways nod from the young officer sent the soldier inside the gatehouse, and soon an order was heard, then the creaking of wood.

When the officer waved them past, Tom and Watson led their mounts into the gloom of the gatehouse that stank of rotting straw and unwashed men, and out onto the fenced bridge across the Vesle to Rheims. As soon as they cleared the gate, it was slammed shut, a hand short of the rump of Watson's big bay gelding.

Whatever else abounded in France these days, it was not trust.

Beyond the gatehouse, a length of road stretched between the river's two branches, up to a second gate, an arch of stone equally half-closed, although less imposing.

They moved towards it at a sedate pace.

Watson waited well after they were out of hearing — and still leant in to speak in Tom's ear: "Would you have believed we'd ever rue the death of Monsieur d'Anjou?"

"Do we?" asked Tom — which was unchristian, surely — but quite honest. Along with Sir Francis, he'd always disliked the prospect of a French prince sitting beside the throne of England.

Watson grimaced. "Well, *in primis*, King Henri would have a likely heir, and therefore France wouldn't be on the brink of yet another little war, and those scarecrows at the gate wouldn't be making ready to stop us — yet again."

"To which, Corydon, I counter: *non sequitur*. Was France an Arcadia with Monsieur d'Anjou alive?"

"A somewhat restless kingdom, I'll grant you, -a ticklish hexagon of lands — but still —"

"But still, what would we have now? A future Catholic King, wed either to Her Highness or a Spanish princess — neither a good thing — and the Guise making trouble just as lustily. At least, right now, the Navarre makes a Protestant heir."

"And unlikely to stay so, if he's ever to have the throne — but…" Watson raised a hand in surrender. "I'll concede half your point: Anjou, rest his soul, is not to be greatly regretted, and France is hopeless — and lo! What did I tell you? They're stopping us again."

Of course they were — more of those city men with the old-fashioned, undented morions.

Another bribe later, Tom and Watson were on the very last leg of this journey: a flagged, fenced bridge thrown across the larger branch of the Vesle, with two triangular cutwaters to break the foaming current. And across the stretch of angry water, the ramparts and the *Porte de Vesle* itself loomed grey and huge.

"Well, well!" Watson laughed. "And don't we believe ourselves a great city!"

Indeed, one would think so, to see this tall gatehouse that frowned down on the arriving traveller so forbiddingly. It had its own drawbridge, a thick portcullis and two round towers twice as tall as the walls. And taller still was the steep slate roof of the gatehouse proper.

Seen this close, the place looked no more genial than it had from a distance — a creature coiled inside its carapace of stone, every iron muscle tensed.

Tom checked an itch to feel for the sturdy dagger that, as part of his mercantile disguise, he carried instead of a gentleman's rapier.

And welcome to Rheims, he thought to himself, as he dismounted again to meet the sentries on watch. To Rheims, where loyalties were muddled, where the English were looked upon askance, where Sir Francis's men were — perhaps — murdered, and where ghosts came back from oblivion.

The stench met them first, just inside the gate.

A stench of rotting fish, smoke, and piss. For all the stately ramparts and towers, the particular business of this first corner of Rheims smelt very much like tanneries and fishmongers's shops.

There was a long street, to begin with — the *Rue de Vesle*, the sentries called it — leading straight up towards the huge ghostly giant that was the cathedral. On the street's right, past a turbid pond, lay a stretch of gardens, wilting for too much water; on its left crawled a thick neighbourhood of poor houses — war or no war, tanners still tanned their leathers in Rheims, and fishmongers gutted their fish.

Bell-towers threw their weak shadows over the red-tiled roofs, more and more frequent as Tom and Watson made their way towards the cathedral — this vast grey giant that stood amidst an honour-guard of belfries.

They climbed up to another gate, at length — an ugly arch, squat and bare of decoration, where nobody stood watch; and there, past this ungainly piece of antiquity, Rheims came to life. A town within the city bustled there, nestled inside long-gone walls. The comings and goings, the commerce, the chiming of bells — all of it was brisk, though not very cheerful. Too many archers patrolled the streets for cheer — but still here Rheims felt alive, if a little sullen. From one side came the hammering of a street full of smithies; on the other, the cathedral loomed, a peak of fretted stone.

Tom stopped a pair of black-gowned students to ask his way, and was directed away from the cathedral, to the markets and beyond. The markets proved to be two adjacent squares, edged by narrow half-timbered houses, shops and hostelries, and filled with stalls and wooden halls. They sold bread and flour in the first, and bolts of cloth in the second. Tom took the latter to be the Marché à la Laine — the Wool Market. They walked around for a good while, and found no sign of the Brebis-qui-File, where the Thibauds kept shop and house. They took a narrow street that landed them in another *ruelle* — where they had to dismount and lead their horses — and then another.

They then had to ask again — or rather, Tom had to, with Watson deeper and deeper in the part of the hired lawyer, deferent to his master.

You lead the way, then, Tityrus, he'd said with a mock bow, on meeting in Soissons and hearing the orders Tom carried. *You lead, and I follow.* And the laugh had been good-natured enough, and after all he must have known since leaving Paris — but...

At the head of yet another alley of half-timbered houses, an aproned man was busy with the shutters of a shoemaker's workshop. Tom asked him for the Rue de la Bûchette, and the fellow jumped on being addressed. Cradling an armful of shoes, he frowned in mistrustful scrutiny of the two men with the horses. Were it their mud-stained appearance, Tom's foreign accent, or the general air of Rheims, the man's scowl didn't lessen a jot.

"That-a-way," he said, jerking his chin. "Up and past the Marché à la Laine, Saint-Hilaire's way." And, having delivered this answer, he turned on his heel and disappeared into the workshop, without acknowledging Tom's thanks.

Ah well. "That-a-way, then," Tom sighed, drawing his horse in a tight wheel, careful not to jostle the shoemaker's wares. "At least he answered."

At Tom's elbow, Watson chuckled. "'Tis your accent that irks them, Tityrus. You sound as English as pudding, these days."

And there — there it was again! The small reminder that things had changed, that Tom was no longer the half-Parisian courier, the youngest in a small fraternity of Service men sharing a roof.

"Why don't you do the talking, then?" Tom snapped, and threw a glance over his shoulder to find Watson with pursed lips and one black eyebrow cocked in question.

Oh Jove, how petty and childish! Tom sighed and clicked his tongue at his horse to follow the shoemaker's directions, hoping to high Heaven that no need to ask again would arise.

The Marché à la Laine, it turned out, was not the same as the Marché aux Draps, nor was it quite a square — but rather a long quadrangle of streets around two isles of newer houses and shops. Most shops were closing for the day — rather early for this time of the year, but there was none of the usual press — the last housewives out to buy one last handful of herbs, the last hopeful peddlers and beggars, and laughing children out of school. All who were about strode with a purposeful grimness, and here and there the *Milice* stood watch, as though expecting havoc to erupt at any moment.

They passed a corner, where a beggar-woman and a peddler bickered over an overturned basket. It was the sort of commotion that in London would draw a crowd of onlookers, laughing and jeering and taking sides. And that had been true of France as well — but here only half a dozen ragged children milled around, and even those scurried back when an archer pushed his way through to quell the small tumult. The woman tried to run, but the peddler grabbed her by the arm, until the archer took hold of her and dragged her away, screaming abuse. The urchins threw handfuls of mud, very impartially, at both beggar and peddler. One of the boys, braying that *Quatre grosses bêtes font an Huguenot*, ran right into the legs of Tom's mare, making her dance and him swear. By the time he'd gentled the animal, nothing remained of the argument, except the forlorn peddler, picking his trampled skeins of tow from the mud.

All told, Tom liked Rheims less and less.

CHAPTER 2

It was a great relief to find, at last, the Rue de la Bûchette and the sign of the Spinning Ewe, where Guillaume Thibaud had lived buying and selling English wool.

It was a handsome jettied house, well-kept and pleasant to look at, with its leaded windows and pointed roof, and its namesake industrious ewe were prettily sculpted in wood, rather than just painted. The commerce of wool must have made the Thibauds a tidy profit — but then, so it did for their Roland cousins back in London.

There were a carriage gate and a house door, both shut tight. Tom knocked on the latter and, at length, a little panel opened high in the door, and a shrill voice asked who it was.

Tom looked up into a young, round face, all the rounder for the white linen coif tied around it.

"I'm Thomas Roland," he announced. "From London."

There was a small shriek, and the panel slammed shut.

"And well-come and well-met, good cousin!" Watson muttered.

Indeed! Tom knocked again, rather harder, until the panel slid open again — although no face appeared this time.

"Did you hear what I said?" he called. "I must see your mistress, Madame Jory." Or perhaps he should have asked for her husband — but then it was Guillaume Thibaud's daughter who had written after her father's death.

No answer came, no face appeared, but through the open panel the sound of voices floated — two of them, pitched in angry whispers.

Oh, Good Lord give patience! Tom knocked again. "Where's Madame Jory? I'm her cousin — she must see me. I will come back with a notary, if I must."

There was a click of the tongue from Watson, who frowned in disapproval. "What if they take you at your word?" he hissed.

Tom frowned back. What if they did? They had papers enough to prove themselves to a dozen notaries — but he had counted on Blandine Jory being eager to see the visitor from London, and here they were instead, being treated like invading barbarians! And it was pouring again, too.

"Now look, will you —"

The rasp of drawn bolts cut short Tom's entreaty, and half the door cracked open to show not the round-faced servant, but a boy.

Oh yes: *a daughter and a son*. Guillaume Thibaud's son must have been no more than fifteen, black-browed and ferocious, with that air of carrying bones too big for him. Also his voice quaked when he presented himself: "I am Remi Thibaud."

He blushed then, and Tom swallowed a smile, remembering the unruliness of one's voice at that age, and the awkward fury that went with it. "Good, then," he said instead. "I'm your cousin Thomas Roland, and it's raining, so if you'll let me in…"

"No."

No? But truly, *no*? "Now see, Cousin Remi, simple civility—"

"You're not my cousin, you."

What passing sympathy Tom may have felt for this child was quickly coming undone in the face of such lip-jutting petulance.

"Even if I weren't, it would be unchristian to leave me in the street like a beggar," he snapped. "But I am. You must know of me, surely — or at least of my father? John Roland of London, your poor mother's cousin."

"That's Blandine's mother, you mean. You're no cousin of mine," the boy squawked triumphantly, as though this disposed of the visitor.

Unus, duo, tres… "Ay, well. I'm still your sister's cousin. Your father's partner in trade —"

"And if you think you can burst in here, and play the master, and —"

"Remi!"

The boy stopped short and shuffled away from the door, letting it open wider. It showed a dim flagged hallway with a vaulted ceiling — and, hastening up along it, a small woman in grey, carrying a candle.

"You churl, what do you think you're doing?" she scolded, coming to slap her brother on the arm — for there was no doubt that this must be Blandine Jory.

She was a dumpling of a woman, plump, small and apple-cheeked, with tiny hands and dainty features that were pretty even when pursed in a scowl.

"Come in, come in," she called, throwing the door wide, and over her shoulder she called for the round-faced servant to have the horses seen to. "But do come in. You'll think us savages … and, Saints keep me, sometimes I believe we are!" This she said with another glare for the sulking boy.

Tom smiled at her as he stepped through the door, uncovering his head. Watson followed, while a stable-boy came running to take the horses.

"And who's that?" Ruffled but unmeekened, young Remi pointed at Watson's long figure.

"Remi!" fumed Blandine.

"John Barnege," said Watson at the same time.

23

But "My lawyer," coming from Tom was what kindled the boy's anger.

"See!" he shouted, turning on his half-sister. "See, a lawyer, he brings — to rob us of house and shop!"

"Enough!" Half a head smaller than the shortest of them, fists on her hips, Blandine Jory stood in the middle of three squabbling men — and they all fell silent under the large-eyed flash of her disapproval. "Go and see that the horses are looked after," she ordered her brother.

He didn't take it in good part. "I'm the head of the family, and if you think I'm looking after the horses while you let us be fleeced of my father's —"

"He was my father too," Blandine cut in. "And you're head of nothing, not until you come of age. Till then, behave like a child, and like a child I'll treat you. Off with you!"

Much to Tom's amused fascination, the boy retreated the way the servant had disappeared, grousing that she was only a woman, and that they'd see once her husband was back — wouldn't they see then!

A rather formidable creature, was Blandine Jory — and there was little doubting that no husband would make much difference. Tom saluted her with a half bow. "Well, *ma cousine!*" he said, and then gave her the phrase that should make him known: "You favour your mother. I remember her well."

She blew her cheeks out, gave a shake of her head and went to open a door on the hallway's right. "Here," she said, leading the way.

It was a small parlour, whitewashed and chequer-floored, furnished sparsely, with a table and a few cupboards, all dark and old-looking — a little dismal in the grey light from the one window.

There was a branched candle-holder on the table — pewter by its gleam. Blandine lit its three fat yellow candles from the stub she held, and motioned for the two visitors to sit.

Seen close, and in better light, she looked much of an age with Tom, a gleam in her large hazel eyes.

"Do you have brothers, cousin Thomas?" she asked, one eyebrow raised.

Tom thought of Ned — Sir Edmund in Scadbury now their father was dead — and of poor dead Guildford. And also of imperious Barbara and feisty Mary…

"And sisters," he said.

Blandine gave a peal of laughter, soft and cheerful — and Tom decided that he liked her very much.

She sobered quickly, though. "Let Remi not hear me laugh with you," she sighed. "He doesn't know, you see. My father never told him he was an agent for the English — God deliver us! He truly believes you're here to claim what's his."

Of course he would. "Needless to say, Thomas Roland has no such intention," Tom said, lowering his voice to match hers.

"He sends his greetings," Watson put in. "And I have the papers to be signed, so that the partnership can go on as before."

Blandine cocked her head in a narrow-eyed study of Watson's swarthy face. "You're truly a lawyer, then?" she asked. "Good. But my husband is away, you see, so it will be a few days before all can be signed." She turned her scrutiny on Tom. "I've been waiting for your visit."

And small wonder she had! "Well, with what you wrote…" Tom prodded. "Tell me of your father, first."

Blandine ran a hand down her face with a sigh — almost a man's gesture. "There's little to say. He took to his bed soon before Easter. He fretted something dreadful that he couldn't send to London. We had the Archbishop himself here, back then — little Monsieur de Guise! — and a garrison to boot."

"I think that we saw some of it," Tom said.

She waved a hand in dismissal. "There are a score left, barely enough to guard the Archbishop's Palace. It's our *Milice* watching the gates now. Lord help us if the King's men ever try to attack — for our archers surely won't."

Tom exchanged a look with Watson. "I thought Rheims was all zeal for the Guise?"

Blandine gave a little snort. "Oh yes — when the Archbishop was here! All the zeal went after him the hour he left. Anyway, my father. As long as the garrison was here, there was no getting through a pin, never mind a cartful of wool bales. So he wrote down the things, you know, and fretted, and on Holy Monday he grew worse. It took him four days to die, *pauvre Papa*, and afterward I could not find the letter. I think he must have burnt it, in fear that someone would…"

For a moment, Tom dreaded that she would burst into tears. "Faithful to the end, poor Thibaud," he murmured, in such clumsy haste that he might have kicked himself.

Still, either the words were what this grieving daughter needed, or the awkwardness of them dragged her away from her grief, because she took a good breath and resumed her tale. "I knew what had been on his mind. He'd told me more than once, and I'd seen the letter. So I wrote down all I remembered, and as soon as he could, my husband made a journey to Calais — and there you have it."

If only it had been this simple! "Your husband … was he not searched?"

Blandine shrugged. "The Archbishop's men had gone, by then. And if anyone ever remembers that my father once fled

France as a Huguenot, they forget again when they need our wool. We're all merchants, in Rheims."

"And what about out of Rheims? We haven't met a King's soldier who didn't stop and question us."

"You're Englishmen. My Jory is just one French merchant going his way on the roads of France. Don't worry, Monsieur: we've been doing this for so many years — in peace and in war!"

And indeed, what had Tom expected? Nothing in Blandine's letter had betrayed a fearful woman, at risk of giving herself away, and them all — and yet, that's what he had half assumed. And he'd been wrong. But still...

"Yes — so you have, or your father has — and whether you can go on doing it, we shall see." He raised a hand to stop the objections he could see tiding up. "Don't take it in ill part, Madame Jory. You must see, if there's reason to question your father's death —"

"Question my..." Blandine's voice rose enough that she slapped a hand over her mouth. "But, Monsieur — question *what*?" she asked, in wide-eyed wonder.

For a heartbeat only the rush and clucking of the rain down a drain could be heard outside, and the slam of a shutter somewhere in the house, as Tom stared at Madame Jory, and then at the round-eyed Watson at his side.

"But you wrote..." He called to mind the letter he'd read twice in Sir Francis's study. "Your father died suddenly, and he'd been visited by this man, Richard Baines, hadn't he?"

"And because of that, you...?" Blandine Jory put a hand to her cheek. "Oh, *mon bon Dieu*! My father took cold, and his lungs went bad! Such a wet spring, we've had... He died of that and nothing else."

Tom found his voice first — and it was to ask a most foolish question. "But are you very sure of this?"

"Am I!" Blandine threw up her hands. "Who do you think nursed him, day and night, as he coughed and spat blood? Why must you think... Saints keep you, Monsieur — is this why...?"

Of course she was sure — and they all, even Sir Francis had assumed...

"Well, well..." Watson said, sounding confoundedly amused. "Come a long way for nothing, have we?"

And now they'd have to go back, and report to Sir Francis that they had all read more than ever was in Blandine Jory's letter. Inside his head Tom went through the letter again, and could find no fault with it. But still...

Sir Francis's voice echoed in his mind: *Even error, Thomas, must be considered and sifted, to determine whether some element of truth may remain buried in it.*

"Still, what of this fellow, Baines?"

Blandine frowned in thought, gathering herself through her disconcertment. "Baines, yes. What of him? You never think he killed my father?"

"I came here thinking so — or, at least, wondering if he had. But if you say it couldn't have been..."

Had she rushed to protest in anger, to dismiss the notion, Tom would have kept many of his doubts. But she sat back to think instead, with brows knitted, and a forefinger to her pursed lips. She considered awhile, and then shook her head, slow and certain.

"No," she said. "The physician said it was a fever of the lungs. *Pauvre papa*, he coughed, and wheezed, and burnt with fever... That was no poison, I tell you."

28

Good sense and a strong head. Small wonder that Thibaud had confided in his daughter.

"*Cadit quæstio*," Watson murmured, most lawyerly.

"So the matter's settled," Tom translated for the bemused Blandine. "If you say it couldn't be, then I believe you. Still, there is the fact that Baines was here, and it worried your father."

"Yes, because *mon père* had thought him long gone." Blandine squared herself in front of Tom, elbows on the table. "The first we saw of him was ... oh, three years ago, when he was sent to spy at the Collège Anglais."

The Collège Anglais, where that papist arch-traitor, William Allen, gathered and instructed the young Catholic exiles from England, turned them into priests and sent them back as secret missionaries. Sir Francis made a point of planting his own men there — and Baines had been one of these gatherers of intelligence. "Only, he was caught."

"And imprisoned. At the Collège first, then the city gaol. When they let him out, he said they'd put him to the rack..."

There was something in the way Blandine pursed her lips.

"But your father didn't believe him?"

She shrugged. "He was hard to believe. One moment he ranted that he'd kill them all for what they'd done to him, and the next he sobbed that they didn't want him — had made him a priest and then thrown him out... Poll-mad, if you ask me. Father gave him money and told him to go back home. He wrote to London that the man was trouble."

"So he did." Tom had seen the letter, unearthed by scribes at Seething Lane. *Baines does not run on an even keel*, had been Guillaume Thibaud's words.

"This was the summer before last — and he never came here again. Father thought he'd gone back to England — and good riddance. And then, at the end of March, up he turns again. It was like seeing a ghost: thin as a rake, ragged, filthy — and not right in the head."

"But did he say why he was still here?"

"A lot of things, he said — and not a word of good sense. He's going back to the Collège, he says, and Father must help him, and in London they owe him, and all sorts of madness. The more Father tried to talk him out of it, the wilder he got. Father wanted to write to London, but by then the League was making trouble, so there was no way — not until after Father's death."

And this was why they'd only known of Baines from Blandine.

"You wrote that he came back."

"I've seen him, now and then, lurking around the house like a stray dog. The other day, he was here."

"But he didn't go to the Collège."

Blandine clicked her tongue. "Perhaps he did — but in all truth, Monsieur, who knows? The man you have there now — Saints keep us!" She raised her eyes to Heaven, as though asking for patience. "A cockerel of a boy, with no sense at all!"

Watson coughed, and Tom didn't turn — sure that, if he did, he'd find him much amused by this description of his young friend. The Good Lord guard them all, the more he heard of Christopher Marley, the less he expected the man to be of any use. The Service, it seemed, wasn't always fortunate in its choice of plants at the Collège Angalis. Still...

"Still, I'll need to see him. To hear of Baines, and of something else — unless he told you. We know that a man called Rafe Lyggon went to the Collège, likely around Easter — perhaps under his name, perhaps not. He went there to see Dr. Allen."

"I heard nothing — and if my father did, he didn't tell me. But in fairness, Monsieur…" Blandine shrugged. "They come and go, like the Fair of la Madeleine — and as for seeing Allen…" Another shrug. "Don't they all do? But perhaps your … what is it that he calls himself at the Collège? Dick Sherbourn, is it? Perhaps he will know…" She pushed upright, went to the door, and called: "Perrette!"

It was a few heartbeats before wooden clogs clattered in the hallway, and the round-faced servant skidded gracelessly to the threshold.

"Shawl and pattens, Perrette," ordered Blandine. "You'll see my cousin to the Auberge de la Fleur-de-Lys. And … wait!" she called, as Perrette made to run away. "Since you go that way, gather a rose or two for *la Sainte Vièrge* at la Tournelle."

This last instruction Perrette did not like. "'Tis wet in the garden," she grumbled.

"You're not made of sugar. Come, come!" Blandine clapped her hands briskly. "Maman's roses!"

The servant trotted away, and Blandine closed the door with a huff of impatience. "Saints keep us — that girl! Mind, Monsieur, she knows nothing. But those flowers, she'll put in a little tabernacle that is in view of the Collège's windows, and they are a signal for Sherbourn to go to the Church of Saint-Symphorien tomorrow between eleven and noon. By the statue of Saint Oricle."

"But is he free to come and go?"

"I told you: 'tis like the Fair. Some of them go to hear lectures at the Université, so they are not observed all the time. The lad knows better than to disregard his summons."

Well, this now! Flowers and tabernacles, and unwitting servant-girls — and at the heart of it Blandine Jory, as brisk and able as the best of Sir Francis's men in Seething Lane!

And Tom had another question for her, just as Perrette's pattens sounded again in the hall.

"What about Baines, Madame? Where do I find him?" he asked in a hasty whisper.

For once, Thibaud's daughter hesitated. "He spoke to Father of a tavern called La Belle aux Pommes — but..." She made that gesture with the palm up that, in France and England, to rhetoricians and housewives, meant 'Heaven knows'.

"And what's he like?"

"Yellow-haired, with a hooked nose, and..." Blandine touched the left side of her jaw. "He has a mark here, like a burn." And then she threw open the door, catching Perrette in the act of stepping close.

The servant stumbled in her haste to retreat away from her mistress's glare.

As Tom and Watson followed her into the hallway, Blandine gave them an unfriendly look. "Well, *mon cousin*, we'll see," she said. "You must come back when my husband returns."

"And I insist that we must see the testament," Watson said severely.

Blandine waved a dismissive hand. "Yes, yes," she said. "Let my husband come home, and you'll see it all you like."

As she spoke, young Remi appeared at the end of the hallway, and came to stand at his sister's side, stealing glances at her and the unwelcome guests, and looking satisfied that there was no friendliness to be observed.

"The horses are ready outside," he announced, so childishly triumphant that Tom would have gladly boxed his ears.

Instead, he bowed ungraciously to Blandine — and to her alone. "As you like, *ma cousine*. I want nothing that isn't mine — but I won't leave until this is all sorted."

She nodded back, just as stiffly, Perrette opened the door to a gust of air, and off they went.

The rain had stopped, and a breeze scoured Rheims in its place now, burrowing in the alleys and tearing the dark clouds above to rags, so that beams of honey-coloured sunlight found their way to finger the city's roofs and spires. People were emerging from doors and gates like moles from their molehills, to gauge whether the rain had gone, or to hasten home.

Perrette led the way at a nipping pace, exchanging greetings here and there, but never slowing. Down the markets she led them, then turned into an alley that grew larger as they passed behind the great apse of the cathedral — and on the girl stamped, lip and chin jutted in the way of one ill-used, one hand clutching a black shawl around her head, the other tight around a posy of roses of an unusual warm yellow. One understood why they would make a good signal.

Tom was wondering how Blandine summoned people from the college in winter, when the bells in the titanic towers started to chime above their heads.

"Oh Saints — five already!" wailed their pouting guide, as she dove into a street on their right. It was a street of good old half-timbered houses, with some traffic of foot and hoof. Halfway down, Perrette scuttled around a clutch of soldiers in fine red, yellow and blue. One of them leered at the young woman, but none of them spared a glance for the two men she led — a very good thing, considering.

"Guise men," Tom murmured to Watson over his shoulder — and turned just in time to walk into Perrette, who'd stopped abruptly.

"Do you want to be trodden, girl?" he grumbled, as he steadied his mare.

Perrette threw him a scowl, and stepped up to the nearest corner. They stood in the back of a cramped square, shaped a little like a horse's head. On their corner, at a height where a man's arm could reach, a tabernacle of limestone showed behind a grate of wrought iron. Within was a painted Virgin Mary — Blandine's *Sainte Vièrge*.

Even in her pattens, Perrette had trouble reaching the effigy. As she tried to stick the roses in the grate with wary little jumps, the flowers escaped her fingers and fell in the mud.

She exclaimed in dismay. "And now M'zelle will burn my ears!"

"Here, here — let me." Watson bent to retrieve the roses, shook what mud he could from the rumpled leaves, and stuck them in place with the ease of long arms, under the flustered Perrette's instruction.

Meanwhile, Tom held both horses and watched the houses across the street, seeking the windows where a man could have a good sight of the tabernacle. Suddenly, half a dozen boys erupted around the corner, shouting and laughing. Apprentices, quite likely, as unruly in France as they were in London. A few yards up the street, a house caught their attention, whose gate stood half open. One man in a three-cornered black hat leant out — an unwise move that prompted the youths to exchange their merriment for something darker. The man disappeared in a trice, and the gate swung shut, but not before the apprentices started to hurl words of mischief and handfuls of ordure from the runnel.

"Perrette, what's that?" Tom asked.

The yellow roses forgotten, Perrette crossed herself. "*Sainte Vièrge*, again!" she cried. "'Tis the place where the English stay. Come, Monsieur, come away!"

34

She tugged at Tom's sleeve, just as shouts sounded from both ends of the street — some of it abuse against the *Anglais*, some calls to desist in the name of the law.

"Our good Collège," Watson said under his breath. "Well liked, are they?"

Perrette stamped her feet. "Oh, but come away! The archers will say it's you who made mischief — and then M'zelle will right murther me, she will —"

And didn't she sound more afraid of her mistress than the archers! But in truth it would be awkward to be entangled in a brawl, to attract the attention of the *Milice*. There was nothing for it but to let themselves be led away, across the little square and down a lane that was already half-dark.

"But why should they think we are to blame?" Watson asked.

Perrette huffed. "Lord watch the innocent — you're English!"

A grave sin, no doubt. And indeed, reckoning by the ado at the college... Tom glanced back over his shoulder. The house itself was out of sight, but a loose throng milled warily in the little square, and just above these busybodies' heads, Blandine's roses glowed yellow in the darkening afternoon, like a tiny beacon. Now Fates send that Marley would see the signal and meet them at the appointed hour.

CHAPTER 3

It was another sign of the times that the Auberge de la Fleur-de-Lys welcomed the two travellers like long-lost sons, with promises of a fine chamber, and a better fire, all to themselves — and the finest supper in the whole of Champagne.

The Englishness of Tom and Watson, once it was uncovered and made certain, quelled the landlord's eagerness a little — but not that of his much younger wife. This dark-haired lady of wide smiles and ample bosom quickly rallied her husband in sharp whispers — surely to the tune that any guest was better than nothing in these lean days — and soon the host was all welcoming cheer again.

In a trice Tom and Watson were ensconced in a largish room, with the promised fire and a flagon of wine. There were also two well-padded chairs by the earth, and in one of those, once he had shed his muddy boots and damp doublet, Tom reclined with a great sigh. He left it to Watson to pour the wine, and raise his glass in a toast.

"To poor old Thibaud, then — who wasn't murdered."

"And to his formidable daughter," Tom added, before drinking. The wine was good, and not watered at all — a small blessing, after the wet day.

Watson sat in turn, long legs spread before him. "Formidable — ay. A pity she can't be left to do the work."

"Can't she, though?" It seemed most unfair — and most foolish. "It would be a shame to lose the Thibauds."

"I don't say it wouldn't, but a woman…?"

"That brother of hers will be a man one of these days."

This sent Watson into a laugh and a pretended shudder. "Heaven forfend!"

"Madame Jory, on the other hand…"

"She doesn't keep much of a Huguenot house, does she? Saints keep us, and flowers for the Virgin, and our sulky little Ariadne crossing herself?"

And this coming from Watson — more than half a Catholic himself…!

"Well…" Tom turned the half-empty glass between his fingers. "Her Roland kin in London are staunch Protestants enough — but out here… She wouldn't be the first to be half and half — and none the worse for it. Not in France, not in the Service."

And if Watson read the acknowledgement for what it was, he didn't show it. He hummed instead, nodding at the flames that clicked and whispered in the embrace of the soot-black firedogs.

"That, or your M'zelle hides her true colours well."

Indeed — and it should have galled Tom that he couldn't tell for sure, but in little, plump, shrewd Blandine Jory, it rather amused him.

"Either way, it works, and what Sir Francis cares for is a ready wit — whether Papist or Protestant and, I dare say, in petticoats or breeches."

A ready wit and loyalty, Thomas — though it is a melancholy fact that, while loyalty can be bought and sold, there is no price that will buy one wits.

"Ay, ay." Watson gave a shrug. "If anyone knows what Sir Francis wants, it will be you."

Was Tom's own mind making up the sour colour in his friend's words? He glanced sideways, to meet Watson's cocked eyebrow.

"What is it, Tityrus?"

And with the words went the old nickname, the skewed hint of a smile. What a petty fellow Tom had grown to be, picking fault where there was none!

"Nothing," he sighed. "Or not much. I was thinking of Baines..." Which was only half a lie, for the thought had been nagging him, ready to fetch right beneath the irritation of resentment. "No murderer, it seems — but still trouble."

It was clear that Baines had not been only in Tom's mind, for Watson hardly missed a beat before asking: "You think he'd truly make lard of Allen's piglets?"

Tom considered. "He's had two years to do it — and nothing happened. Yet, now up he turns, promising vengeance... I wonder where he's been all this time."

"Begging in the streets, thin as a rake and filthy, by your fair cousin's account?"

Before Tom could retort on the assumed kinship or any other matter, there was a knock at the door and Madame Raulet bustled in, followed by a pair of food-laden servants.

"Now you see us as good as deserted, Messieurs — but the Fleur-de-Lys can still serve a tidy supper to such gentlemen as you," she cooed, a hand to the snowy partlet that covered her bosom. She only stopped to scold one underling busy with a plate of pastries, and then went back to gush on her guests. "I wish you'd seen us when we kept a full table, Messieurs. Ah, but *le bon Dieu* knows, Rheims is no longer what it was. The Fairs — ah, Messieurs, they've gone down to naught, and we see precious few travellers these days — and small blame to them! No, we're no longer what we used to be..."

"We saw an ugly scene," Tom said, the first time he could put in a word edgewise. "A pack of boys attacked a house..."

Madame Raulet threw up her hands. "Savages!" she cried. "And you'd think, with the streets full of archers — but ... ha!" The lady's fine dark eyes flashed with contempt. "Things were better, you know, when Monsieur de Guise's men were here. Now we're left with these *patauds*, and honest folks must fear for their lives in their own houses — I tell you: in their own houses!"

It was Watson's turn to push his way through the landlady's torrent of words. "A man said it was the Collège where the English exiles live," he said.

"Oh, those!" She tossed her head. "I should say nothing, because Monsieur de Guise brought them here, and they are your countrymen — but..." She stopped, with more head-shaking, and much biting of full red lips.

"Does it happen often?" Tom ventured.

"What would you have? They're English!" she said. "Not heretics, they say — but these days people have no Christian charity. One day it's the English, the next the Huguenots, then those who are for the King, then the Leaguers... Sad times, Monsieur — that's what these are. I tell you: sad times!"

And with this melancholy conclusion and one last look to satisfy herself of the laid supper, Madame Raulet shooed off her servants like poultry, and followed them out.

As soon as the last step had died away, Watson gave a soft whistle.

"Well, well," he said. "We'll do well to watch our step while we're here. I doubt they'd care how French your supposed father was."

"I doubt they'd even ask." Tom went to sit at the well-laid table. "The one good thing is, since there was nothing foul about Thibaud's death, there's not much left to do here. We talk to your friend Marley, we find this Baines, and off we trot, to Calais and home, before the truce ends."

And it was to this prospect that they drank, before falling on Madame Raulet's much-lauded supper with the appetite of two men all day in the saddle.

The landlady, it turned out, had not boasted unduly: the larded pigeons were roasted to perfection, and the pastries golden and soft, and the cheese more than decent. There was even a bowl of strawberries and cream. Still, the long day's fatigue was enough to make even the fine fare something of a chore. It wasn't long before Tom pushed back from the table. "Lord, but I'm tired," he muttered around a yawn — and would have quipped about old age, but Watson preceded him.

"You've grown soft, Tityrus!" he laughed. "It took a good deal more to undo you, when you were a hardy little courier… It must be an easy life that you well-born folks have in Seething Lane, eh?"

There — there he went — again!

And, of a sudden, it was once too many. The tired haze burnt away, Tom sat upright. "And you won't let me forget it, will you?" he snapped. "I was called back to London, ay — and put to work there. Do you think I asked for any of it?"

"Now —"

"But no — you think, like every other soul, that it all came to me through my name and nothing else!"

"Tityrus —"

"Enough of that!" Pushing back his chair, Tom strode away from the table. "That was a name for when we were friends. Phelippes doesn't call me that anymore, don't you know? Ever since he came back to London himself, I've become Mr. Thomas. A half-stranger to bow to! We're the Thomases no longer, had you not heard?"

"I've heard now — and so has half of Rheims."

Tom clicked his tongue, turning away — half in anger, half in shame. What would Sir Francis think of such unseemly fulminations, and in the middle of a French inn!

But Tom missed the companionship they'd shared in Paris, the three of them — himself, and Watson, and little Phelippes the cypherer — Tityrus, Corydon and Philippus to themselves, the Thomases to all at the Embassy. He missed it fiercely — and whatever he'd expected on being reunited with Watson… A dunce — that's what he was. A soft-minded dunce!

And there Watson sat, eyes sad and watchful. "We knew…" he began, and stopped — biting off, no doubt, the old Paris name. "We've always known it was to end. You were never to be a courier your whole life — you've always known that. Paris was a season to us all. Away from there…" He shrugged, with a little sad smile. "You're what you are, Mr. Thomas. I'm just too good at taking liberties — and I shouldn't, strange as it is to be under the command of little Tityrus." He held up a hand to silence Tom before he could protest. "But it matters little, for I'm thinking of leaving the Service."

"Leaving the Service!" Tom exclaimed. "Does Sir Francis know —" And devil pinch him for a fool! What business had he sounding this stern and reproachful?

Watson's smile strained thin. "Oh, Mr. Secretary won't lose his sleep over me. Know this, though, Mr. Thomas: I've never believed it's just your name —"

A knock at the door cut him short. Tom called to enter, and they watched in silence as the two servants cleared the table, and the silence stretched when they were gone.

There was no taking up the conversation again. Tom found he'd rather cut his tongue, and it was a great relief that Watson was just as quiet.

Full of aches, more mistempered than not, and awkward with Watson was not a good way to wake in the morning. It was in a sullen disposition that Tom broke his fast on bread and cheese, and it seemed to him that, whenever he looked up from his plate, he caught one of the household averting curious eyes in great haste.

Had they heard the quarrel last night? Had they grasped any of it? Or were they just wondering, all and one, what had bitten the two Englishmen overnight to make them bearish — it being a well-known fact in France that all the English were not right in the head?

Or, in fair truth, it could have been Tom's own conscience, nagging him into seeing things that were not there. He would have given much, this morning, to have held a tighter rein on his tongue — and all the more because Watson followed him so quiet and obsequent.

It felt fitting that, even on a sunny morning, Rheims should coil around itself just as skittishly as it had in the rainy evening, and La Belle aux Pommes, as it turned out, lay just off Rheims' den of debauchery, the Rue Tire-Vit. Tom had to ask his way, once they plunged into the maze of filthy alleys behind the cathedral — and in truth the place lacked even the deliberate disorder of a maze. It was a knot, a tangle of runnels where one waded ankle-deep in all sorts of ordure, and men scurried about hugging the mouldy walls of houses that, in spite of never rising higher than two storeys, all but met at the eaves, blocking out the light of day. Had it been always like this, or had the wars stamped their mark of poverty and fear?

A bang overhead shattered all glum philosophies, and Tom had barely the time to dive out of the way as the contents of a piss-pot went to join the filth underfoot.

"Oy, call out at least!" he shouted, but the offender had shut the window and disappeared.

He'd jumped out of the way, but not out of harm entirely, and the spatters showed on his boots. Across the alley, where he'd slid for shelter, Watson was grimacing at his own breeches and looked up to meet Tom's eyes, and they both burst out laughing.

Tom felt a little better for it.

In the end, tipping a rapacious urchin proved the only way to find La Belle aux Pommes, which lurked in the darkest corner of a dark, foul little courtyard. It boasted one smoke-blackened room where an old fellow, oak-like in colouring, gnarled limbs, and robustness, presided over a huddle of painted women.

There was a price to be paid, of course, for a jug of atrocious wine, and nothing in the way of intelligence.

A man named Baines? What manner of name was that? English? Pah! Englishmen were a dime a dozen, these days. How was one to remember them? And all with a manner of shuttered slyness that Tom had seen before in this sort of creature — the sort who made a living out of knowing nothing at all.

Devil pinch the fellow! For all Tom knew, Baines could be hiding somewhere in this stenching burrow, perhaps up the stairs that climbed along the room's long side. He ran a scowl of deep displeasure around the place. On the far wall, someone had painted the fair maid with the 'apples' — or so he assumed from the patches of colour that showed under years' worth of soot. Under this crude decoration, two young women sat in tired, careless disarray around a flickering stub of rush-light.

It took a light tug on his girdle to alert Tom to the presence of a third siren, who had slipped behind him in the gloom.

He closed a hand where his purse would have been — but that he always kept it in his sleeve — and with the other he grabbed for a thin wrist, earning a chuckle and a jaded look from silver-pale eyes.

"If I wanted to rob you, Milord, you'd never know it 'til you were fleeced," she purred. "Come and sit with us. I like myself an Englishman."

"Do you?" Tom couldn't help but smile. "You must be the one soul in all of Rheims."

She chuckled again, throwing back her head to expose a throat curved like that of a none-too-clean swan, and threaded an arm through Tom's, tugging him towards the table.

Tom let himself be tugged. Who knew what these women knew — and could be bought into revealing? He only paused to glance over his shoulder at Watson, who stood lingering by the door.

The young woman did not miss it. "Your friend, too, if he likes. There's three of us, you know — not that I couldn't mind you both."

How did one respond to this, but with a laugh? Impudent brat — and she no more than eighteen! Watson made his way to them, his wide white grin in place, and they sat with this questionable bevy. A still younger girl, with a maidenly brown braid slung over a most unmaidenly naked shoulder, was sent to procure more of the nasty beverage they called wine — which she fetched beyond a curtained door under the stairs. The landlord, notably enough, had made himself scarce — hiding, perhaps, to keep an eye on his mermaids.

Once they were all cosily sat, in a haze of bad liquor, sweat and the cheapest perfume, and once they'd laughingly drunk to French ladies and English gentlemen, the third woman all but leant across the table, elbows and bosoms on display, and tipped a sharp little chin at Tom.

"'Tis Dickon Baines that you seek?" she whispered.

"Barbe!" protested the one with the braid, only to be cuffed on the arm.

"What?" Barbe hissed. "Papa Fricque plays deaf and mute, and we don't."

"But —"

"We owe Dickon nothing."

"Speak for yourself!" Tom's silver-eyed friend said, from where she leant against his shoulder. "I owe him a bruise, me."

This drew a sniff from her with the braid. "Fair's fair, Lison: you'd filched away that cross of his — and you scratched him!"

Which was easy to credit, as Lison lunged, nails forward, and would have scratched her fellow too, had Watson not grabbed her fingers.

"Ladies, ladies," he tutted, holding tight as the woman squirmed to free herself.

Tom tapped on the table and, when he'd obtained silence, turned from face to intent face. "Say that you owe Baines nothing," he said. "On the other hand, you might owe us, might you not?" And he reached for the purse in his sleeve — and found nothing.

Oh, Lord guard fools — most of all when such a woman is around! He glared at Lison, who gave another of those dove-like little laughs and, having freed herself from Watson's grasp, dangled the purse from her quick fingers. "Didn't I say you'd never know?"

With a sigh and a shake of his head, Tom snatched back the purse and weighed it in his hand. He did not carry much in it — but still enough to be a temptation to the likes of Lison.

"Don't fear, Monsieur." This from Barbe, together with a pointed look. "She knows better than to rob you. And don't mind la Néné, either. She's sweet on your Dickon."

Néné tossed her braid, mouth twisted. "He made me sorry, poor wretch — but sweet on him — tchah! He was the oddest fellow."

"Well, then…" Tom fished for a few sols and carefully set them in the middle of the table, where they glinted in the rush-light's greenish glow.

Three pairs of eyes sought each other, brows were cocked, lower lips were nibbled.

Tom added another coin. "The oddest fellow…"

If he had doubted who was chief in this little bunch, the answer was Barbe's hand shooting out and closing on the coins. Lison curled against Watson and giggled, looking greatly satisfied with the commerce.

"I carry no purse, Mademoiselle," Watson murmured, earning an arch smile.

Coins secreted away in her unlaced bodice, Barbe drew Tom to her side on the bench against the wall, and Néné nestled against him.

"So…" he prodded.

It was all it took: the three women began to expound on Dickon Baines in soft murmurs and little laughs.

There had been ducks in the moat back at Scadbury — the delight of Tom's sister Mary, who guarded them fiercely against hunting — if not always from the cook. They would huddle close sometimes and chatter softly among themselves. The three mermaids of La Belle aux Pommes, once started, sounded just like that.

"Always preaching, he was."

"We're all sinful filth, you know."

"Him most sinful and filthiest of all."

"For all that he called himself a priest."

"A priest my foot!"

This drew a chuckle from Watson. "Oh, but he is."

The women were startled into laughing exclamations — more duck-like than ever — with much clapping of hands to mouths.

"Why, and him wanting to kill this and that…"

Now, this was promising.

"Who was this and that? Did he say?" Tom asked.

The mermaids exchanged doubtful moues.

"A priest, he said."

"*All* priests."

"Papa Fricque." This with a three-sided burst of laughter.

"All the English — but he never meant…" This from Néné, who tapped her temple. "'Twas the devils in his head, you know."

"Devils or no, he was always at it."

"When he wasn't crying on his sinful soul!"

"A good thing that he scuttled."

Ah — now… "And when did he scuttle, then?" Tom asked.

"He didn't." Lison's pale eyes twinkled in malice. "Papa Fricque kicked him out for a mad dog when he hit me."

"Ay — and beat him too," Néné said — still Baines's champion. "And it was all your fault, Lison. If you hadn't filched his cross…"

"Yes, yes," Tom cut in, before the argument fanned itself to flame again, and turned to Néné. "So, when did Papa Fricque kick him out?"

The woman considered, tweaking at her braid. "'Twas la Quasimodo, or the day after, maybe. There were still soldiers around, and Dickon picked a fight."

"A week after Easter, then — and he never came back?"

That there were three shakes of the head all at once, with none of those glances of consultation, Tom took as a sign of uncorrupted truth — for once. He turned from woman to woman, smiling as winningly as he knew.

"And you would tell me, if he did? Find where he is now, perhaps?" And, because winning smiles were bound to count for little here, he added, "It would be worth your while."

This time, they did look at one another — although only Néné's eyes showed a hint of trouble, and for the first time it occurred to her to ask in a small voice, "What is it that you want with him?"

Not one to be so bothered, Lison slapped her friend on the arm. "What do you care, you goose?"

Which Tom took to mean assent — at least on Lison's part.

Whether it was at Lison's mercenary heart, or at Tom's handling of harlots, Watson looked vastly amused when he asked a question of his own: "And before la Quasimodo, had he lived here long, your Dickon?"

Barbe took a thoughtful sip from her pot. "I don't know that he did. He'd drink, have one of us — la Néné, mostly, for she let him weep all he liked — and then he'd sleep it off in the yard."

"He had money, then?"

"From our late friend, I'll wager…" murmured Watson.

More of Guillaume Thibaud's well-meaning succour, given for the journey back to England — and soon gone in a place like this.

A shrug from Lison. "When he had no more, he did some little service — for us, or for Papa, and once —"

"Once he threw out a drunk who was beating me," Néné cut in. "So there. And after that, Papa Fricque let him sleep under the stairs. And clean pots for his keeping."

"Oh, didn't that gall him!" Lison giggled, looking suddenly much younger, like a spiteful child. "Him a gentleman, and a priest, and a learned man, scouring piss-pots for a bunch of whores!"

And, however much or little of a gentleman Baines was by birth, wasn't this a steep fall, poor fellow!

"But how long had he —"

The rest of the question was drowned when Barbe laughed of a sudden and threw her arms around Tom's neck, drawing him in for a kiss. Over her unkempt head, Tom saw Lison running her hands through Watson's hair — and, behind their backs, lurched Papa Fricque, come to see what his girls were up to.

"Enough's enough, you geese!" he grumbled. "We know nothing here."

"Barbe…" Tom prodded. "How long?"

"A month — more, near on two," she murmured against his jaw.

"Do you know where he went?"

He could feel her pout against his cheek. "To do the Lord's justice, for all I know! And we've beds upstairs, you know?"

But that was not Tom's notion — not in this place, not with this woman, who was likely to bring worse to a man than a ready wit and willing body. He disengaged himself and squeezed past Néné. "Another time, *mes belles*," he said, a little more breathlessly than he liked — for, in spite of all, his body had some regrets. He threw another coin on the table, and this time the huge landlord was there to grab and pocket it.

It was nothing to the leave-taking of Watson, who bowed extravagantly, leaning to kiss Lison's hand. "Now that we know our way…"

It was not until they were out in the alley — the stench of this sirens' lair still clinging to their clothes, that Tom raised his eyes to the Heavens. "*Now that we know our way!*" he mocked. "The way to a dose of the clap!"

Watson laughed, and countered: "Well, you started it. *Another time, mes belles!* What would Sir Francis say to his little cousin…" He stopped short with a wince, glancing askew, gauging if Tom was going to take it in snuff again.

But Tom didn't. "He'd say," he sighed instead, "that his cousin spent a good deal of time and money to learn precious little. Ah well. Come now. 'Tis Saint-Symphorien for us at eleven, and your friend Marley."

CHAPTER 4

They'd been waiting by the statue of the beheaded Saint Oricle for a while, and Tom was beginning to wonder if Blandine Jory's roses could have gone unseen, when a man threw himself on the kneeler by his side and remained there, breathing hard.

A slight, dishevelled young man, clad in black, with a black hat squashed under his elbow. A three-cornered hat. Of his face little showed beyond splayed hands, except cheeks red with effort.

"*Aequam memento in arduis...*" he panted.

"*...Rebus serbare mentem,*" Tom answered duly — Horace on keeping one's head when trouble arose.

With a great gulp of relief, the man — the lad, for he looked even younger than his one-and-twenty years — turned to sit on the kneeling step. "God's nightgown, I thought I wouldn't make it," he breathed. "One wouldn't believe there can be so much harping on the doctrine of Purgatory, and —"

"And if we were the wrong men, Kit Marley, you'd be dead," hissed Watson, leaning over the lad's shoulder.

"He said..." Marley twisted around, and broke into a huge smile of happy recognition. "Why, Watson!" he exclaimed, scowling when both Tom and Watson shushed him.

Oh Lord save and deliver! What had Madame Jory called this one? A cockerel with no sense...

Nobody seemed to be paying them any mind, for a mercy, not even when Watson cuffed young Marley.

"Be quiet," ordered Tom. "Have they taught you nothing?"

The lad gave him an unfriendly glare, but gathered himself in a hunch — head lowered, elbows on knees — that could pass for praying zeal.

Watson murmured introductions: "Kit, this is Mr. Thomas Walsingham."

Which was unneeded and ill-advised, and if it was meant to impress the lad, utterly useless.

All Marley did was arch one eyebrow to give Tom a cold, level scrutiny. "Mr. Secretary's boy."

Even if Tom had missed Watson elbowing Marley in the back, there was a colour of recollection to the words, enough to set one's teeth on edge. Was this how Watson discussed him with strangers? But then, Marley was no stranger to Watson, was he? The young friend he'd recruited in Cambridge, a peer he'd never have to bow to…

Tom straightened. "I go by Roland here," he whispered, in that manner of cold command Sir Francis used at times — because wasn't he in charge here, by God? "I hope it's understood."

"When it's just us —"

Tom cut right through the protestation. "I've called you here to ask about a man. Two men, in truth. One is named Rafe Lyggon."

Without the smallest pause for consideration, Marley shrugged and shook his head.

And after all Tom must have possessed a good deal of restraint, for he swallowed his flare of anger. "He was at the college at some time in April."

"Think well, Kit," Watson said.

Another shrug — but, at least, the lad sucked his teeth for a heartbeat or two before answering. "Never heard of him —

but then, I only arrived a week before Easter. And if he was there under another name… What's he like?"

What, indeed? "I rather hoped you'd know. Forty years or thereabout. A gentleman."

"There are some older students…"

"This one would have come and gone."

"I wish you luck, then!" Marley snorted. "There's always someone coming and going. Dr. Allen never turns away a soul. Never know where you could find a martyr-to-be."

"Or a spy of the Queen of Scots," Tom groused. "For the future, take some note of these birds of passage, will you?"

It went with all the rest that the brat should whine: "But there's a host of them…"

A host! Tom glared at the young fool. "You'll make the effort." And then, hopeless as it seemed… "Now for the second man: one Dick Baines."

And look how Marley shot upright at that, bright-eyed and hitting a fist to his own knee. "God's wounds! At last, someone listens!" he exclaimed, loud enough that Tom and Watson both shushed him again. But who the devil was the dunce back in London, choosing the men to send to Rheims?

People were gathering in the transept. When a thick-faced matron turned to scowl at them across the nave, Tom half-bowed in apology, grabbed Marley by the elbow, and hauled him towards a side chapel near the door, Watson keeping the rear.

Once they were out of view, half hidden behind the reclining stone effigy of some dean of old, Tom pushed Marley to sit on the tomb's socle, and hovered over him, fists to his hips.

"Soft and fair, now: you know this Baines, I take it?"

"Know him! He wouldn't leave me alone!"

Tom traded glances with Watson, who reached to shake Marley's shoulder.

"What the devil do you mean?"

"That he's been following me, I mean. He caught me near Thibaud's house, the day I reported there."

Blandine had said the fellow haunted the house. And yet... "How did he know you for one of us?"

"He..." For the first time the lad looked away, and blushed. "He must have..."

But Watson knew his Marley, by the way he sighed through his nose. "Kit..." he prodded.

"Oh, go to Hell! He called to me in English. He called me a College Rat — and I turned, and..."

Oh, Jupiter above — as though they had time for this! Tom waved it away. "Ay, ay — and what did Baines want of you?"

"He told me to run, said they'd find me out, put me to the rack, that your uncle would throw me to the wolves the way he had —"

"Cousin."

Marley blinked, perplexed into sudden silence — and Tom could have kicked himself that still he must insist on this so. And of course now he had to explain.

"Sir Francis is my father's cousin, not my uncle. Go ahead."

And see if the lad didn't seek Watson's eyes as he resumed his tale in growing excitement. "Well, after that I saw him again outside the college. He begs in the street, or by the Church of Saint-Étienne. That's where we go to hear Mass on Sundays, and he'll be there, staring at us when he thinks no one is watching. And I told Thibaud — but did he listen? That old lack-wit —"

"That old lack-wit is dead, Kit," interrupted Watson, with a choir-master's severity that was seldom seen in him.

Not that it meekened Marley in the least; if anything, it made him look up in triumph. "Ah! You see — you *see*? God's nightgown — if only... When was it that he died?"

"Right before Low Sunday." This from Watson again, together with yet another shushing.

Marley nodded — Wisdom Vindicated. "See? And I'd been there right after Easter — and that infernal daughter wouldn't let me see Thibaud, for he was ill. She scoffed when I told her. Why, she sent me away — and if only she'd —"

"Whist!" It was becoming tedious to shush the little hellion at every step. "What the devil is it that you told her?"

And, for once and for a mercy, Kit Marley lowered his voice to a hiss to impart his breathless tidings: "I told her that Baines has done murder!"

So now it was plain and indisputable: the Service chose its men for Rheims in the Bedlam.

"Murder." Tom wove all the disbelief he knew into the one word.

Which made Marley shoot to his feet, and he would have stalked away, had not Watson pushed him back to his stony seat.

"Now, Kit..."

And he could have been speaking to the long dead dean, for all the good it did.

Christopher Marley twisted where he sat, for all the world like the cockerel Blandine Jory had called him.

"Plague take it all!" he rasped in a savage whisper. "What's the use of sending men to risk their heads, if you won't believe—"

The rest was lost when the bells of Saint-Symphorien began to strike noon overhead — a pair of them at first, then more, and then, like echoes, many others from the churches all around. It sounded different, heard from inside the church, each big chime shivering through bones and teeth. Tom strolled around the tomb, out to the nave, where the sun streamed through the stained-glass window to paint jewelled patterns on the flagged floor. In the transept some midday Mass was about to begin. Even across the whole church's width, silver and gold glinted around the altarpiece. *Ex voto*, no doubt, to some miraculous saint or other — one of many such shrines that could be found all over France. If war broke out again, much of that wealth would soon be gone, seized to feed the armies of one faction or the other.

As soon as the bells' clamour began to dwindle, Tom turned back to the tomb. Watson stood keeping watch. Marley sat against the tall sepulchre, hands fidgeting on his knees, head thrown back. He sat straight to narrow his eyes at Tom.

"Then tell me what it is that I should believe," Tom said. "What murder did Baines do?"

It was plain as day that the lad would have liked to shut his mouth and say no more. *It doesn't matter, if you're not going to believe me, does it?* Or something to that effect. Perhaps he'd already said so, judging by Watson's mutter of "Now, don't be a fool, Kit."

There was an intake of breath, some more rebellious scowling, and then a stormy torrent of words. "At the college, back at the end of April. He poisoned a man — and now you say Thibaud is dead, so that must have been Baines, too…" He raised pleading, furious eyes to Watson first, then to Tom. "Plague take you, don't you *see*?"

What Tom saw was how fiercely certain young Marley was of his charges. On the other hand…

"Thibaud wasn't poisoned. He wasn't killed at all."

"How do you know?" Marley started — far too loudly — and stopped short, lowering his voice. "How do you know that it wasn't Baines?"

It was not to be suspected that 'because the daughter says so' would do much to convince Marley — whose place, though, was not to question what he was told.

"Because you have to be in a place to poison someone there," Tom snapped. "Did you ever see Baines at the college?"

"No — but he must have been there, mustn't he, seeing that Hugh Downes is dead?"

And the fellow was at Cambridge, reading for his Mastership, no less!

"Fallacy!" called Watson, like a master overseeing a disputation.

And it was unchristian, surely, to find it amusing that the overeager brat should blush?

Tom couldn't help himself. "Don't they teach you, at Divinities, that you can't explain the effect by the cause and the cause by the effect?" he asked, and held up a hand to forestall the protestations he saw mounting. "And, if you don't mind, who was Hugh Downes, that he should be murdered?"

It was perhaps some consolation that, given a choice between defending his rhetoric and pursuing the matter of murder, Marley settled for the latter.

"One of the students," he said. "Not a very bright one. A good fellow, though. Seven or eight-and-twenty…"

"How did he die?"

"He caught an ague, so they put him in the infirmary. Then one night, before Matins, we all hear a great cry. We run, and there lies Downes, at the foot of the staircase, all broken. Dead. They said he must have wandered in his raving, and fallen to his death." Marley shook his head when Tom opened his mouth to object. "But falling down the stairs won't make you blue in the face, will it?"

Or would it? Tom thought of dead Frenchmen at the Embassy in London. *Blue inside the mouth*. Not that he'd ever seen that particular body…

"Blue in the face or inside the mouth?"

Eyes narrowed at the ugly memory. Marley touched his chin and jaw. "The face — and not truly blue. A red so dark, it was almost purple."

"And couldn't that have been the bruising from the fall?"

"I don't…"

"You say it was night; you were all still sleeping. There would be no more than a few candles. How could you tell the colour of the face?"

"It was all dark, I tell you."

"The lips, too? The tongue?"

"I don't…" Marley grimaced. "Not the tongue, no. Not inside the mouth. He was… The mouth was open, as if to scream, and his tongue…" He swallowed hard, before looking squarely at Tom. "'Twasn't dark."

So not hemlock, most likely — although this meant little enough.

Watson pulled a doubtful face. "I don't know," he said. "It seems to me it could have been the fall."

Which was very much Tom's own thought. "Little enough to throw the blame on Baines."

Marley looked up with the upward palm and the victorious smile of one closing a disputation. "Ay — but he said he'd do it."

According to Watson, Kit Marley's father was a cobbler in Canterbury. Surely the cobbler must have often taken the cane to his insufferable brat — and so must have sundry masters, at grammar school and in Cambridge?

Tom grabbed the boy by the shoulder. "Were you keeping this for sweetmeats?" he snapped. "How do you know?"

"He told me, that's how!"

"He sought you, and said he'd kill this Hugh Downes?" asked Watson, disbelief plain on his face.

Marley clicked his tongue. "*I* sought him. The first time I saw him at Saint-Étienne, I slipped out and went to talk to him."

"You never…" Tom laughed bitterly under his breath. "But of course, of course you did!"

"Kit, Kit, Kit!" Watson blew out his cheeks. "What if you were followed? Or seen?"

And didn't the little dunce have the cheek to shrug it off! "What then? Can't I take pity on a beggar, want to give him a coin?"

Oh, Lord smite all arrogant pups! "Ay — and what if it was anyone who knows *him*? Don't you know he was at the college himself, two years or so before you?"

There was a blink, a flicker of doubt — but it was swallowed in a heartbeat, burnt away by that damnable assuredness again. "If anybody saw, they can't have known him — for nobody challenged me…"

Watson held up a hand. "Or else, they knew him only too well, and now know what you are, and bide their time —"

Marley ignored him altogether. "And anyway, Baines told me again to run, for he was going to poison them all. He would poison the well and kill Allen and his whole gaggle of black devils!" *So there!*

Wanting to kill this and that, the mermaids had said. *All priests, all the English…*

Across the church, the good, simple folks who didn't have to deal with murderous madmen were muttering their Latin in answer to the priest.

"But you didn't believe him," said Tom.

Marley stamped a foot. "Believe him? Laugh in his face, I did! But then Hugh Downes died…"

He ranted that he'd kill them all for what they'd done to him… But still, madness was one thing, and…

"Don't you reckon," Tom asked slowly, "that if he'd poisoned the well, there would be more dead than one?"

"Ay, but others have been unwell — Dr. Allen for one, and another priest."

And while Allen himself might be interesting… "Hardly a massacre, is it?"

There would have been protestations — but just then the sacring bell knelled from the gold-studded chapel, making Marley stiffen like a hare scenting a hound.

"God's shirt — I must go!" He crammed his hat on his head, and tore it away again. "Dr. Barret isn't one for strictness, but someone will notice if I'm not there for dinner."

"Wait!" Tom grabbed him by the arm. "Watson may be right; perhaps they know you for one of us, by now — or they suspect. Keep your head down, and your eyes well open — and, for God's sake, do nothing. Be ready to leave."

"But —"

Tom shook his head. "Off with you, now — and mind, do nothing."

The boy's nostrils flared mutinously — but he gave a half-hearted nod, and hastened away.

"Lord watch us," Tom sighed, and raised an eyebrow at Watson.

Watson shook a rueful head. "I know, I know — he's bright but... He has the sort of mind that will paint things in large strokes. Calls himself a poet."

"So do you," Tom pointed out. "And, young or not, were you ever this skip-brained?"

There was another grimace. "Still, he's no fool — and if this fellow died... Downes, was it? And Baines made threats. Told the Thibauds."

"Told half of Rheims, it seems."

"You reckon he could have done it?"

"I reckon we'd better find him," Tom said. "And ask Madame Jory if she's ever heard of this Downes."

The Mass was over by then, the faithful flocking away along the sun-chequered nave, and not a soul raised an eyebrow when two men joined their loose ranks — which went to prove that Thibaud's way of doing things was a good one.

It stood to reason that, if Baines was keeping an eye on both Allen's people and Thibaud's house, he must have some place or other where he kept watch, both at the Marché à la Laine and by the college. It also stood to reason that the scarecrow Blandine and Marley described would not go entirely unnoted.

"Ergo," Tom concluded as they picked their way along a muddy alley, "there are places where we can seek him, and people we can ask."

And to his own ears he sounded pedantical and officious, and oh, how Watson would have teased him in their Paris days. This other Watson, though, this fellow who called Tom *Mr. Secretary's boy* to strangers, just nodded with a wary cheerfulness to set one's teeth on edge, and asked where would they begin.

Since it was close, they began at Saint-Étienne, little use as it was bound to be, for Baines had no reason to go there, except to spy on the men from the college — who in turn had no reason to go there but for their Sunday worship. Still, the man could hardly spend all his days around the college without being noticed at some time — and, if he truly was reduced to begging, the vicinity of a church was a more likely place. Especially one by a square where the citizens of Rheims bustled all day about their pious or worldly affairs.

But Tom didn't truly expect to find Baines there — and was not overly disappointed when he didn't. Or, at least, he didn't see him, much as he studied the Place de Saint-Pierre, with its well-tended trees. But the fact remained that, here or elsewhere, Baines could be hiding and watching — unseen.

The same thoughts must have held Watson in play, for, as they made their way along the Rue des Anglais — by which the college and Saint-Étienne were in easy reach of each other, he expressed a wish that Baines were a madman of the witless sort.

"But I have my doubts of it, for it occurred to me that, if he riddled out Kit by seeing him at Thibaud's door…"

"He may have done the same with us, ay." Tom gave a small skewed smile. "Well, if either of us tumbles down the stairs at the Fleur-de-Lys to lie in a blue-faced heap, the other will know that your friend Kit is right."

There was a flash in Watson's eyes that could have been guilt or vexation, and he shook his head. "What he said," he sighed, "I never… Oh, Hades seize it, Tityrus! We all know that you're the son Sir Francis never had — that's all I ever —"

Oh, this now — this! Tom bit down a bitter laugh — and should have bitten down the bitter words with it, but… "Is it?" he snapped. "Why, then you have it wrong. Sidney is the one you mean — not I."

Sir Philip Sidney — Sir Francis's son-in-law and friend, knight, soldier, courtier, diplomat and scholar, whom Tom couldn't help but grudgingly admire, much as he would rather do otherwise, and who had no discernible fault, other than ignoring his clever wife, Tom's Cousin Frances. And who, most surely, would never go and expose his own petty, childish, ill-advised jealousies — if he had any, and why should he, being all that he was?

"I reckoned you must be friends with..." Watson blurted, round-eyed, and then, for a mercy, clamped his mouth shut.

Not that Tom was of a mind for prizing mercies.

"Come now," he ordered. "And keep your eyes well open." And, as though he hadn't made enough of a fool of himself, he strode away, disregarding his own counsel and leaving Watson to follow if he cared.

He slowed down soon enough, though, watching for beggars, and seeing very few. Was it the time of day, or were they all afraid of the archers? Of those few, most could be, at a first glance, the mad-eyed starveling that Blandine Jory had described, and one of them was youngish, and all of them were so dirty that any mark would be lost under the grime. And in truth, beyond the words of three harlots and an overeager poet — all more spiteful guessing than fact — there was no certainty that the man begged in the streets. Why, perhaps he sold some manner of wares at corners, or earned a few sols as a servant, for he must eat somehow — ergo all peddlers and servants were to be observed.

Needles and haystacks, indeed, and every chance that needles were all very much alike, and the Mass at Saint-Étienne was still four days away — supposing the truce held that long.

Tom stopped at the corner of the small square. The Collège Anglais was well in sight from there, with a stone escutcheon carved atop the lintel of the black gate. Nobody showed at the windows. Passers-by went about their errands — citizens and vendors, priests and cartmen, and women always in twos or threes, unless they were escorted. This was one thing: women didn't go about alone in war-threatened Rheims, and men had a circumspect briskness in their step. Only the urchins showed no care, darting this way and that, splashing in the rain-swollen tracks of endless wheels. Child, man or woman, though, no one had a look to spare for the Collège Anglais. The eve's burst of violence might well have happened a thousand miles away, and the death of Hugh Downes, either by illness or murder, might never have happened at all.

Also, as far as Tom could see, either up towards Saint-Étienne or down towards the city walls and the river, there were no beggars in the Rue des Anglais.

There was, however, a painted sign next door to the college, a gaudy thing depicting a yellow beast that might bear some resemblance to a goat. Could that not be a fine place to keep an eye on the college…?

Watson was observing the sign in turn.

"Perhaps…" he murmured.

Tom nodded. "Perhaps."

The Chevreau d'Or, it turned out, was not a tavern but a stabling — with a long, narrow yard dotted with puddles separated from the college by a wall. Tom was considering the gnarled fig tree that grew close to the wall when a black-bearded man in an apron hastened across the yard, calling, "Messieurs?"

"And wouldn't it be lovely if Baines knew about horses?" Watson asked under his breath.

"Let's find out," said Tom, just as the bearded fellow reached them.

He looked to be of an age with Watson. A farrier, reckoning by the leather apron, and the leathery cheeks of one who spent his days bent over a fire.

"What will you want, Messieurs?" he asked.

"You hire out horses?" Tom asked. Which, together with the morning's conversation at La Belle aux Pommes, was going to make for an expenseful day — but then...

Knowledge, Thomas, is never too dear, had been one of Sir Francis's first instructions, back in Tom's early days — and a very useful one.

Supposing that the farrier complied — which seemed none too certain. For a while he studied these possible customers head to toe, sucking his teeth with eyes narrowed and soot-stained brow knitted. Anyone who saw him would think Tom had asked for his daughter's hand in marriage, rather than a horse for hire.

"You'll have to see my brother for that," the fellow announced at length, and led the way across the long yard, calling aloud for Pierre. A boy with a pitchfork, far too young to be the farrier's brother, threw open one half of a double door at the yard's far end, nodded, and disappeared again into the gloom of what must be the stables proper.

"One good horse," Tom said, "for one day, or perhaps —"

Before he could explain further, another, equally black-bearded man appeared. The farrier went to meet him, muttering at some length.

"Foreigners," Watson murmured. "English! Don't like the look of them, *mon frère*. Can't trust the English. Eat hired horses, the English do..."

Which was likely a shrewd guess. But Pierre must have been of a less mistrusting disposition — or perhaps a greedier one — for he dismissed his brother's mutterings with a shrug, and stepped around him to meet the two dangerous foreigners with a ready smile.

"Hire a horse, would you, Messieurs?" he called. "Couldn't have found better. The finest horses in Rheims, we have. Come and see for yourselves."

And he led the way to the stables, showing great cheer in contrast to his scowling brother — Vulcan and Bacchus tending to French nags.

Still singing the praises of his beasts, the fellow ushered his customers into the stables. And the finest horses of Rheims they might be — although Pierre's enthusiasm seemed somewhat over-liberal — but there were precious few of them. This perhaps explained the man's disregard of his brother's misgivings: war, or even the threat of it, harmed the business of stabling just as it did any other.

"One horse, you said?" Pierre went to stroke the white face of a sturdy roan. "This is Dragon. Strong, good-tempered, and a good galloper at need…"

"He will do," Tom said, and, as Pierre waxed poetical about his gelding's many virtues, he paced down the length of the stable, fair-sized but uninhabited.

"You look at my empty stalls, Monsieur?" Pierre asked, as he unlatched the half door and coaxed out the placid-looking Dragon. "Ah, but these are unchancy times! Those who could leave Rheims, have done so — gone to the country with their horses and carriages. A mistake, if you ask me — for we have walls here, and soldiers, but out in the country, what have you, I ask?"

In truth, Tom had no interest at all in the empty stalls, and very little in the horses — but he had much in whatever two-footed animals may be inhabiting the place. So far he'd only seen the two brothers and the boy with the pitchfork, who was now amassing hay at the stable's far end. And certainly, the business didn't look brisk enough to require another groom.

"But is there anything you seek, Monsieur?"

Tom turned to find Pierre behind him, his cheerfulness shadowed.

"We have other horses, if you don't like Dragon — poor Dragon!"

And to hear him, one'd think Dragon must take offence at being discarded, and perhaps fall into a melancholy for it.

"Oh no, Dragon will do." Tom looked the fellow square in the face. "I was told that all your horses are excellent. A man I used to know in England told me. Sang such praises of your beasts... Perhaps you'll know him: Dickon Baines."

Faces, Thomas, speak as much as tongues.

Right now, the stable-keeper's face spoke very clearly of deepest mistrust, making him look much like his brother.

"I don't know anyone of that name," he said. "Why do you ask?"

"Oh, nothing but curiosity." Tom took his most innocent air. "It must be true that abroad one seeks his likes — so it came to me to wonder about my friend is all. You don't object, do you?"

But perhaps Pierre was more of his brother's brother than he affected, or perhaps all French stable-keepers were suspicious in their hearts. Or else, there was a chance that the fellow knew Baines and meant to protect him, for he nodded, slow and glum.

"These days, Monsieur, I take objection to everything and all — and so do the archers. If I were an Englishman, and thank *le Bon Dieu* I'm not, I wouldn't go about Rheims with a curious tongue in my head." He squinted past Tom's shoulder, to the open door where Watson stood. "And it is growing late now.

We close at this hour. Come back tomorrow, Monsieur, if you really want a horse."

Of which, it was plain as daylight, good Pierre had his doubts.

Ludicrous as it was, there was no use in pressing. Pierre shouted for the boy to return Dragon to his stall, and escorted the unwelcome visitors to the gate himself. The farrier emerged from his forge to keep a watchful eye on this ejection, and without ceremony Tom and Watson found themselves in the street, the gate of the Chevreau d'Or slamming shut on their heels.

"Well, well," Watson tutted. "What have you done, vilified that poor Dragon?"

"I doubt I showed rapture enough to content our Pierre — but no: 'twas when I asked of Baines that he lost all his cheer."

On hearing the tale, Watson whistled and glanced over his shoulder at the shuttered gate. "You think he's there, then? A pity you didn't take Dragon, after all. We could have gone back tomorrow —"

"And found neither hide nor hair of Baines — if he ever was there." Tom bit down on the flare of irritation. "Would you keep him under your roof, knowing those who seek him will return?"

"We can hardly storm the place and tear it down. Perhaps they count on that."

"I don't know..." Tom shook his head and watched the sky over the tiled roofs. It was darkening again. "They sounded less than fond of the English."

Watson snorted. "What, here in Rheims — not fond of us? *Mirabile dictu*! Still..."

"Still, Madame Jory can send her husband to the Chevreau d'Or when he returns. He'll find some business to discuss with

Pierre — and, as he does, rail against the English and see what comes of it."

Little enough, in truth, and of doubtful use, and likely to be too late by the time Jory returned.

The bells of the cathedral began to strike four, and Saint-Étienne answered, and what must be Saint-Symphorien, and then more churches all around. Swallows and sparrows took flight, circling in the sonorous sky. Did each call of the bells frighten the birds the way the rumours of war frightened men — no matter how accustomed they ought to be?

Fanciful thoughts, from which Tom shook himself. There was another sign across the street, a few doors down, depicting a pig's head. "I'd wager that's a tavern, down there — and I'm famished."

A tavern it was, and since they'd gone dinnerless, it was good to sit down with bread and cold meat, and a jug of decent wine. Good and opportune, since the common room's window offered a good view of the college. But discreet questioning bore no better fruit than it had at the stable. Not that the young waiter dared to throw them out, but he lost all loquacity behind a low-eyed, pinch-lipped mask — wariness personified.

And the same happened in a nearby bookseller's shop, and then a few doors up, where Watson pretended to a broom-wielding servant to have dropped a ring in the mud. And with each rebuff, Tom's particular suspicion of the men at the Chevreau d'Or abated.

"They can't all be sheltering Baines, can they?" he asked, after a very demure little servant-maid with a basket all but ran from them. "No, that jolly Pierre is right: in Rheims it doesn't pay to have a curious tongue in an English head."

Which, in truth, meant all but nothing — or, worse, it meant one thing.

"We'll never find him, if you ask me," Watson sighed — and small blame to him.

Only…

When you are in command, Thomas, it is your duty to comfort the doubt of others, and never vent your own.

And, being in command, Tom could only square his shoulders and play as resolute as he knew, as he said there was still the Marché à la Laine tomorrow. He then directed his steps back to the *auberge*.

CHAPTER 5

Head low and shoulders hunched against the beginning of another squall, Tom was deep in thought as he reached the door of the Fleur-de-Lys. Deep in thought of Hugh Downes, of his death, and of the questions he had not asked of Christopher Marley. And, in fair truth, also of Baines and his murderish boasts.

As he crossed the *auberge*'s threshold, something made him blink out of his musings.

A voice.

An Englishman's voice, shouting in barbarous French — and, in between bursts, the retorts of Madame Raulet.

Across the sparingly lit hall, the landlady stood, waving a wooden spoon under a man's nose.

"I ain't coming back later none, Mistress," the Englishman bawled. "And if you wasn't a woman…"

And, for all the world…

Watson laughed aloud. "If it isn't the Faithful Dolius! You taught him French, then!"

Which was greatly to exaggerate the case — for few would call what the fellow spoke French — but there was no doubt, no doubt at all, that there, arguing with a fiery-eyed Madame Raulet, stood Nicholas Skeres: Sir Francis's servant, and sometimes Tom's own.

"Skeres!" Tom called, stepping forth with a mind to quell the hubbub.

Skeres turned, and his minotaurish face, scarlet with outrage and the effort of making himself understood, broke into a large grin. "Master!" he bellowed, and then turned back to Madame

Raulet. "See?" he shouted in English. "See? This is Master Tom! Told you 'e was 'ere."

And, because the landlady, having caught little of the speech, seemed inclined to take offence, he raised his voice yet louder. "MY MASTER, SEE? MAS-TER ROW-LAND —"

"Quiet, Skeres!" Tom ordered, greatly relieved that the lad had not been throwing about the wrong name. Having obtained some sort of grumbling silence, he proceeded to offer both explanations and apologies to Madame Raulet — and how like Skeres that, in spite of understanding little enough, he kept trying to interfere, nodding knowingly and blaming all that was wrong on the landlady, the inn's folk, every soul in Rheims, and the whole of France.

It was a mercy when Watson stepped in, and Tom could leave him to placate the woman, grab Skeres by the arm, and drag him towards the stairs.

"Must you make such a noise?" he hissed.

And see how the Minotaur looked away, and pouted. "Confounded woman said you weren't 'ere, and I must come back again. But the girl at the shop said the Floor Delice, and—"

Oh, Lord give patience... "Yes, yes, never mind. But what the devil are you doing here at all?"

Skeres opened his mouth to answer, and then closed it in thin-lipped enmity, eyes hardening as they fixed on something behind Tom's shoulder.

And Tom turned to find Watson coming to join them, eyes alight with laughter.

"You very nearly talked us all out of supper, bed and roof, Faithful Dolius."

One didn't expect Skeres to join in with laughter at his own expense — but such a hostile glower!

72

"'Tis Master Barnege, Skeres, you remember him," Tom prompted, only eliciting a grunt. "When did you leave London?"

"Day after you did, late-ish." The Minotaur offered this information with far more truculence than it deserved. "Thought to catch up — but no, you must go as an 'are."

"Had I known you were following…" And then Tom let it go, for Nature had apparelled Nick Skeres with Achilles's own armour, when it came to sarcasm. "Well, you've caught up now. So what is it?"

"Day after you left, there was…" the lad began in the hurling that passed for a whisper with him — only to fall to scowling silence when Tom and Watson shushed him as one.

And sure enough, when Tom turned, there they were: the Raulets, hugging each a jamb of the kitchen door to eavesdrop. The husband disappeared on finding himself caught; the wife did not. In fact, she stepped forward, still brandishing her spoon.

"Monsieur Roland," she began, "I told your friend —"

"Yes, Madame — yes," Tom interrupted — for eavesdroppers surely deserved no manners. "I'm sorry for all the clamour. This man is my servant, and he'll sleep in my room. A pallet will do. Now we'll go upstairs, and I'll thank you for some supper for us all."

And, without waiting for the landlady's answer, he marched his little troop up the stairs.

"And I call it rank unfair that she'll take it from you and not from me!" Watson murmured under his breath. "Is it the blue eyes, do you reckon?"

Tom called him a zany, marvelling when no thunderous snort came from Skeres, and then he stopped just short of the gallery — one hand on the newel post, the other raised in warning. For their door, just at the head of the stairs, should have been closed — and instead stood ajar, thin yellow light glowing through the fissure.

For a heartbeat there was silence on both sides of the door — then…

"'Od rat it!" muttered Skeres — which sent whoever was in the room scurrying noisily.

And, there being no doubt left, Tom threw open the door and charged through, unsheathing his dagger, with Watson and Skeres on his heels.

"*Qui est là?*" he called, just as the intruder snuffed his candle. The room was plunged in the blue half-darkness of twilight, and all there was to see was a shadow, backing towards the window, where it showed against what light lingered outside.

Steel hissed as Watson and Skeres drew in turn, and the shadow raised something far too thick for a blade, and held the wrong way. A cudgel.

"Give up, Baines!" Tom ordered in English. "There's three of us — all armed."

And just as steps sounded running up the stairs, and voices called to know what was wrong, and the first fingers of candlelight slid through the open door — that's when this singularly witless burglar took it into his head to rush a whole crowd, howling and whirling his cudgel high over his head.

Tom raised his arm, shifting his grip to take the blow on the forte of his blade — but before he could, there was a bellow of "Master!" and he found himself thrust aside hard enough to crash backwards into the chair.

There was hammering, and growling, and a shrill cry to let go, and then the whole household burst through the door, Raulet bravely at his people's head, carrying a branch of candles and a stick.

"What's this, Monsieur Roland?" he demanded.

And what was this indeed! Tom disentangled himself from the upturned chair, sheathed his blade, and took stock. Skeres sat on the floor, an arm around the throat of a much smaller man. The hammering was made by the fellow's heels as he tried to free himself.

"*This* is, I think, a thief," Tom said — for whether this was true or not, whether it was something far worse, he'd find out for himself, and not in front of all these good people.

The landlord was moving his branch about, surveying the room's disarray, the upset chair, the open clothes-press, the papers strewn on the floor, and…

"We have no thieves at the Fleur-de-Lys," he had the cheek to say.

To which Tom burst out laughing, Skeres gave his most minotaurish snort, and Watson exclaimed: "And what do you call this fellow, then — one of the Three Kings?"

"Monsieur!" Madame Raulet pushed her way through the small crowd, stopping only to berate her husband in a quick hiss, and came to lay a hand on Tom's sleeve. "Oh, Monsieur Roland — what my husband means is, we're an honest house. Mother of God, Monsieur, you mustn't think we're one of those places where guests are robbed blind!"

"I think nothing of the sort, Madame," said Tom, and look at the doe-eyed gratefulness this woman could affect! "But still I'd like to know…" He turned to the two on the floor, and shifted to English. "Don't choke him Skeres, will you? Get him up."

There was some scuffling and cursing as Skeres climbed to his feet, dragging up his prisoner — who, with each whimper, sounded more French, and younger, and shriller, and not like Baines at all.

And, when Raulet came forward with his branch of candles, what must the light show, but the tear-stained, blotched, scowling face of Remi Roland?

Oh Good Lord! What Tom had done to deserve it all, he didn't know. Much to the landlady's round-mouthed disquiet, he cursed with a passion, in English and French, grabbing Remi's shoulder and shaking him.

At which, of course, the silly woman must grow motherly, and throw herself between them. "Monsieur, the poor child!" she cried. "Leave him be — you and your man!"

"No, I won't leave him be, if you please, Madame," Tom said through gritted teeth, and then to Remi, who was bristling at being called a child, "What do you think you're doing here, you confounded brat?"

It was the landlord's turn to push in the middle, gaping from Tom to young Remi, with all the air of one seeking to lay the blame at someone else's door. "You know the thief, Monsieur?"

"He is…" Tom took a deep breath through his nose, and let it out. *Unus. Duo. Tres…* All they lacked now — *all* they lacked was for Raulet to make a row, and call in the *Milice*. "He's not a thief. He's my cousin —"

"I'm not!" cried Remi, ending in a yelp when Skeres cuffed his head for him.

The audience murmured — and small blame to them, for truly, truly…

"Well, his half-sister is. And, relation of his family though I am, young Remi doesn't like me much, and thought he'd play an addle-headed prank —"

"It wasn't —" squeaked Remi.

"Quiet, you dunce!" Tom roared. "And wait until your sister hears of this!"

And whether it was Tom's sudden ferocity or the notion of Blandine's wrath, the boy was struck dumb at long last — and glory be. He deflated in Skeres's grip, and suddenly looked like the child Madame Raulet had wanted to defend.

Tom hadn't the slightest particle of charity to spare for him. On the other hand, he had a small and perplexed crowd to dismiss.

"So you see," he said, unleashing all his persuasion on the Raulets, "there was no theft after all. And you'll forgive us the commotion. I'm not very well blessed in my family, I fear…"

He'd seen Sir Francis use this manner of smiling, steely courtesy on Peers of the Realm, Privy Councillors, bishops, and foreign princes. Little wonder that it worked on this gaggle of French inn-folk. He left Watson to shepherd them out, and went to loom, arms crossed, over the boy.

It would have been too much, of course, to hope the little dunce was cowed for good. He stared back, all childish defiance — only to flinch when Tom uncrossed his arms.

Watson had talked the host out of his candle-branch and put it on the table, so that the room showed in all its disorder.

"I ought to cane you — and soundly!" Tom said, leaning over young Remi. "What is this all about?"

Behind him, Watson was moving around the room — trying to see, no doubt, what the boy may have filched or found.

"You'd like to know, eh?" the brat nodded with such smugness that Skeres gave him a good shake.

"You mind your manners!" he growled — and then, to Tom, "Do I trounce 'im, Master?"

"No, you don't," Tom said. For one thing, he didn't relish the notion of restoring a battered brother to Blandine Jory. And for another, there was one thing alone Remi might want to steal from his father's English partner. "I know what he was after, don't I, Remi?"

Across the room, where he knelt on the floor, Watson held up his paper-case. The ties were undone. In his other hand he held a handful of tightly written pages.

"You didn't want me to see them, did you?" Remi brayed, face alight with malice. "But I've found them, and now I know. I know everything!"

The cursed papers, showing that nothing had been changed between the Thibauds of Rheims and the Rolands of London, and therefore disproving Tom's disguise as a quarrelsome Thomas Roland…

"How did you read them?" Watson stood, waving the disordered pages. "They're in English."

Remi blinked, gawping at the papers. "I have English enough," he stammered. "My father had me learn, for I'm to run the business…"

Which was all fiddlesticks, and he couldn't have read the papers — or he would have known they were in French.

Tom smiled. "Well, if you know everything, then there's nothing more to tell, is there? Skeres, show young Maître Thibaud the door."

Seldom had the Minotaur obeyed an order with more zeal — or he would have, but Tom stopped him.

"No, wait. It's near dark." He fished for a coin and flicked it to Skeres, who caught it awkwardly, one-handed. "Have Raulet send someone to see him home."

This Remi must have liked the least, for he squawked as Skeres manhandled him through the door, cries fading down the stairs.

Tom shut the door and leant against it. Had he ever been this pestilent, even at fifteen?

"Too tender-hearted for your own good — that's what you are … ah!" Watson exclaimed in satisfaction at finding on the mantelpiece the unscathed flagon of wine and the glasses.

"Tender-hearted to that brat! But his sister wouldn't be happy to find him in gaol tomorrow morning."

Watson raised his eyes Heavenward in mock piousness as he poured for both. "And behold, O people of Rheims, how the fair Blandine strikes terror in unruly children and seasoned intelligencers alike," he murmured.

The clown. "*And* he's mad as a wasp now. If he runs into the *Milice* alone, there's no saying what trouble he can make."

"Amen to that." Watson raised his cup in a toast. "We don't lack trouble as it is." He sipped thoughtfully. "You called him Baines at one point."

Give up, Baines. There's three of us. But that had been before the whole household had barged through the door, hadn't it? "Let's hope nobody heard. This place is an Argus — but with a thousand ears."

"True of most inns," Watson mused. "We believe that Baines did murder, then?"

Did they? Did he? Tom looked down at his glass. In the candlelight the wine gleamed black as iron gall. "In truth, I don't know. Why would Baines kill, of all people, just this Downes?"

"If he meant to kill them all…"

"But only two fell ill, and one died. Why Downes? Was he around when Baines was caught? Did Baines blame him? Or did Downes die by chance, in someone else's place?"

"Allen's, perhaps? Allen one would understand. Why, Sir Francis himself…"

Tom raised a forefinger in mock admonition. "Ah, never! Sir Francis doesn't believe in making martyrs."

"While Baines, I'll wager you, doesn't know how to think that far ahead. And then there's the priest."

"Supposing that they all fell ill at the same time — which we don't know." Tom kicked half-heartedly at the upturned chair. "We know next to nothing — not even truly that there was murder done!"

With a sigh, Watson bent to right the chair, and sat in it. "Well, one thing we do know," he said, stretching his long legs before him. "Baines didn't slip in here to murder us both."

Yes, well — there was that. "And also that young Remi didn't see what he should not." Tom glanced up. "That was well played, Corydon."

And see how warily Watson smiled, wondering whether he was forgiven, surely. "Pot-headed brat! He doesn't know all the ill he's doing, I'll grant — but still … all the wits must have gone to the sister."

Tom smiled back, raising his cup in salute. "And behold, O people of Rheims, how the fair Blandine strikes with admiration all seasoned intelligencers…"

They laughed together at that, and there was barely time enough to mark how very much it felt like the old Paris days, before the door burst open and Skeres stood on the threshold, brow knotted in grim disapproval.

"Someday, Nick Skeres, someone will have to teach you to knock at doors. Someone else — for I surely failed."

Skeres didn't budge — nor did he try to excuse himself. "Stable groom wanted more to take the boy 'ome. 'Ad to fork out meself."

"How much?"

"Two solds."

"Sols," Tom corrected — more out of habit than hope — as he took the two small coins out of his purse. "Value his time, does he?"

"An honest trade, to get rid of young Remi," said Watson — and Skeres, as he collected his dues, scowled all the blacker.

Underlip jutting, he checked the two coins this way and that in the candlelight, buffed each in turn against his sleeve, and dropped them carefully into his purse — and all the time he never looked up, never said a word.

Tom waited until the purse was restored to the boot where the lad kept it for safety, and then, because nothing seemed to be forthcoming, he asked, "So, Dolius. Why the devil are you in Rheims?"

There was an unclenching of shoulders that could be relief or impatience released, and finally the lad looked up for a heartbeat — but not quite at Tom. It was a skewed glance, and a dance of the bushy yellow eyebrows, both directed Watson's way, in a manner that perhaps he imagined subtle. "Letter," he muttered out of the corner of his mouth.

And he four years a Service man! Not for the first time Tom wondered at the recruiting of Nick Skeres — and held out an impatient hand. "And can I have it, do you think?"

With the letter came more rolling of eyes Watson's way — so artless that Watson burst out laughing.

"Worry not, Dolius," he said, climbing to his feet. "I won't spy over your master's shoulder. Why, I'll go and sit on the stairs if you like."

With a huff, Tom broke the seal, unfolded the note, and angled it toward the branch of candles.

Dear son Thomas, it began — not quite coded, but couched in the guise of an innocent letter from Thomas Roland's mother. The supposed good lady hoped her son was well, and informed him that his sister's confinement was going as was to be expected — which meant there was no prospect yet of a continuation of the truce. Ah well, not that they'd really counted on it, and it was nothing to warrant its own letter, was it?

Tom's stomach clenched as he read on, seeking what had had Sir Francis dispatch Skeres in pursuit.

I pray that your business will let you be back before her time is due, the false Mistress Roland went on. And then: *We had word from my cousin in Hampstead.*

And what could be in a letter from Ambassador Stafford in Paris that concerned Tom so urgently?

He advises that your horse Corydon has grown ill-natured and untrustworthy.

Tom's heart sank, and it took all his restraint not to look up at Watson.

Corydon...

He hasn't thrown his rider yet — not that my cousin knows — but he plays tricks, and one of the grooms, a Scot, was bitten. It is my thought that an animal of such disposition should be sold before it causes harm to you or others.

Not a traitor, thank the Good Lord — at least not that. Or perhaps just not yet. And ... *he plays tricks*. What had the idiot done?

I know you are fond of the creature, and I regret that you must deal with this matter — but I fear that it cannot wait.

Slowly, Tom folded the letter, smoothing each crease between his fingernails.

"Have you seen to your horse, Skeres?" he asked.

"Ay, when I got 'ere —"

"Well, then, go and make sure they fed him. That groom must be back by now."

"But —"

"And see to it that they have it saddled and ready, first thing in the morning."

"Never sending me back, are you?"

"Mr. Barnege's gelding too."

"And yourn?"

"Just the two."

That Skeres made no other protest, had to be counted as a great wonder. Tom waited until the door closed behind the lad, and listened as the stairs creaked under the heavy steps, before looking up at Watson.

"What have you done, you fool?"

And there it was, crossing the dark, vivid face like clouds through a March sky: the impulse of lying, of laughing, of denying, of brazening it out... Oh, Tom had seen it often enough — and it was quick, but Tom knew the man well. He held the masked gaze and waited, until Watson looked away and nodded his chin at the folded letter.

"What does it say, that you should turn against me like this?"

And it could be wounded bitterness, or it could be an attempt to talk himself out of it. Or, in fair truth and this being Watson, it could be both.

"Stafford found out," was all Tom said.

"And he had to send to London, had he? Without even hearing me?"

Without hearing him, yes — because Watson, the player of tricks, had been away, off to join Tom first, and then headed for London. But still Watson had not been heard, so perhaps, perhaps...

"I'll hear you," said Tom.

"Will you!" Watson threw his glass in the empty hearth, where it smashed. "After all these years ... they could let me slip out quietly — but no! Kicked out, I must be — and of all men, Tityrus, of all men, it must be you!"

It did seem cruel. Tom swallowed the thought, and made himself wait without a word. It wasn't a long wait.

"Doesn't Mr. Secretary tell you?" Watson asked.

No. Not half of it. I want to hear it from you. Defend yourself, explain. "What have you done?"

An innocent man... What would an innocent man do? Not throw himself into the chair like a petulant child, surely? Not grouse that Tom needn't look that virtuous?

"You've lacked money yourself often enough, haven't you? But people will fall over themselves to give a gentleman all the leeway — especially..." *Especially when he bears the name you do*, he didn't say. "My kind ... we make do. There was this fellow — a witless popinjay if ever there was one — and how was I to know he was the Scottish ambassador's stepson?"

Here was the bitten Scottish groom, then — and look at the cheek of Watson, playing ill-used! Again, Tom waited.

Watson had never been good at this. "Lovat is a fool. He rifled through his stepfather's money-box — twice," he huffed. "And the second time he was caught at it, and by then it was too late."

"You never..." Tom's heart began to sink, for cards were forbidden in France, unless it was at Court — but there were exceptions. Unless... "Were you caught cheating?"

For the first time Watson looked ill at ease. He stood and went to the window. "It wasn't cards," he said, his back to the room. "I cozened him into backing a voyage to the Indies. And to make him trust me, I told him I was Stafford's man of business. And..." He lowered his voice so that Tom had to strain to hear. "And good friends with Mr. Secretary Walsingham's own cousin."

Tom exhaled slowly. *Good friends, ay. Oh, Corydon.* The man he used to trust, to look up to. *I regret that you must deal with this matter...* But he must nonetheless. Part expediency, part instruction, part trial, no doubt — for this was how Sir Francis tempered his men.

"When they caught young Lovat, who knows what he told his stepfather? That I was spying on him, that I tried to buy him, God knows what else — and it all came under Stafford's eyes. Ever since I found out who it was I'd cozened, I've been waiting..."

Watson was blathering now. Most of it likely enough, none of it of the least use — and he must have seen it for himself, for he fell quiet at length, head low and shoulders hunched. Waiting, indeed.

Few things will serve you better, Thomas, than an ability to make a judgment quickly and unwaveringly.

"You'll leave for London at dawn." For a mercy, Tom's voice stayed cold and even. "You'll go to Seething Lane. They'll pay you. Settle your expenses."

Watson blanched. "To Seething Lane —"

This took some work to ignore — the voice whispering that, in Watson's place, he would just want to fade away, never face a man from the Service again. Tom squared shoulders and voice. "You'll travel as Barnege."

"With your bully-rook to guard me? Where are you afraid I'd run?"

This, too, Tom ignored. "I want your courier's pass, and Stafford's packet."

Watson dithered, shifting his weight — too old a hand at couriering to betray where he held his papers by a gesture or a look — but Tom knew his friend's tricks.

Or did he, in truth? He'd thought so — but now...

"Don't make me take them, Watson. Please."

There was a long, dark, pleading look — then Watson sighed. He slumped on the bed, unclasped his eating knife, and began to unstitch the lining of his hat, enough to take out a paper pleated to a thin strip. Then there was his sleeve, and a pocket in the paper-case.

That all of them were familiar, came as a relief. A thin, stunted, most foolish relief.

It was not long before Tom pocketed the Ambassador's packet and two passports — Watson's own, and one that was to serve for Baines. "Is there anything else you're carrying?" he asked, and when Watson just shook his head, he left it at that. He should have asked about the Scottish popinjay's money, by right, but he didn't. Through his own doings, and deservedly though it was, Watson would be very soon out of wages.

Perhaps Watson saw through the omission, and resented it. "Do you know what I think, Mr. Walsingham?" he asked slowly. "Had it not been for you, had I not used your name, I wouldn't be paying the devil's own price for this bit of mummery!"

Had it not been for *him*...! Tom gaped, speechless at the impudence. Teach him to feel sorry for the man.

And just then, Fates be thanked, Skeres reappeared, sparing Tom the fight that was sure to ensue.

If Ovid's winged Sleep — or was it Virgil's? — visited Rheims that night, waving his branch dipped in the river of oblivion, he gave Tom a wide berth. Perhaps that mildest of the Gods meted out wakefulness as punishment to those who hardened their hearts against their friends? Then his justice was of a fickle quality for, by the sound of it, not only was Nick Skeres snoring away on his pallet — as well he should, being innocent — but also the culpable Watson, stretched in his chair, was breathing with the ease of untormented sleep.

And, because he didn't want to wonder how many witless popinjays had been cozened with the Walsingham name, Tom lay wide-eyed in the darkness and rehearsed the many things he didn't know about the death of Hugh Downes.

CHAPTER 6

The cheek of the French, when one thought about it! Ever complaining of the English rain — as though France were instead an Eden of endless sunny days — and here another day was rising grey and windy.

Out of charity with France, the French, and mankind in its entirety after a sleepless night, Tom waited in ill-humoured silence as the groom saddled the horses. Meanwhile, Nick Skeres kept an eye on Watson with such wary ferocity that, after a while, Tom beckoned to the lad and led the way to the yard. Skeres went to stand where he could watch the door.

"He isn't going to run, you know," Tom said.

Skeres only shrugged.

"It would take a madman to become a fugitive in the eyes of the Service. And besides, he'll want his wages."

"What for, if they give 'im more?"

"And who would *they* be?"

Skeres looked over one shoulder, then the other, like a villain at the play, then leant close to hiss in Tom's ear: "These cursed French, the Spaniards… Shiploads of gold, the Spaniards 'ave. What if they give some to your friend to loosen 'is tongue?"

What if they did? Would they try, once Watson was back in London? And if they did, would Watson take the bait? Yesterday Tom would have taken offence on his friend's behalf. It saddened him that all he had to say now was: "I doubt he knows much that's worth buying in Spanish gold."

"'E knows —" Skeres began, loud with impatience — and then, wonder of wonders, checked himself without having to be told. "'E knows who you are, for one thing, and what you're doing 'ere."

That, and — more worryingly — he knew of the Thibauds, and of Kit Marley at the college...

Oh, baggage — ugly, petty baggage! Had Tom not known the man long enough to still have this one certainty of him?

"He'd never do it. And you've no call to look all philosophical."

Skeres shrugged again — he did a good deal of that. "Ay, ay — you know 'im and I don't — but I tell you: if I could let 'im out of me sight, I'd stay 'ere — and no mistake." And see how wisely and knowingly he nodded...

"No, you would not," Tom snapped. "You'd follow your orders."

But it took more to meeken the Minotaur, who raised his hands more in patience than in submission. "Don't take it in snuff, Master. I'm going — and why you must stay, you'll know and I'm not asking. Still, going I am, for, say what you like, your friend's right madded, and what's to keep 'im from tattling on you to the first French soldier 'e finds, eh?"

"You are, Dolius — not that I believe he'd ever do it, mind."

"Oh, pittikins!" Skeres shook his head in disgust. "'E doesn't believe! You weren't born no fool, Mr. Tom — but bless you, sometimes you need watching like a newborn babe!"

Swallowing a huff of laughter, Tom slapped the lad's shoulder. "Why, thank you, Dolius! You make me almost sorry to see you go."

And see how he lit up. "You want me to stay, then?"

"No, I don't. Go see whether that fool of a groom has saddled himself by mistake, will you?" And, as the lad grumblingly obeyed, another thing occurred to Tom. A shout of *Master!* Followed by a mighty shove… "Dolius, when we found the boy upstairs last night, you pushed me out of the way…"

Stopping on the door, Skeres lowered his eyes to his rather black fingernails. "Didn't know 'twas a runt of a boy, did I? And you were going for 'im all but blind…"

And Tom found that, after all, he was truly rather sorry to see this faithful Minotaur go.

Once he had seen Skeres and Watson trot down the street in the grey light, and disappear around the corner, Tom took stock of his circumstances.

Three things he'd been sent to do: to look into Guillaume Thibaud's death; to find Baines and, if possible, return him to England; and to instruct Marley to learn how much of Mary Stuart's post went through the Collège Anglais.

Now it seemed that Thibaud's death had been nothing that it shouldn't be, and that Thibaud's daughter was more than capable of keeping up her father's work. With that set to rest, Tom rather wondered what good would come of instructing Marley — and there was still the conundrum of Baines. Now not only was the fellow nowhere to be found — but Kit Marley would have him a murderer. Now, the death of a Catholic student was no business of Tom's *per se*, and yet … what if it truly was Baines's doing? Or — and this was something of a new thought — could Downes's death be anything to do with the Scots Queen's letters?

Why you must stay, you'll know and I'm not asking, had grumbled Nick Skeres. Well, it seemed that Tom had still much to do in Rheims.

And since finding Baines was one thing, and securing another conversation with young Marley was another, Tom directed his steps towards the Rue Bûchette.

Nobody minded him, as he made his way through the morning crowd of sellers, priests, schoolchildren, monks, peddlers, and black-gowned students of the university. In his soft-crowned hat and sober travelling clothes, he could well be yet another citizen, staidly going about his business. It was when, in the proximity of the Marché à la Laine, he began to spy for his quarry that things changed. Just as in the Rue des Anglais, here too questions only earned tight-lipped glares. In one thing Watson had been right: after two years back in England, Tom's accent had gone astray, and most of those he addressed knew him for a foreigner — and worse, an Englishman.

Had Watson been there still, Tom could have had him do the talking — for all that, much as he liked to jest about it, his accent had never been quite as good. But there would never be any jesting with Watson again — over Tom's French or anything else.

Oh, Tartarus seize it! Tom shook himself. Fancies and melancholies. A season, Watson had called the Paris days. A season, come and gone.

Off he set again, exploring every street, courtyard and alley that might let a man keep an eye on the Thibauds' house. It was a good while before, at long last, a pair of elderly lace-makers remembered a yellow-haired man who spoke very poor French, and loitered about as no honest man should. And yes, Monsieur, he'd been around just the other day, hadn't he? Or was it the day before? But certainly not before that, for the sisters' pet cat had not given birth yet... Tom sat in the small shop with the two ladies who, unlike their fellow-citizens, had no qualms about talking as they worked at their lace, wax-white fingers never once slowing. He wouldn't have sworn on the sharpness of their pale eyes, and they seemed keener than he liked on egging each other on — but Tom had learnt from Mr. Secretary himself the art of teasing out his answers piecemeal, and of sifting truth from lie and from delusion. By the time he took his leave of the amiable sisters Maubin, he had little doubt that the yellow-haired man was Baines, still haunting the Thibauds within the last three days.

It wasn't much, but it was something at last, and it gave substance to Tom's notion that the fellow used at least a few perches in his watching. And on the strength of that, one could allow himself some late dinner.

Rheims was too provincial a town to boast what in Paris they called *cabarets*, places where customers sat at a table, and ate and drank much in the way you did at a fine inn in London. Paris was a-swarm with these new-fangled places. Here, for the most part, if you had a thirst, you bought a pot of wine in a *taverne*; if you had an appetite, you might find yourself a *rôtisserie* — and so did Tom, not far from the square tower of Saint-Hilaire, just as the bells chimed two.

It was late enough that all they'd give him was a thick slice of *pâté en croûte* — the crust having grown rather soggy since the halcyon hour of its baking, but still savoury enough. Here too he tried, over his wine, a few cautious inquiries with the *rôtissier*'s boy — only to find this greedy-minded youth would say nothing unpaid, and, if vailed, anything he thought would please.

So it was fortified in body and cynical in mind that Tom took to the street again, under yet another fall of rain. It was light and lukewarm, for once, the right sort for late May — the sort that, in the Kentish countryside, would carry a green scent of summer. It was less pleasant between walls, thickening the air with dampness, rotting greens, and piss — but it fell softly enough, and Tom didn't mind it as he walked back towards the Rue Bûchette, considering what to do next.

And next was either more of the morning's search, or a visit to Blandine Jory for more yellow roses to lay at the Virgin's feet. He was reckoning how long it would take him to do both of these things — and in what order — when he caught something at the corner of his eye. A flash of dark movement that was gone the moment he turned. And perhaps he had been wrong — or perhaps not…

There wasn't much of a crowd in this particular street — two youths carrying a cask between them, a grey-habited monk, and a schoolboy with a satchel and the air of playing truant. Tom stopped in front of a tailor's shop — more a mender than a maker of clothes by the look of it — and made a pretence of peering inside. Nothing showed at first — but then the tailor came to his threshold, offering his services. And while the fellow chattered away … there! There it was. A manner of carrying the shoulders, the tense awkwardness of one ready to bolt… Not a very good watcher.

Tom thanked the tailor and moved along. Had he been prone to fancies, he would have said he could feel the pursuer's eyes on himself as he picked his way among the dirty puddles. He swerved out of the way of a hasty servant-girl, and there it was again — or was it?

Ah well, there was one way to know: a narrow alley yawned a few paces ahead, and down that Tom plunged. It was little more than a passage, gloomy and ill-smelling, so rutted in its centre that rainwater and ordure pooled ankle-deep. It was also deserted — bless the Fates — and, a dozen yards ahead, it crooked in a sharp bend.

Flattening against the wall just past the corner, with dagger drawn, was the matter of an eye-blink. To keep splashing his boots was something Tom had heard once from an older Service man — and half believed a jest. Well, a jest it might have been — but it worked: hear the fellow's steps enter the alley, waver a heartbeat, then pick up again with an effort at stealth. Tom slowed his pretend march and stopped. There were steps, a shadow reflected in the disturbed water of the runnel — and hard breathing, closer and closer.

Tom grabbed the man by the front just as he turned around the bend, and spun him in a half circle to pin him against the wall, hand to throat, dagger point under the chin.

"Shall we have a quiet word?" he asked in French — and took a good look.

Haggard, all arms and legs, the man pressed against the wall, squirming away from Tom's blade. The hair that hung limp under a ragged cap would perhaps look straw-coloured once washed, and the mouth worked in an ill-shaven face, all knobs and hollows, marked by a burn scar on the left side of the jaw. Close enough to Blandine's description that Tom shifted to English.

"And for one thing, Richard Baines, I want —"

The man gave a snarl and flailed, and nicked himself on the chin before Tom could draw back.

"Stop, you lack-wit!" Tom caught again the man's front, hard enough that something tore in the worn doublet.

Baines went quiet of a sudden, touched the cut on his chin, and gawped at the bloodstained fingers in such puzzled fear that...

"'Tis a scratch," Tom found himself saying. "You won't die of it."

For the first time, Baines took a good look at the man who'd caught him. "How many spies must Allen send?" he asked hoarsely.

Allen? Tom shook his head. "I'm sent from London."

"London…" Baines murmured, as though a name once heard and half forgotten.

"London, ay — where you should be. Or anywhere you like in England. In fact, anywhere but here."

And see how the man strained again against Tom's grip. "Thibaud, was it?" he hissed. "'Twas Thibaud that tattled on me! The cursed, poxy capon — Lord rot him, I'll kill him, I'll—" and then his face crumpled, and he turned away, sagging against the wall and crossing himself. "*Parce mihi Domine,*" he muttered again and again. "*Parce mihi…*"

Both poor Thibaud and Lison had been right: Dickon Baines did not run on an even keel. And yet…

I'll kill him…

"The Lord may forgive you — or he may not — but kill Thibaud you won't."

Baines looked up, an ugly spark of half-hope, half-terror in the sunken eyes. "He's dead?"

"Has been these four weeks past — as you should know, since you've been stalking his house."

And there the madman went again — bursting into laughter. "*Dabit Dominus inimicos tuos…*" he chortled breathlessly. "*Deus confringet capita perambulantium in delictis suis…*"

Madman indeed … Bedlam mad. Tom suppressed a shiver. "And just how does the Lord smite your enemies?" He gave the man a good shake — and lo! Baines looked back, sane-eyed and smiling.

"Told that unchristian daughter," he explained, all reason and mildness. "You persist in sin, the Lord will crack your proud head."

"And you do the Lord's work yourself, sometimes? Not Thibaud, for he died of a lung fever — but Allen and his people at the college —"

Before he knew it, Tom was on his back in the runnel, the dagger flying from his hand, Baines leaping away... He twisted to reach for the man's ankle — and Baines trod on his hand in a skewed step before he went sprawling.

With a savage curse, Tom threw himself on the fugitive, landing in an awkward heap. "Thank your stars that *I* found you, and not —" He gritted his teeth and went no further, when a knee buried itself in his stomach. Curled on his side, gasping for breath, all he could do was curse some more as he watched Baines scramble towards the alley's mouth and disappear. There. So he would be laughed out of the Service for a dunce, and later go to Hell for a blasphemer, no doubt — and, worst of all, what would Sir Francis think?

Tom climbed to his feet, hissing in pain when he tried to brace himself on his trampled hand. Just as he staggered, in search of his dagger, someone entered the alley at a run. Baines, perhaps, back to help the Lord smite another foe of his?

It wasn't Baines.

It was a tall, red-bearded man, who studied Tom from head to toe, reached towards him and then stopped, looking uncertain.

"Are you well?" he asked — and, while he spoke in French, there was no mistaking the English colour of his words.

What had that soldier said, of Rheims being lousy with the English? *Can't throw a stone but you hit one of them*, he'd said — and it seemed that he hadn't been wrong. What with that and the scuffle with Baines, Tom very nearly burst out laughing in the man's face. *Ay, let him think you are the Bedlamite, for good measure!*

"Yes — yes, thank you," he managed, with as much dignified civility as a man could muster while covered in mud and rotting lettuce. "I think…" He looked around, caught sight of his dagger, and went to retrieve it. When he bent to pick it up, and wavered, he found himself steadied by a firm hand.

The stranger raised an eyebrow — but, for a mercy, didn't remark on Tom's unsteadiness. "A fellow Englishman!" he said instead. "Were you robbed?"

Tom patted his girdle — where he never carried his purse. One didn't live long by trusting Samaritans — no matter how solicitous and gentlemanly dressed. "I was warned against French cut-purses — but not half enough, it seems." A grimace, a shake of the head. "Ah well, I thank you, Sir, for coming to my rescue."

The rueful chuckle was of the sort one likes in a friend, and drew laughter lines in the man's face. "Why, it seems to me that you rescued yourself. That fellow shot out of the alley, all bloodstained, looking for all the world like a fleeing murderer. You see that I had to make certain…" He frowned again. "But are you sure he was a cut-purse? I've never seen one use such violence…"

No fool, this one. Tom shook his head in his best bemused manner. "Ay, well, this isn't England. Who knows what's in these heathens' heads?"

"True, true…" The man bent to retrieve Tom's hat, and held it by the brim. "I wouldn't wear it, in your place," he said.

No — nor the doublet, if Tom could choose. His good travelling doublet! Teach him to lay his ambuscades in filthy alleys. Still he smiled at the stranger, and gingerly took back the hat. "Not until it's sponged and dried and brushed," he said.

"If nothing else, French inns have decent servants," was the answer, and with it came another of those searching frowns. "But … are you injured? I should see you to your inn, I think. Is it far?"

And there it went — something so minute it was hard to name. Was it really a sharpening of all this eager solicitude? Perhaps it was true that a suspecting mind found all suspicious — but still…

There is less danger, Thomas, in fearing too much than fearing too little.

"Oh no, I'm quite well — and I'd better be about my business." *And you about yours.* "But I'm very much in your debt, Sir." Tom took a small bow — and there was the awkwardness of neither offering, nor asking for names.

Or there would have been — but this most courteous of Samaritans just bowed back, not put out in the least.

"Not at all, Sir. Not at all." And was it a touch of amusement that glinted in the grey eyes?

And that was why, once on the street again, Tom didn't turn his steps towards the Rue Bûchette. And since, by the same token, he'd rather not go back to the Fleur-de-Lys, he took a different direction.

At least it had stopped raining.

Redbeard, if he was following, was much better than Baines at the game. There were no suspicious movements, no awkwardly poised watchers. Which was all the more reason to walk to the Porte-aux-Ferrons, and from there to the Marché au Blé, where Tom remembered seeing a couple of large *auberges*. He plunged into the first he found, at the sign of the stag, and was glad to find it a busy Post inn. The hall had a fire roaring in the hearth, and men sat on benches in twos and threes, drinking, or waiting, or eating. Now let them all just ignore him long enough… But no, of course. Down the stairs bustled a young woman in a blue kirtle. A very pretty young woman she was, and any other day Tom might have wished all those old stories of the host's daughter welcoming the guest with a kiss were true. Right now, he could have done without the attention.

Monsieur was most welcome, and would Monsieur be wanting a room? But … oh! (And see how she brought her hand to her ripe-cherry mouth!) What had happened to Monsieur?

As bitterly, as pitifully, as feelingly as he could, Tom explained that yes, he'd been set upon and robbed, and now he was seeking a friend of his here at the *Grand Cerf*. Would Mademoiselle please have Monsieur such and such fetched? And he gave a made-up name that threw the young woman into some confusion, because she did not think… Tom gave another name — that of his counterfeited friend's equally counterfeited travelling companion. The woman pouted, beckoned a servant-man and sent him to fetch her father.

"But, Monsieur, the war!" she explained as they waited, leaning forward a little breathlessly. "There is this truce — but the Good Lord knows. Perhaps the soldiers stopped your friends… Ah, but here comes *mon père*. He'll know."

Of course, the *père* had never heard of either traveller, and had no great amount of charity to spare for mire-covered Englishmen — at least not until his daughter begged him to hear what had befallen *ce pauvre jeune homme*! So there was nothing for it but to repeat the whole rigmarole of robbery and missing friends, and then the host began to bemoan the ills of war just like his daughter had done. And all the time Tom kept an eye on the door and windows, and what he could see of the market square through them.

Of Redbeard, if he had followed, there was neither hide nor hair.

When the host came to the end of his lamentations, Tom gave a mournful shake of the head, and looked about himself like one at a loss. "Then I don't know…" he sighed.

It was enough to move the young woman, if not her father: the host might have been less hospitable, but his daughter, who clearly led him around at her will, sat Tom on a bench near the fire with a pot of wine, all the time cooing that perhaps Monsieur's friends would arrive yet.

Tom drank the good claret, and waited long enough for Redbeard — if he was watching — to decide that his quarry lodged at the *Grand Cerf*. Then, as soon as neither father nor daughter were in sight, he left his bench — finding himself rather stiff and sore — and sneaked out through a back door.

The sky had cleared by then, and the afternoon was lighter.

As obliquely as he knew without getting lost, Tom made his way back to Thibaud's house at the Brebis-qui-File and knocked at the door, hoping that anyone but Remi would answer.

It was the servant Perrette, in the end, looking uncertain, until she took a good look at the visitor. "Monsieur!" she exclaimed, round-eyed. "Come in, come in — I'll fetch M'zelle…" She dragged him into the hallway and, chewing her bottom lip in some perplexity, went to knock at the small parlour's door.

It was a moment before the door was thrust open just a hand-span, with enough force to make Perrette jump back.

A scowling Blandine Jory peered out. "I told you —" she began and then, over the servant's shoulder, she caught sight of Tom — and gaped.

Oh, but he must look a fright...

"Help and deliver us!" Squinting in the hall's greyish light, Blandine took her supposed kinsman by the sleeve. "What have you done now?"

And wasn't this the rankest unfairness — as though it must of necessity be his fault!

Before Tom could protest, Blandine was already acting. She had Perrette take his doublet and hat, for sponging and brushing, and dragged Tom himself into the parlour.

"It's good that you're here," she said. "I was about to send for you."

And, as she closed the door, a man leapt up from the table.

"God's shirt — here you are!" he blurted in great agitation. It was Christopher Marley. He strode around the table like a charging lion, shoving aside a chair. "What have you done with Watson?"

"*Barnege*," Tom amended, not looking at Blandine. "And he—"

In the middle of waving the correction aside, Marley stopped short and stared. "What happened to you?" he asked, in a manner that had Tom raise a hand to his own face.

He hissed, finding that the hand hurt, and the cheekbone hurt even more. A madman's strength, it seemed, was no figure of speech. "Baines happened," he said.

Both Marley and Blandine exclaimed.

"You found him?" she asked, her whisper rising to a squeak.

"Yes..." Tom struggled a little — and honesty won. "Or at least, he found *me*."

Blandine Jory took a sharp breath, and Marley looked at her in triumph before turning to Tom.

"Then you're lucky to be alive," he said. "For Baines just did murder again."

"How the devil do you mean? Begging your pardon, Madame Jory."

Marley breathed through flaring nostrils. "I mean," he ground out, "that there's a man dead in Allen's pantry. Poisoned."

"Oh, Saints help — tell it the way it is!" Blandine swatted the lad's arm before turning to Tom. "He knows naught of poison."

"Well, Downes was poisoned, wasn't he? And Thibaud, and now this one —"

Tom and Blandine both shushed him.

"My father wasn't poisoned, I tell you!" she hissed.

And because Marley was ready to explode, Tom held up a silencing hand.

"He wasn't — and of Downes we don't know. As for this other ... who is it? Not Allen, I'd imagine. This priest, you said — the one who fell ill?"

"Of course not! It's Fettiplace!"

As though only Fettiplace could lie dead in the pantry — a fact only ignored by the very dim.

Unus ... duo ... tres...

"And, out of your goodness, who would Fettiplace be?"

To his credit, the lad checked himself. He turned away, burying his chin in his own shoulder. "Ay — well. You know Sir Francis Yates?"

"Yates of Buckland — recusant among recusants? I thought he was in prison."

"Well, his son is not. A boy of twenty, not very sharp-witted…" A shrug. "Zachariah Fettiplace was young Yates's man — and now he's dead."

"Baggage!" Tom frowned. Knowing themselves spied, some of the exiles rechristened themselves even within the doubtful safety of the college walls — and surely, one whose family was so notorious… "Yates's son is never here under his own name?"

A shake of the head. "Just passing through. Kept Easter with Allen — said his father would like that — and left after a couple of days."

"Leaving his servant behind?"

"Fettiplace came back late this morning, they say, and now—"

"Why did he come back?"

What stores of patience Marley owned were running thin. "How do I know? But can't you see?" He leant on the table with both hands splayed. "Once back in Rheims, he must have fallen in with Baines, and Baines must have told him what he told me — and then Fettiplace ran to warn Allen —"

"Did he?" Tom asked. "Did Fettiplace warn Allen?"

"I don't know…"

"And besides," Blandine asked of Tom rather than Marley, "wouldn't Baines kill this man before he went to the Collège?"

To this Marley had no answer — besides giving Blandine a murderous glare — but it was a most sensible question, all the more so since Baines had shown no qualms about laying into a foe in the street. Which also raised another question… "When did this Fettiplace die?"

Again, Marley floundered. "I don't know. They found him an hour ago or thereabout…"

"And had he been dead long? Was the body cold? For, an hour or two past noon, Baines was well away from the Rue des

103

Anglais, chasing after me." And, in fair truth, raving of how the Lord would smite his enemies… "So, you see, much depends on when Fettiplace died."

"I don't know!" Marley slammed both palms on the table, pushed away, and stalked to the window. "But two men are dead at the college, and Baines swore to kill them all!"

And this was a fact. Three facts, in truth, and while there was little enough to prove they tied together, it was growing difficult to exclude that they might be. If it was indeed Baines — a Service man, doing murder…

"Very well, then —" Tom began, and at the same time Marley asked again: "Where's Barnege?" He strode back to the table. "He must come to the college, see for himself —"

Watson, yes. Oh, Lord.

"Barnege left for London at dawn."

Tom caught Blandine's worried frown, and Marley asked, "But why?"

Because he's a fool of unfaithful character, who betrayed Sir Francis's trust — and mine.

"He was summoned back," was all Tom said, and it would have to be enough for both these people who were now all he had in the way of friends in Rheims. He gazed from one to the other.

"But…" Marley began — and stopped at that, though with burning eyes that promised plenty of questions later.

Blandine, for her part, nodded a little, frowning. "Your servant that came yesterday asked of him," she said slowly — and then clicked her tongue. "And I'm afraid that my brother…"

"Your brother we'll have to discuss. Meanwhile…" Tom turned to Marley. "Perhaps it's not the worst of notions that you've had: I'll go to the college —"

"You?"

"But, Monsieur…"

It was half-comical to see the two pairs of eyes go round at once. Marley's jaw slackened in astonishment — which could still be blamed on him knowing who Tom was. To Blandine, on the other hand, he had no other name beyond the false one of her cousin, and her patent worry stung rather more.

"But won't they… You're never a Catholic, Monsieur?" she asked.

At which Marley gave a disbelieving chuckle. "No, I'd wager you he's not."

And just what did they think he'd done, through his years in the Service, trained by Sir Francis himself?

"Are *you*?" he snapped at Marley — although the boy was Watson's friend, and to say that Watson had a recusant's past was to put it generously. Yesterday Tom would have said it didn't matter, but now…

And look if the brat didn't smile — though it was little more than a twitch at the corner of his mouth. "I'm no Papist, I swear to you," he said. "But then…" *But then I'm not Mr. Secretary's own kinsman.*

As though religion must hang heavier on the shoulders of a Walsingham. Heavier, thicker, harder to dissemble.

Petty as it was to be sour about it, it was more than Tom could help. "And, if it lightens your misgivings, I won't be going as a rabid Catholic looking to priesthood. Something easier will do. Something in between."

"Yes — yes!" Marley snapped his fingers. "We have those all the time. The teetering sort. Let's say…" Head tipped back, forefinger raised, he narrowed his eyes at Tom — a painter studying his model. "Your mother was a Catholic. Come from a family of recusants. Couldn't resist giving you a taste of the

Old Faith, poor lady — all in secret. And mind, you had a good Protestant education — but underneath you kept a soft spot for Rome in your heart. Then at Cambridge you fell in with a Popish crowd —"

Tom shook his head. "It can't be Cambridge — nor Oxford, for that matter. Most men in the college will have fallen in with Popish crowds there. How would none of them have ever met me?"

"Right, right. Then…" Marley paced round and round, snapping his fingers in the air again. Not a painter — no: a poet, conjuring a character out of thin air. "Scotland?"

"Italy. I doubt many of them will have done their studies in Padua." And neither had Tom, in truth — but he knew enough from Sir Francis and from Watson.

"Oh, men!" Blandine came to stand between them, hands on her hips. "Why can't you just be a small merchant's son, who never studied anywhere?"

Marley turned on her. "Because in Italy he lived among Catholics, and then went back to England, found bigotry and persecution, his friends gone into exile, his mother old beyond her years with fear — and that filled his heart with rage, and now he seeks battle — that's why!"

"Battle!" Blandine threw up her hands. "He needs a story, not a *chanson de geste*!"

"What would you know —"

"Quiet, both of you!" And Tom was pleased that he obtained silence. "Where was Downes from? And what was he?"

"A yeoman's son, I think — from Kent. Why?"

Which was good and promising. "Where in Kent?"

"Around Chelsfield. But why?"

Lord give patience! Tom's younger sister Mary had been like this — at the age of five. *Why? Why? Why?*

"Because," he explained, with the slow patience that had so maddened the child Mary, "if Thomas Roper must ask questions, he'd better have known Downes at least a little. After all, Downes is part of why he came to Rheims…" And, even as he spoke, the life of Tom Roper took shape in his mind, like a handful of coloured pieces sorting themselves into a picture, for all that he was no poet. Did Marley, who was, see it for what it was? Surely enough, he was ready to ask questions.

"No." Tom held up a hand to forestall him. "The less you know of Roper, the better. You never met him, mind. You never met *me*."

Whatever else the cobbler's boy had learnt in Cambridge, it never was subjection to his betters.

"What do you take me for?" he groused, with a sullen shrug.

A conceited cockerel — among many things. "Go back now, before they miss you."

"With all the uproar, they wouldn't miss Dr. Barret himself. Mind Barret, by the way. Superintendent of the Studies, Allen's pup, very pious, very eager to prove he's a good, clever soldier of the Lord."

"I'll bear it in mind. Now go. I'll follow soon."

"And what if they won't have you?" asked Blandine. "With all the uproar…"

Yes — what indeed? What if they said, *We're too busy now: come back in the morning?*

But Marley snorted, and motioned to Tom with a rhetorician's gesture. "Look at him, poor lad. Battered and bruised and robbed of all his earthly goods… Wouldn't you take him in, out of Christian charity? Why, with any luck, they'll put him in the infirmary!"

107

With any luck, ay! "Right where Downes was killed?" Tom asked.

And, for the first time in their short acquaintance, Christopher Marley laughed. A boyish, bright-eyed laugh. "You want to ask questions, Tom Roper," he said. "Where better? Oh — and mind you cross yourself now and then."

And he laughed again while Blandine pushed him through the door and followed to see him out.

Save and deliver them all — the brat was enjoying himself.

With a sigh, Tom sat in a chair by the wall. Lord, but he was sore, and his left hand throbbed when he tried to flex his fingers. Not enough to be broken — and thanks be for that.

Baines, prowling and hiding out there, mad to the marrow ... but a murderer? The roving eyes, the mutterings, the psalms, the snatches of utter reason, the sudden violence... Would such a man slip in and out of a house to poison its dwellers one by one? And *quæstio vexatissima*: why Downes? Why Fettiplace? If Downes could have been a mistake, this Fettiplace certainly was not. The servant who had come back to Rheims after a month. The servant of a notorious recusant. What if it wasn't Baines at all? Then Downes too, perhaps...

Tom startled when the door clacked open, and Blandine's back pushed past it. He leapt to hold it open for her, and she turned, showing that she carried a trencher in her hands and Tom's doublet on her arm, his hat squeezed under her elbow.

"You may as well have a bit of supper," she said. "I misdoubt they'll feed you much, in there."

Tom took a hasty bite of cheese and a sip of wine as he prepared. He half emptied his purse and moved it to his boot, after Skeres's way, and discarded his dagger — because Roper had been robbed, and would carry no more than his eating knife. Blandine promised to send someone to the Fleur-de-Lys to gather Thomas Roland's things, since he would be staying with his cousins.

"And there's the matter of your brother..." Tom said at last.

Blandine choked with rage to hear what lay behind the boy's fibs. "Kill him, Monsieur — that's what I'll do! Just let Jory come home, and there will be such a caning!"

Much as Tom agreed... "In fairness, though, he doesn't know what harm he might have done. You know your brother best — but wouldn't it be safer to tell him?"

"Saints keep us! He lacks both wits and sense. You wouldn't think him my father's son!"

"Well, think on it, Madame Jory." Tom rose, a little stiffly. "I'd better go, now, if I hope to learn anything."

She handed him his doublet, still damp and rather muddy. The hat was even worse. "Perrette had sponged it too well, and I had to undo her work a little. And that hand, I'd like to bind it proper — but..." She produced a strip of rough linen, and briskly tied it around Tom's hand and wrist. "A maid did this, at the *taverne* where they brought you. You don't remember where, for you're new to Rheims and became lost..." She stopped, clicking her tongue. "Saints — listen to me, teaching *you* these things!"

"All very good notions," Tom said, smiling. "Your father taught you well."

Blandine Jory did not smile back — why, she looked downright grim. "The good Lord keep and guard you against the murderers, Monsieur," she said. "You, and that young runagate of yours."

And, with this cheerless valediction, Tom took his leave of Blandine Jory.

CHAPTER 7

At the college, a servant was closing the black gate.

"Wait!" Tom called in English. "Wait, please — is this…" He looked over his shoulder, lowering his voice. "Is this the English College?"

The servant's face twisted in ill-humour. "What do you want?" he asked.

"I was robbed. I … I was coming here — and then…" Tom shook his head, striving to look hapless.

Like the people at the *Grand Cerf*, like the servant Perrette, like Marley and Blandine Jory, the servant squinted at Tom's face, then down at the roughly bound hand, then up again. "And you were coming here?"

And now relief, a sagging of the shoulders. "Ay — for I was told —"

The fellow waved him silent. "Come in," he ordered, and drew the wicket open, just wide enough for a man to squeeze through.

And this was how Thomas Walsingham stepped inside the Collège Anglais of Rheims.

Or he stepped, at least, into a narrow whitewashed entryway that opened at its end onto a courtyard, and took all its light from there. Its light but not its noise: from somewhere inside the house came a rumble of men's voices. There were also two doors on either side of the passage, and, as the servant bolted the gate, a man in a black cassock strode in from the one on the left, calling for "Carter!"

He stopped short on seeing Tom — and even against the light the man's scowl could not be mistaken.

"Who's this?" he asked in a harsh voice, thick with displeasure.

"Father Immes!" Carter limped to meet the newcomer, and chattered to him with much hand-waving agitation. Both men looked at Tom, then Father Immes nodded.

"Go ahead, Carter. And fetch Rudd on your way."

And, as the servant scurried away, this bearded, scowling man who was one of the traitorous exiles came to stand before Tom, caught him by the arm, and turned him towards the blue light from the court.

"What is your name?" he asked.

"Thomas Roper."

And, of all things, laughter flickered deep in Tom's throat. Foolish, damning laughter — oh, Lord! Sir Francis Walsingham's own cousin entering the Collège Anglais under an alibi. Ulysses in lamb's fleece, stepping into the Cyclops's lair. If he were caught... Had Baines truly been put to the rack?

Faces, Thomas, speak as much as tongues.

Whatever Tom's face was telling, though, this particular Cyclops misread, for he shook his head.

"Don't fear," he said — more in impatience than charity. "We won't throw you into the street. It's just that you come at a moment..."

Another burst of voices erupted. Immes, with a click of his tongue and a sigh, steered Tom through the door.

"Wait there," he ordered, pointing to a row of benches against the wall opposite, and he disappeared as briskly as he'd arrived.

Again, laughter itched in Tom's throat. Fear made men do strange things. Had Marley, conceited peacock that he was, been afraid as he crossed this threshold? Had Baines? But then, neither of them was what Tom was. What would these aspiring traitors do, finding a Walsingham in their hands? And even if they never did, what would Sir Francis say when he learnt of the risk his cousin had taken? Let him not have blundered too badly...

It would have been some consolation to think he shook himself out of such morose thoughts — but, in fair truth, it was the nearing sound of voices that cleared his mind.

The yard was a huge, flagged rectangle. On the long side across from the house was a wall grown with ivy and a few creeping roses, and ... was it a fig tree beyond the wall? The yard of the Chevreau d'Or, no doubt. The other side had a two-tiered gallery, with a fine row of arches. Under this gallery a door led inside the house, and from there the voices came, together with the wavering ruddy light of several candles.

As quietly as he could, Tom stepped near this entrance, striving for an air of natural curiosity rather than stealth. The door stood open, a skewed rectangle of light showing a scene out of Virgil: two servants carried a plank, and on it a body lay shrouded in a piece of sacking that only let a man's booted feet to be seen. All around crowded black, murmuring shadows. The servants awkwardly handled the plank and what it bore, bending to lay it on a bench under two rows of shelves full of jars, pots and baskets.

"Are you sure, Catesby?" asked the round, crisp voice of a man out of sight — the Pluto presiding over this domestic Avernus.

Allen himself, perhaps? But the voice sounded young — and younger still that of the answering Catesby, out of the murmuring black crowd.

"I didn't hear it myself, Doctor. He was already dead. It was Elliot that he told, wasn't it, Robin?"

"Ay…" said another young voice, breaking on the syllable. The man who stepped forward cleared his throat. "Ay — but not that he was ill. That he felt unwell, that's what he said…"

And at that moment one of the servants half dropped his end of the plank, which slammed on the bench, to a chorus of drawn breaths and exclamations. The sacking slipped, and one arm slid out, lolling in the way that is only of death.

"Careful!" Pluto warned, striding into view, just as one of the shadows looked towards the door and caught sight of Tom.

"Who's there?" this fellow called, pointing, and Avernus dissolved in a gaggle of round-mouthed faces — some fearful, some angry, some caught in astonishment.

Mind you cross yourself, now and then…

Tom stiffened, hand half raised in the sign of the cross. Round-eyed himself, he hoped. Frightened.

"Who are you?" Pluto asked. "Show yourself."

And there went Immes — harsh voice curbed into obedience. "I've let him in, Dr. Barret. He came asking for shelter."

Dr. Barret nodded, never taking his eyes off Tom. "You come upon us in a sad hour. Are you from England?"

"Yes, Father. From Kent. I've —"

"Doctor," Barret cut in. "'Tis *Doctor* Barret. And you won't be sent away tonight." Again he never looked away as he raised his voice to call: "Colson. Take him to my room."

Colson proved to be a curly-headed boy of seventeen or so, who bowed to Barret and, arming himself with a rush-light, trotted away along the gallery, with no more than a jerk of the head for Tom.

Tom bowed his head in turn to the two priests, letting his gaze slide behind them, where one of the youths had bent to tuck the dead man's hand under the rough shroud.

"Thank you…" he murmured, and followed after young Colson at the more sedate pace of weary bones.

"I say that Dr. Allen ought to be told —" said a new voice behind his back.

"And disturb him again!" This was Barret, quite brisk, and then the door clapped shut.

Richard Barret, then. *Superintendent of the Studies, Allen's pup, very pious, very eager to prove he's a good, clever soldier of the Lord…*

"Come along!" Colson, young face greenish in the light of his rush-candle, was waiting at the foot of a staircase. "What's your name?"

"Thomas Roper."

"I'm Will Colson," the boy said, and started up the stairs two steps at a time.

Tom followed, careful not to stumble. There was still light in the yard, but the narrow windows let in little of it, and the stairwell was dark. The boy's dancing shard of light did little to relieve the gloom, particularly as he kept half a dozen steps ahead.

He stopped at the first storey. "Come along!" he called, bouncing on his feet as he waited on the landing. "I must go back before the Marie rings."

A woman — here? There were all manners of tales about the ways of Romish convents, but… "Who's Marie?"

"What are you thinking?" The boy stifled a giggle. "Our bell, the Marie is! We've named it for the Queen — and old Bénoit rings the Hours. Dr. Worthington will skin me alive if I miss Vespers."

"Well, Dr. Barret sent you…"

Will Colson snorted. "Ay — and Dr. Worthington'll skin me. Hurry, now — you're not that old."

Tom smiled to himself, thinking of the time when three-and-twenty would have seemed a mature age to him — but he sobered before entering the rushlight's dim halo, for it was a grim question that he wanted to ask. "That man downstairs — is he...?"

Young Will sucked his teeth. "Poor fellow. A servant, they say. Was here with his master — that was before my time — and came back. Noll Catesby says he was ill, Lord rest him."

A child playing out a man's words and grave manner — the latter not too well — as he led the way along the gallery. Opening one in a row of dark doors, he showed Tom into a whitewashed cavern of a room — tall and cold, with a writing table and a chair for all furnishings. Colson went to light a candle that sat on the one window's sill. It must have been better than the boy's rush, for the flame burnt a clear yellow, enough to show books heaping on the bare table, and half a dozen stools pushed against the walls.

Colson pointed to one of these stools. "Jump when Dr. Barret comes, though," he said, "or he'll eat you alive."

Tom smiled in spite of himself. "Lionish, is he?"

The boy pulled a face. "You said you're from Kent. He doesn't much like Kentish men, I reckon. Or perhaps 'tis just Dick Sherbourn that nettles him."

Ay, well, *this* Tom had no trouble believing, if Kit Marley's alias was half as vexing as the boy himself. "Does Hugh Downes nettle him too?"

And of course, if young Yates's visit had been before Will's time, he may never have met Downes — but there was more than just unknowingness in the boy's eyes as he repeated: "Hugh Downes?"

"Kentish as an apple, is Hugh. He's here, isn't he — he must be, surely?"

115

But what the boy might have said Tom was not to know, for at that moment the door opened, to show Richard Barret on the threshold. He carried no candle.

Mindful of Will's warning, Tom made haste to rise. Beside him the boy shuffled, shifting his weight from foot to foot.

"Vespers, Colson," Barret said. "We have much to pray for, tonight."

Young Will bowed his head and scurried away, barely nodding in answer to Tom's word of thanks.

Barret sighed, shook his head, and closed the door, then moved the candle to the table, so that both he and Tom were in full light. A church's bell began to ring somewhere beyond the shuttered window, answered by another, much smaller, inside the house — Colson's Marie, no doubt, named for the Queen. For the time it took six chimes to toll, Tom and the priest watched each other.

Richard Barret was a tall man, with a scholar's stooped shoulders and a long, youngish face. But the eyes were what stood out: hooded, large, clear-coloured, with a steady, searching brightness.

"Sit, sit," he said at length. "They'll have some salve for those bruises of yours in the infirmary. Roper, is it? And you were robbed?"

Having sat down, Tom let Kent thicken a little in his speech, and told his tale of being set upon, of losing all but the few coins he kept in his boot for safety, and the clothes on his back.

Leaning against his table with his arms crossed, Barret listened and watched until Tom fell silent.

"And your letter was also lost?" he asked. "You must have had one, if you were coming here."

And there went the snare, for the lie would have been convenient — *oh yes, I had a letter from such and such, and it was lost* — but easy enough to disprove.

Confusion would be safer. "But I had none…" Tom shook his head. "I didn't know."

"Those who come to join our ranks, for the most part, are sent here by some friend, some faithful soul."

Not quite the truth, surely — for many would not trust to write such a letter, nor to carry it — but… *A pretence of ignorance, Thomas, can be a very good mask.*

"I didn't know." A sagging of the shoulders, a hanging of the head. "I just… My father disheired me as a Papist. I've no family, no friends —"

"And are you truly?"

Tom looked up to find Barret leaning forward, the searching eyes fastened on him — and there was a colour of scorn in his voice when he asked: "Are you truly a Papist as your father claims?"

A deep, deep sigh, a bitter smile. "That's what he called my mother when he was angry. She was of the Old Faith, and he'd rail at her for teaching me Latin prayers, the Rosary, and such … so he sent me away to London when I was still a boy, 'prenticed me to an uncle. I never forgot, though. When I came back, my mother was ill. I believe it gave her consolation that I prayed with her. She was a meek, gentle soul…" A thought passed through Tom's mind of his own late mother, whose soul had been neither meek nor gentle, and who'd have had much to say about her youngest son's falsery. "Then she died, early this year, and I believe it was also of the cruel things she saw done against the Faith. The same day, my father said he never wanted to see me again."

117

"And you thought you'd come to us." It was no question, and the clear, sharp gaze rested full on Tom, waiting, gauging.

Was the hand to the brow too much? "Ay — for there's this man, we used to know each other as boys, and he..." Tom looked up, as one fired with a sudden thought. "I'm a lack-wit, Doctor! You have a man here who knows me."

It was no more than a heartbeat, but Richard Barret looked wrong-footed. This he must not have expected. "You have a friend here, then?"

"Ay — ay! I'm a fool for not thinking..." Tom smiled as though in relief. "Hugh Downes will have a good word for me!"

"Hugh Downes..." Like young Will Colson before, Dr. Barret also hesitated.

And to this hesitation, Tom Roper would insist, no doubt: "He *is* here, surely? I asked the boy before, but..." Roper would stop, frown. "He's never left?"

Another might have looked away — but Barret did not. He took a breath, let it out, and shook his head. "It pains me to give you such news, Roper. Your friend is dead."

One he'd known as a boy. One he'd admired — but not a close friend. Not one whose loss would give deep grief.

"Dead," Tom repeated in a small whisper.

Barret inclined his head. "He's been this past month. Of an illness."

Again, a good deal less than the truth — for, murder or not, Downes had hardly died of his fever. Also, it was worth noting, Barret didn't look much touched. Perhaps it was his natural manner, or perhaps Will had been right, and the man cared little for the Kentish. Either way...

"Lord rest his soul, poor Hugh." Tom shook his head, looking away, like one not knowing what to say.

It was a surprise when Barret laid a hand on his shoulder, the sharp gaze softening a jot. "A bad day, and a worse end to it," he sighed. "Come and have supper. Then there will be a place to rest. Tomorrow you can pray for your friend, and we'll decide what to do with you."

Lighting a rush from the candle, which he then carefully snuffed, licking his fingertips to douse the last tiny ember on the wick, the Superintendent of the Studies led Tom downstairs without another word.

A man was crossing the courtyard, and Barret beckoned to him. Candlelight proved him a servant carrying a pail of water, and there were instructions given that Roper should have supper in the kitchen, and a cot for the night.

Out of the way of the students, then — at least for now. Ah well, Tom was the last who could grudge these people some wariness. Just let them not throw him out in the morning.

Barret gazed at him again, up and down, with the slightest frown.

"I wish you could have had a better welcome under this roof, Thomas Roper," he said. "God give you the good night."

And with that he was gone.

The servant, a sturdy, sandy-haired youth who named himself as Rudd, led Tom past the yard, into the entryway and from there into a kitchen where a fire burnt low, and the air smelt of soot, and tallow, and onions cooked too long.

"There ain't much left," Rudd announced, after inspecting a pair of large pots. From one of them he scraped something into a bowl — which he made up by the very simple means of slopping into it some of the water from his pail. More of this water he poured into an earthen cup — and with bowl, cup, a chunk of brown bread and a spoon, Tom found himself sitting at a corner of the table in the centre of the kitchen. That he could see near nothing, he counted as a minor blessing as he swallowed his broth — which tasted of soot, and tallow, and of onions cooked too long. At least the barley bread, though old, was good.

I misdoubt they'll feed you much, in there... Blandine Jory didn't know what a true oracle she was!

And whether it was chance or the habit of the Collège Anglais with strangers, Rudd was off on his errands before a conversation could be struck, and appeared again only to lead Tom to another room, no larger than a cupboard, where a pallet and a blanket awaited.

"'Tis just the night," Rudd consoled. "They'll put you with the others tomorrow."

Or so it was to be hoped very much, Tom thought, as he struggled with his boots in utter darkness. Otherwise, how could he observe the joints and flexures of this deadly affair?

He sat and waited for a while, listening as the house went to sleep. If nothing else, he reckoned this small cupboard of his must be close to the pantry where poor dead Fettiplace lay. With any luck, he could filch a candle stub from the kitchen and take a look at the body.

It was a feat to keep himself awake, but at length the Collège Anglais descended into silence. Tom rose and, in stockinged feet, felt his way to the door — and found it bolted from the outside.

Tartarus seize the Cyclops and their distrustful sheep!

There being nothing for it, Tom lay down to snatch some sleep. The blanket was clean, for a mercy, but thin and worn, and the pallet hard to bruised flesh and weary bones. The night was going to be as miserably penitential as supper had been in this lair of zealous traitors.

Let the zealous traitors not doubt him — at least not too much, at least not too soon. Let him do better work of unravelling this tangle than he'd done so far. And this very improper, very heartfelt prayer was all Tom could manage before the day's weariness claimed him.

CHAPTER 8

24th of May

The Collège Anglais stirred well before cockcrow.

When sounds of alacrity began in the kitchen, and Rudd went to free him, Tom left his cupboard to find that night was just beginning to pale.

He tried to peek into the pantry, for a fellow could lose his way in a new place, surely? But the pantry was occupied by a bald, elderly man who waved the trespasser out to the courtyard.

The yard was alive already, with the students milling around the well in the corner, doing their ablutions in the brisk, smoky air. They talked low between themselves as they waited for their turn, sombrely enough, and that could well be a consuetude of cheerlessness — although there was something unquiet about it. But then, whatever the manner of Fettiplace's death, they would have to be a little more, or a little less than human, not to feel the weight of it.

Yawning, Tom went to join them, and even as he hovered at the outer reaches of the group, found himself an object of curiosity.

That Marley was the first to address the newcomer, was no surprise at all. At least it wasn't done too awkwardly.

"Where from, in Kent?" he asked, approaching with a few others — and, on seeing Tom's perplexed look, he shrugged. "Little Colson, here, is all mouth."

Being one of Marley's curious fellows, poor Will blushed pink and spluttered.

"Chelsfield," Tom said.

"Canterbury myself," Kit Marley said. "Dick Sherbourn."

"Thomas Roper."

"We know, we know…" The brat smiled sideways at Colson. "Here's Draycott, Talbot, Elliot, and this big fellow is Catesby. Colson you know. Then Norris, and that's *Dominus* Thurstan Hunt…" He raised his voice just a little for the benefit of a tall, broad-shouldered man who stood apart, rubbing his wet hair with a cloth. "Not that he'll mingle with us lowly students now he's ordained."

But there was no bite in Marley's words, and Hunt took it in good part, smiling as he made his way to them, much in the manner of an older brother. He had a hand raised to clap Marley's shoulder, but lowered it of a sudden at the sight of a thin, long-faced man bearing in on the little group, cassock flying about him like the feathers of a crow.

"Sherbourn!" this man called.

"Why can't you stay out of trouble, Dick?" Hunt asked under his breath.

"Too fond of his own wit!" muttered big Catesby — and perhaps it came out louder than he meant in the sudden silence of the students.

The crow-like fellow suffered from no deafness — nor did he mean to affect it. "And you're too ready to find fault with others, Oliver Catesby," he snapped, before turning his displeasure on Marley. "Not that you don't deserve it! Not even death will teach you that levity has no place among us? " He jerked his head Tom-wards. "What will a stranger think of us, if you show him such childishness?"

Head and gaze lowered, Kit held himself with a stiffness that belied the humble pose — and here came on his shoulder the hand of Thurstan Hunt.

"He'll pray to the Lord to mend his ways, Dr. Bagshaw," the young priest said. He was a head taller, and full of a gentle firmness that the other lacked. They both looked to be about the same age of thirty, but Bagshaw, who must have held some rank within the college, only had a barely concealed irritation for them all.

"See that you do, Sherbourn," he ordered. "And so will Catesby. So will you all — for your companions and for yourselves. Pray that the Lord purge us of all unworthy thoughts —"

And he would have preached longer, but that the Marie began to chime.

He clapped his hands twice then. "Lauds and Mass now. Quick. Don't tarry," he barked, and the students hastened towards the gallery and the back of the house — Kit Marley with the others. Tom couldn't see Catesby's face, but there was no mistaking the bunching of the thick-muscled shoulders. At his side walked a younger man, golden-haired and anxious, murmuring and shaking his head.

When Tom made to follow, Bagshaw moved abreast with him.

"After Mass, you'll go to Dr. Barret's room," he said.

So they were not content with last night's scant examination — not that it was to be expected. This morning Barret would bend his back to it in earnest, and perhaps someone else. Even Allen himself?

Tom nodded with a meekness he was far from feeling.

They passed the stairs and entered a vast hall at the back of the house.

It looked as though it might have been a stable once, long and low-ceilinged, and with few windows. Now the place was whitewashed and panelled waist-high, with a small pulpit halfway down its length. A large crucifix hung between the two windows on the short side, over a table mounted on a dais and dressed as an altar. On it gleamed two white wax candles in silver holders, and a scant array of liturgical gold. Dozens of black-garbed men stood in rows before the altar, filling the place.

Tom stopped just inside the threshold, looking around, breathing in a smell of frankincense, wax and, for some reason, cabbage. Was it a sin to attend a popish Mass, when it was done in the Queen's own cause...?

Bagshaw, for one, was scowling.

"'Tis a long time since I've gone to Mass..." Tom murmured. "My poor mother..."

A very long time indeed, since he'd never gone, and what Tom's mother, even from Heaven, would have to say bore no thinking. With a sigh of great vexation, Bagshaw shoved Tom into the nearest row of students, and ordered him to open his heart to the Lord and pray, in the way he'd send a man into battle.

With that done, Bagshaw went to stand at the front of the assembly, just as a sacring bell tinkled. Teachers and students began to sing psalm after psalm, and litanies for the conversion of England and Dr. Allen's speedy recovery, and then the Mass proper.

The priest on the altar was another of Hunt's ilk — in fact, what Hunt would become in half a dozen years, if he did not end at Tyburn before: stately in body and carriage, with greying temples, and a manner of gentle fervour as he intoned the Latin formulae.

All the time Tom stood with bowed head and joined hands, murmuring his answers — for he'd read the old rites as part of his training, and knew his Latin. Of those who watched him —

and no doubt there were a few — the charitable would think him overcome. The suspicious would doubt — but then, so they would whatever he did.

One thing he could not do was watch in turn, for fear it would be observed. Only once, catching a flicker of movement out of the corner of his eye, he turned — and met a pair of eyes in a white face. Large black eyes, they were, and shifty. As soon as he saw himself caught, the fellow looked away, but the wordless exchange had not gone unmarked. Catesby, two rows behind, was watching sharply — and Tom's next neighbour, a stocky young man, cassocked and tonsured, glanced sideways with a cocked eyebrow. He seemed amused, rather than suspicious, but still prudency and a lowered gaze seemed a safer course.

When it was time for the communion, Tom hesitated like the fool he was. Should he...? Surely, if he must pass himself off as a Catholic — what had he been thinking? And see young Marley, filing with the others as though he'd been doing it his whole life.

"Won't you...?"

Tom blinked to find the young priest's worried eyes on him.

"I'm not..." Tom groped in his mind for something that would excuse such agitation. "I'm unshriven..."

There was a silent "Oh" of understanding, a repeated nod, and a hand to the elbow. Then the priest strode to the head of the small procession, leant to whisper in Dr. Barret's ear, and Barret nodded. Another matter for discussion later, no doubt.

What remained of the Mass Tom spent rehearsing in his mind Tom Roper's heart and mind for the interrogation to come — until the men around him began to sing a hymn.

They did not sing especially well, apart from two or three better trained voices, and the high treble of a few boys. Most of the others just followed the lead with more fervour than skill — as soldiers might sing their prayers before a battle. And from it the hymn took some manner of rough, stirring beauty.

It was full day by the time they walked out to the courtyard, and to the scent of freshly baked bread. Carter, Rudd, and the bald old servant from the pantry waited there with baskets full of brown loaves, which they broke into pieces and handed to the students — and this was the breaking of fast, accompanied by a cup of the weakest ale.

The teachers did not partake, heading upstairs instead. Would they have manchet bread and butter waiting in their rooms, and roasted herrings on a Friday? Sour tales abounded of the hypocrisy of Catholics when it came to the comforts of the flesh.

The young priest from Mass, for one, didn't have the look of one who fasted much — although, seen closer when he sought out Tom, there may well have been more sinew than fat under the faded cassock.

"Dr. Barret says not to fret about the Communion," he said, "and to go upstairs to him when you're done." He had a slow, West Country voice, a thatch of straw-coloured hair, and a wide freckled face that broke into a smile. "And I've no manners, have I? Christopher Hodgson."

Tom strove to swallow his mouthful of bread.

"I know, I know — don't choke yourself, Tom Roper." Hodgson's eyes danced. "'Tis the way here: what one knows, we all know very soon. Eat now. Don't keep Dr. Barret waiting."

And was there the slightest shade of contempt in the exhortation?

Tom always liked to think of a problem as a number of coloured pieces that he had to find and put together until they made a pattern: that Hodgson held no great fondness for Dr. Barret, he tucked away as one of these pieces; whether it was useful, he would see in time. Meanwhile, in whatever spirit the exhortation had been given, it seemed prudent to take it to heart. Having washed down the last of the bread, Tom found his way upstairs, seeking the room he'd visited last night.

The gallery, that had seemed to stretch far in the darkness, looked a good deal shorter in daylight, and the doors along it less numerous. One stood ajar — a set of maws, waiting to swallow an unwary spy. And from it came the voices of two men, not quite arguing, but not in agreement either. Tom crept close.

"…Not Dr. Allen's — yours," one of the arguers was saying. "You take too much upon yourself." And surely it was the voice of the priest who had said Mass — though with an edge it had lacked when coming from the altar.

"I only follow his lead: welcome all who seek our door — in faith, in doubt, or in confusion." And this was Barret. "Roper seems like a simple enough fellow — but the Lord's vineyard has need of all, not just the scholars."

A simple fellow, really! And one may have striven to give just that impression — but still…

"Dr. Allen can tell false-hearted rogues from good men. Can you?"

"We all know I'm not Dr. Allen — nor do I pretend to be. As for this lad… At worst it will be a deed of charity, for those bruises are no pretence."

There was impatience in the other man's sigh. "We'll see. But I'll say this again, Richard: you take too much upon yourself."

"Because I didn't turn away a man —"

"*And* because of that poor Fettiplace. Even if Dr. Allen were absent, I'd say 'tis not yours alone to decide — but he's not."

128

"And do you think he'd want the *Milice* here —?"

"What are you doing?" A sharp whisper came from behind Tom's back.

He spun around. Caught eavesdropping…

But, Fates be thanked, it was only the boy Colson, looking from the stairs, more curious than alarmed.

"Will!" Tom exhaled. "You gave me a fright! Dr. Barret sent for me — but…" He looked from door to door. "I'm lost."

With a soft huff, the boy pointed to a nearer door, and then ran off down the stairs, two steps at a time, waiting for no thanks. In the other room the two men were still talking, although the voices had moved away from the door.

Oh Lord!

Had young Colson been possessed of a louder disposition or a distrustful mind… Before anyone else could catch him at fault, Tom made haste to knock on Dr. Barret's door. When there was no answer, he knocked a little harder, as one innocent of snooping would.

It was no more than a heartbeat before the door that was ajar swung open, and Barret appeared on the threshold.

"Oh yes, Roper." He gave Tom one of those keen gazes. Behind him was, indeed, the stately priest. Seen close, he had a face that went well with his Mass voice, rather than the waspish conversation: full of warmth and gentleness, with a long Roman nose, liquid eyes and a soft mouth. A liar's face, Tom's mother would have called it — and she would have disliked the man on sight, as much as her son did.

"Will you join us, Dr. Worthington?" Barret asked.

And look at the kindly smile! "Oh no — I'll leave you to your work," he said and, with a nod at Tom, retreated to what must have been his room.

Without a word, Barret led the way to his own. Sunlight filled it, warming the bare whiteness and showing, in a corner, a little door that must have led to Worthington's room. Would the priest hover behind it, listening in on this colloquy? Ah well, it mattered little.

Barret motioned Tom to the stool, and leant against the table.

"You just came from England. You know the sad state of the Faith," he began. "I'm sure you understand that we must know more of you." He waited, fixing Tom with eyes that, seen in daylight, were of the most startling blue.

Of course, would have been the gentleman's answer — but Roper was no gentleman.

"If you don't believe —"

Barret held up a hand for silence. "Were poor Downes here, he would vouch for you. More than once he said there were many young men in his parts, eager to join us. Are you one of them, Thomas Roper? Do you look to priesthood?"

Softly, now. Not too much zeal. Tom looked down at his hands. "I don't know."

And this earned one cocked eyebrow. "Most of those who come to us, think that they do know — one way or the other. A good few do not, in truth, but not many freely admit to such a doubt. Do you possess a philosophical soul, lad? Or a weak one?"

And which would be the worse sin in this man's eyes? Tom took a deep breath. "I have nothing and no one left, Doctor. My father's a mercer in Chelsfield. I was his journeyman, and was to inherit the shop, in time. Now I'm left so penniless, I can't even afford to be a recusant."

"Were you before?"

Well, it wasn't to be expected that Barret should be a fool. Let him just be a fisher of souls.

"The years I lived in London… I was a very silly lad, eager to please my father. But after I came back to my mother, after praying with her in secret, day after day… After she died, I found that I can't turn my back on the Faith again."

And wasn't this as fanciful as Marley's angry physician out of Padua? Oh, how Blandine Jory would scoff! But Barret wasn't scoffing. He rubbed at his chin in thought.

"Are you your father's only son? He could yet change his mind."

"My sister is his heir, now. She and her husband will see to it that he doesn't."

"You could go at law."

"Against my own father!" And perhaps Roper would have shown anguish at this point — but Tom knew himself no player: bitter sadness would have to do. "And then for what? My folk turned their backs on me for a Papist, those of the Faith at home mistrust me for being raised a heretic — and I don't…"

Barret hummed, like one who heard nothing new, and then asked the question Tom had been expecting: "Were you baptised a Catholic?"

"My mother said I was. In great secret, as a babe."

"But you have nothing to prove it."

A shake of the head, a hunching of the shoulder. "I've nothing, Father. Only that weak soul you say: when I found myself shunned, I couldn't stand it. I thought of Hugh, then, and…"

And Barret was caught! The sharp blue gaze softened a little, and the crisp voice grew warmer. "Perhaps you've little need of your father's inheritance: you have a far more precious one from your mother. Stay a few days, Roper. Rest, think, pray to the Lord for guidance, talk to our people, know yourself among friends. Then we'll see. Dr. Allen, if he's well enough, will think what to do."

A few days. Not so caught, then — but a few days would have to do for now. Tom rose, full of relieved thanks, and was dismissed. He was already on the threshold when Barret called to him.

"Have you some French, Roper? Some Latin?"

The useful mask of ignorance… "I went to grammar school for two years or so, in Chelsfield. I'd little head for it, though, so they 'prenticed me early. As for French, I picked up a few words along the way."

"*C'est une langue de sauvages, n'est-ce pas?*" Barret asked, with the most barbarous accent. Not caught by half, then…

Tom frowned, as blank-eyed as he could make himself, and wished he knew what it was that made Richard Barret smile — doubt satisfied, or suspicion confirmed?

Whether in welcome or out of distrust, Tom was sent to Dr. Worthington's room where, together with a dozen others, he sat through a lengthy expounding on the Sermon on the Mount.

The lecture was in English, and that he himself was there, together with Will Colson, as well as Catesby and Robin Elliot, marked it as meant for the less learned of the students. Those lesser labourers in the Holy vineyard that Worthington held in some contempt. Not that one would have guessed it — not to see the priest explain the Holy words with such gentle, bright-eyed zeal, such care for his little flock's understanding, such pleasure in each lamb's good answer.

It would all have been rather tedious, but for the exercise of seeking fault in Worthington's assumed manner — for it must be assumed, surely — and finding none. Why, the man even went into raptures over the Lord's entreaty to turn the other cheek. Which, truly, coming from those who would murder the Queen and burn all Protestants at the stake…!

Then again, perhaps not all the students were of a mind with the Lord — or at least with the way Worthington spelt the Lord's mind.

Take Oliver Catesby, for instance, bouncing his knee as he listened, grimmer and grimmer, until…

"Even when we're done injustice, Doctor?" he asked, breaking through the teacher's speech. "Even then we turn the other cheek?"

That it was asked not in question but in challenge, Worthington affected to ignore. "Indeed we must — more than ever."

"*Blessed are they that suffer persecution for justice,*" a ruddy fellow quoted, with a great air of righteousness about him.

Worthington nodded solemnly. "*Blessed are ye when they shall revile you, and persecute you for my sake…*"

"Blessed, ay!" Catesby wasn't silenced, red-faced and oblivious to Elliot's pleading hand on his sleeve. "But still, *eye for an eye* is in the Scriptures, also."

The ruddy one must have been waiting just for this. "*But I say you not to resist evil,* says the Lord…" he said, forefinger held up, so smug that Tom felt sympathy for Catesby.

"*Blessed are the meek,*" piped up young Will, only to shrink and look away when both Catesby and the ruddy man glared at him.

It greatly consoled the boy that Worthington was smiling.

"And I think our Colson cinched the matter for us all," the priest said, looking at each man in turn — and Colson beamed, and some nodded in accord, and some did not. This was the game, them: to gauge each student's humour and inclination as much as to instruct the group. And, because a newcomer must be especially worth gauging, Worthington had his eye on Tom, when another man spoke.

"'Tis all very well, Doctor, and I'll turn my cheek no matter what's done to me — but what if I see mischief done to others?"

A few nodded and murmured — Catesby the first and fiercest, hitting a large palm upon his knee.

Worthington ignored them all, except the asker — a strong-boned fellow of seven or eight-and-twenty, with close-cropped hair like a bronze helmet.

"A sharp question, Savage. A soldier's question. And not an easy one." And then he turned to Tom. "Let's hear your voice, Roper. What would you answer to Savage?"

"I…" Poor Tom Roper would know nothing of disputations. He'd grow flustered, not knowing what to say, and he'd say it clumsily when it occurred to him. "Well, there's that about laying down one's life for one's friends… Perhaps 'tis about defending those who can't defend themselves —"

Savage leant forward on his stool. "What if we see something done that will harm many others — a cruelty, a betrayal? What if the cheek that we should turn is not our own?"

There were more murmurs, a shuffling of feet. The ruddy fellow clucked most fowl-like, and Catesby quivered, eyes bright with hungry challenge.

Again, Worthington ran his eyes over the circle of young faces. It could have been the gaze of a fond father — although Tom was ready to swear that sharp calculation lay hidden behind that benignity. And, it was worth noting, the good Doctor offered no answer — to Savage's questions, to Tom's own fumbling answer, or to Catesby's defiance. He exhorted them all to think on what was said, instead, and to consider the Scriptures — and then, with the Marie chiming, he dismissed them to their dinner. And, to see and hear him, one could have thought him the gentlest heart and the very pink of benevolence.

CHAPTER 9

What had been a chapel at dawn was now apparelled like a very spartan dining hall, with two long trestles where several dozen men sat in small groups. On the dais was now the high table, where Worthington joined Barret, Bagshaw and Immes. In the middle, an empty chair marked Allen's absence.

And dinner, at last, would allow some questions. Tom hesitated just past the threshold, wondering where conversation might prove most fruitful. There John Savage sat with a few others — Savage, who held a belief in striking first. What if Downes had been a threat to him, what if...?

"Come, Roper. Never look so lost."

A hand closed around Tom's elbow, and he turned to find Hodgson smiling at him. "We wait for no invitation, here. You sit where you will, and eat what you're given."

So much for sounding Savage, then. Hodgson steered Tom to another place, where Marley sat with Catesby, Elliot, and the shifty-eyed fellow from Mass.

And of this individual Hodgson asked, "Make our Roper welcome, will you, Gib?" And since Gib would not look welcoming, he turned to Marley, "And you, Sherbourn."

Marley scooted on the bench to make room. "Sit here, then. We'll make our own small Kent."

Across the table, young Elliot smiled a little. Catesby did not — and in truth he looked like one who seldom did. He was perhaps Tom's age or a little older, huge and thick-necked, dark of complexion, with dark-shadowed eyes that scanned the newcomer. At length he said, "Laying down one's life, eh?"

Tom made a show of being flustered, and Elliot chuckled.

136

"Roper's had his first taste of Worthington's Scriptures," he explained.

"Has he?" Hodgson shoved aside the glum Gib to sit by him. "And how did it like you, Roper?"

Catesby snorted, and perhaps Marley thought he had to rescue Tom, for he cut in.

"Why, *Dominus* Hodgson! Here with us humble knaves? Won't you be missed at the high table?"

The high table… Was this young, earthy priest one of the teachers?

Whether he was or not, Hodgson just shook his head in all good-humour — and it was Gib who took it in snuff.

"If he has the charity to sit with us, you're not one to sneer!"

And never be it said that Marley left the last word to another. "Oh, but he's welcome — both here and up there. Are you, Deacon Gifford? I never see you sharing your bread and salt with the exalted ones."

"Peace, peace!" Hodgson patted the shoulder of the outraged Gifford. "We all sit where we choose. Let's not be quarrelsome, Sherbourn — or what will Roper think?"

Not that Marley was silenced. "Can he still think at all, after a morning of Worthington? It would have been more charitable to make him start with Barret."

Hodgson pulled a face that had Marley huff and lean in to whisper, "And don't say Barret is a puppet of the Jesuits, will you? What do you call Worthington, then?"

"I call him nothing," Hodgson said. "Nor Barret. I just say, give me Dr. Allen, and I'll be content." He turned to Tom. "But truly, how are you finding us, Roper?"

Any need to pretend confusion or timidity was spared, for at that moment the students began to rise, benches scraping on the floor. Barret, from his place on the dais, said grace, and

137

then a thin, pale man went to the pulpit to read from the Scriptures in a reedy voice, for the edification of them all as they ate their boiled onions and bread in pious silence.

A commendable exercise for the soul, no doubt — but how one was to untangle murders and conspiracies without asking questions, Tom truly didn't know. Had he thrust himself in the midst of the exiles for nothing? For it was one thing to observe the comings and goings day after day — although Marley seemed to have done precious little of that in near on six weeks — but it was another thing entirely to sound out the joints and flexures of what perhaps were two killings, and perhaps were not.

"*Unde bella et lites in vobis?*" the reader intoned.

From whence are wars and contentions, indeed — and Tom only had Barret's few days, and the onions tasted vile.

It must be a sin, surely, to be so little edified by the reading of the Scriptures — and so relieved when Catesby half leant across the table to ask under his breath: "Friends with Hugh Downes, were you?" Even in murmuring the man had a square manner — demanding answers rather than asking — and never looked away, not even when Elliot would have elbowed him silent.

"We used to know each other as boys, back at home." Tom sighed. "Poor Hugh. A fever, Dr. Barret said."

"A fever, ay," said Catesby, no more forthcoming than Barret had been, and rather more brusque. When Gifford glared in admonition, he resumed his methodical eating.

The college closing ranks? Or were the Cyclops's sheep just pressing together in unknowing disquiet? There was nothing for it but to try — and Tom Roper could be a most stolid fellow.

"Poor Hugh," he murmured again after a while. There had been this man at home, back in Scadbury, who had taught the Walsingham boys to lay a trap for coneys, and he... "He had an ague once, as a child, and lived through it. So he'd laugh, and say that he knew what wouldn't kill him..."

And see how Elliot startled — a lock of golden hair falling across his forehead — and took a breath to talk.

"Robin," whispered Catesby without looking up.

"'Tis just ... he never said, not even..." Elliot choked into silence when Catesby grabbed his shoulder in rough comfort. "He never said."

"They were good friends, Elliot and Downes," said Hodgson. "And Noll, too. Now, be quiet, listen and eat."

Friends! Tartarus take Kit Marley — hadn't he thought to mention this? Then again, Tom himself hadn't thought to ask. Better keep the inventions few and small — nothing that a teller of tales, if Downes had been one, would share with his new friends. Good enough friends, it would seem, to have young Elliot fighting tears. Tom caught Kit Marley's frowning glare, and met it with nothing more than Roper's stolid worry.

"I'm sorry that —" he began, and stopped when Gifford hissed him quiet, with a pointed look at the spoonful of onions on Tom's trencher.

"We do not scoff at the Lord's gifts, here!"

With as penitent an air as he could muster, Tom went back to his dinner.

On and on the reader tirelessly droned. Tom hardly heard him, busy as he was considering whether he'd learnt anything at all — and who of the men who sat with him was minding St. James the Apostle, and who was lost in his own thoughts on the matter of Hugh Downes's death.

Dr. Barret took the pulpit after dinner, to explain Saint James — and Tom had to agree with Marley: if made to choose between the two, he'd rather have Richard Barret's clarity over the sentimental transports of Worthington. Still, at the end of it, he was very glad to be rid of both, and to be led, together with a dozen others, through a small door in the back of the refectory, out to the garden that stretched behind the house.

It was planted with beds of herbs and a few apple trees, with roses in bloom that crept up the brick walls — none of them of that rich yellow of Blandine Jory's. Tom looked about himself, as though admiring the place, seeking... Ah, there it was. In the wall, down at the very back, was a narrow door with two bolts. Not a way in, then — unless there were times when it was left unbolted? The dining hall had no windows on the garden side, but there were three of them upstairs — this side, unlike the rest of the house, only having two storeys... Anyone using the garden door could go unobserved — or they could not.

Surely not at times like this, with the students scattering in little groups among the verdant beds. A pleasant place — but even that was no recreation, for the students were put to tend the vegetables and herbs.

And, it seemed, not only the students.

"Good for the soul," Hodgson explained with a huge grin. "And for cultivating patience. Dr. Allen likes a garden. Works here himself, sometimes." He discarded his doublet as he spoke, rolling up his shirt sleeves and smiling at the blue sky. "Come, Roper," he said. "Do you know how to gather peas?"

How fortunate that the child Tom and his little sister had liked to help their nurse in the kitchen garden — for Tom Roper would know for sure. Doublet doffed, and sleeves rolled in turn, he bent his back to it, side by side with Hodgson, half-kneeling in soil that was black and heavy with the rain of the past days. And had anyone told him that he'd find himself gathering peas in the cause of the Queen…

We never know, Thomas, what the Service will require of us — and therefore it will serve you best to be prepared for all things. And, in Tom's mind, Sir Francis's voice sounded far more amused than its wont.

Only, it had never felt this hard back in Scadbury. When Tom straightened to stretch his aching back, he found Hodgson watching him with a raised eyebrow.

"Ah, but I've lost the knack!" Tom laughed. "It's been so many years. We used to do it skipping, my sister and I." No — Roper's sister. The one who had turned her back on him, and grabbed for his inheritance. Lord, but it was hard to always be another, always on guard! With a sigh, Tom went back to the peas.

Hodgson wasn't smiling anymore. "My father was a farmer," he said. "We kept a garden, and you wouldn't find a finer one in the whole of Lancashire. Such peas, Roper. Such chives! Sometimes…" He shook his head, and resumed his work.

And it struck Tom that this Papist zealot was homesick. A farmer's boy who'd traded all he knew for his faith, and could never go back, unless it was in treason, and iron, and fire.

"Find us another basket, will you, lad?"

Hodgson's smile had grown sad — and Tom wished he liked the priest less.

When he returned with a wooden bucket, Marley had joined Hodgson, and Thurstan Hunt with him. Marley squatted by the bed, poking at the swollen pods with a curious finger — and wouldn't one think him a lordling, new to the very notion of working with his hands! Hunt hovered, until Hodgson waved him to a bit of masonry nearby — once the base of a fountain, perhaps, or a sundial.

"Sit, Hunt. Sit down before you faint away."

"I'm not fainting away," Hunt said, but the protest was mild, and he obeyed all the same, squinting in the sun. And he did look ill, wan and short-breathed.

Dominus Hunt, Marley had called him: was this the priest who had been ill? When the man wiped a hand across his sweating brow, Marley glanced at him askance in worry.

"Hunt was ill, the other week," he said, with a pointed look, and Hunt sighed like one who'd rather talk of something else.

But here was a chance, at last — unsubtly as it was won — and Tom looked up from the peas. "A fever? Like…?" And he stopped short, as though Tom Roper had thought, all of a sudden, how inconsiderate the probing was.

"Like poor Downes — rest his soul?" Hunt shook his head, sad but untroubled. "Only a sickness of the stomach."

"A nasty one," muttered Hodgson. "For days and days he could keep nothing down. Not even a cup of water."

Hunt grimaced in memory. "I won't call it pleasant — but nothing like…"

He let it trail, and for a while they all went back to their gathering, heaping handfuls of bright green pods into baskets and buckets.

A sickness of the stomach… It could have been poison — but nothing like what had befallen Downes.

"What ails Robin?"

Tom looked up to find Hunt studying another group of gardeners. The ruddy, righteous fellow was there, and Catesby, who tore the pods as though they'd offended him, and young Elliot, all hunched on himself.

Hodgson sat back on his heels. "He's badly shaken, our Robin."

And here the door was open for more of Roper's thoughtless blurting. "Ay, that he'll be, poor lad. Hugh first, and then Father Hunt — not that you died, Father, thank the Lord, but still — and then another of you yesterday, poor fellow…"

See how Hodgson shook his head with a little sigh, and Marley raised both eyebrows.

Hunt, it seemed, nothing discomposed. "…And Dr. Allen with the stone. What you must think of us, Roper!"

"*I* think of you…?" Oh, to be able to blush at need! "Oh, but…"

Hodgson patted Tom's shoulder. "Don't fret, lad — it's not the plague."

But something else was on Hunt's mind. "We hardly knew him, poor Fettiplace — Lord rest him. Why, I misdoubt Elliot ever had a word with him, that he should be this grieved…"

"Robin is tender-hearted," Hodgson said. "And it was his cousin found the body." He caught Tom's questioning frown. "Noll Catesby. You wouldn't know by seeing them, but they're kin, and closer than brothers. Never find one without the other." He pushed to his feet and picked up the full bucket. "Come, Sherbourn, these go to the kitchen."

They walked away with their burden. Tom rose in turn, brushing bits of soil from his breeches — and oh Jove, his knees! Perhaps Watson was right, and the life in Seething Lane had made him soft.

Hunt was still watching Robin Elliot, and how desolately he shook his head at whatever his cousin was earnestly whispering to him.

"Perhaps he knew the servant from back home?" Tom suggested, half to himself and half to Hunt.

"Sherbourn travelled here with Fettiplace's master. If anyone knows anything of that poor man, it would be him."

Would it, now? Tom swallowed a bitter laugh. Oh, devil pinch Kit Marley — and pinch him hard! Was the boy a natural, not to have told this? And what else he'd kept to himself, Tom would very much like to know.

But there was no chance of talking to the heedless brat — nor of stealing a look at Fettiplace's body — for more readings and more prayers followed the work in the garden, until the Marie called its flock to prayers and then supper.

The hall had a golden dimness in the thick yellow light of late afternoon, more chapel-like now, with the rush-lights burning on the tables. Once more Tom paused just across the threshold, trying to get his bearings. Cornering Marley among this crowd would be less than useless — but nothing bad could come from posing a few careful questions to Savage, could it? Not that Savage was anywhere in sight...

And then Will Colson, entering the hall breathless and furtive, smacked into Tom, who steadied him by catching one shoulder.

"Did I miss Vespers?" the boy gasped, almost slumping in Tom's grip when he received a shake of the head. "Don't tell, Roper! Barret sends me to the school of the *Bons Enfants* — hopes I'll learn some French there, but..." A puffing of cheeks. "I don't, and they make me stay longer, and it's a race to be back in time... Don't tell! I was just..."

The young imp! "Just practising your verbs, I'm sure. But won't Carter tell?"

"I didn't come in through the door..." The boy stopped short. "You're not going to tell, are you? Barret doesn't know how to be strict, but Worthington..." He glanced over his shoulder at the high table, and leant in to whisper in Tom's ear: "There's a stabling next door. The gate, they shut it late. And there's a tree in the yard — just by the wall..."

There was a brisk clapping of hands as the milling students moved to find a place at the tables, and young Will clung to Tom's arm.

"But I only do it when I'm late for Vespers. You're not telling?"

Oh, the beaming smile that split the young face from ear to ear, when Tom shook his head — for he had no wish to see the boy caned, and surely even Barret, no rigourist though he might be, would have much to object — and besides...

When young Will dragged him away, Tom went without protest, half amused at having made a steadfast friend so easily, half musing on what he'd just learnt. So there *was* a way in, from the Chevreau d'Or. Not out — not the same way, for there was no tree in the yard of the college — but still. Considering the import of this, he followed the boy to the same table where he'd sat for supper. Marley wasn't there, nor Hodgson — but the two cousins were, and the unamiable Gifford, and Father Hunt.

Ah well — perhaps something could be drawn out of Oliver Catesby, on the subject of finding Fettiplace's body.

They all stood for the long prayers — a portion of them for the restoration of Dr. Allen's health, a much smaller one for poor Fettiplace's soul. Colson prayed with a fervour that came no doubt from relief. Elliot was desolate, and Hunt and Catesby soldier-straight — and Gifford, too, though he lacked both Hunt's serenity and Catesby's fire.

More broth and bread followed, and more reading from the Scriptures — but no whispered talk and no questioning, for Gifford seemed bent on hissing down each word in strictest discipline. His authority was not much helped by the way he kept his eyes stubbornly lowered on his bowl, ignoring Catesby's contemptuous stares. Only once Hunt gave the poor fellow a glance, and it was one of impatient pity, and it struck Tom that Gifford might be of the unlearning sort in such matters.

And so must be, in the matter of cooking, whoever kept the college's kitchen, for the broth was even thinner and more tasteless than the night before. Young Rudd's recipe of adding cold water came to mind. Oh, for Madame Raulet's well roasted pigeons — or, indeed, a nice wedge of cheese — and a pot of wine! Following the example of his tablemates, Tom crumbled the bread into the broth for thickness, if not for flavour, and listened to the Apostle James's admonitions against judging one's fellow men.

At length, the reader came to the end of his labours for the day.

"'Tis Worthington explaining," whispered Will Colson — an admirer of the man, reckoning by the colour of his words. But instead Barret took the pulpit.

"A word, before the explanation," he said in his crisp voice. "I have a great joy to announce for some of us, who are to receive Holy Orders in sixteen weeks' time. Yaxley, Greene, Pattenson, Osbaldistone and Jackson will receive full orders; Charnock will ascend to deaconry, while Gerard and Sherson will be made subdeacons. I entrust these brothers to the prayers of you all…"

There had been murmuring across the hall with each name, and up near the high table one very young man was sobbing with joy among his smiling companions.

"That milksop!" Catesby snarled. "That mewling babe a deacon, and Sherson, too, and —"

"Be quiet!" ordered Hunt, over Gifford's shushing hiss.

Elliot clutched at his cousin's sleeve, but Catesby did not heed.

"One to talk, are you, Hunt? A priest already! How long have I been here? I study and pray, and ask for nothing better than to go back to England —"

"Noll, don't —" whispered Elliot, peering anxiously around.

"Even our Gifford is a Deacon, for all that they threw him out of the Seminary in Rome!" With a bitter chuckle, Catesby nudged Tom roughly. "Would you believe it, Roper? This weasel made a deacon by the Cardinal of Guise himself!"

Poor Gifford spluttered in disbelieving rage, and Colson gawped, and men were turning and rising.

Oh, but the fellow was a penance!

"Softly now!" Tom caught Catesby's forearm, holding him down when he would rise — too imperious for Roper, perhaps, but here was the man who'd seen Fettiplace's body, looking to get himself expelled. And Tom could have preached moderation to the doorjamb, for all it helped: the ox-strong idiot just shook himself free, eyes afire.

"There goes Catesby, whining again," someone said, just loud enough to be heard.

"Who says I whine —?"

Hunt half rose, both palms on the table, mouth thin and eyes hard. "Noll Catesby, enough!"

"What's this?" Cassock billowing around his ankles, Father Immes descended on them. "Again, Catesby? What will Dr. Allen say?"

"I —"

Immes waited for no answer. "Is this the obedience that you show? The patience, the charity, the meekness?"

"Ay, meekness! What is it you want for the Lord, Father? Soldiers or sheep?"

"Be quiet, young fool!" Immes commanded. "Will you never learn that a soldier is one who obeys his orders?"

"I obey orders, I do all I'm told, I shell peas, for God's sake — and yet you won't…"

"Noll!" Elliot whimpered, white to the lips, and Catesby clambered to his feet, jostling both his cousin and Tom off the bench.

Elliot caught himself on the table, hard enough to gash his palm on a corner. "Noll…!"

"Ay, Robin," Catesby sneered. "That's the way. Weep, and they'll order you tomorrow. Why, any half-heretic beggar they'll order. See if they don't make Roper a deacon before me!"

And he shoved Tom's shoulder, sending him against the table, hard enough to upset the rush-light. Oh, what a good few days — Baines first, and now… Tom shoved back just as Catesby came for him again. Catesby — who was half as big again…

"Enough!"

It was Thurstan Hunt stepping between, standing tall even as he panted in his weakness.

Tom found himself held back — Colson on one side, Kit Marley on the other — as though *he* were the one doing mischief. Bleeding though he was from his gashed hand, Robin Elliot held tight to his cousin, and Hunt glared at them all, until white candlelight fell on them all, like figures in a painting — Catesby breathing hard in his cousin's hold — and there went Barret and Worthington.

"Go to my room, Catesby," Barret ordered. "And you, have that hand bound, Elliot."

It seemed like a long time before Catesby looked down, and let his cousin lead him away.

Nostrils flaring, Barret took a deep breath. "And what of you, Thomas Roper?"

Had Tom Walsingham broken through for a moment — the fleece slipping off Ulysses's shoulders? Was it suspicion in the ring of faces all around? What would Roper, the mercer's son, do?

"He pushed Catesby," Gifford offered a little breathlessly — and why he should was beyond saying, seeing as Catesby had been the one to revile him.

But there went Colson, loyal lad: "Noll pushed him first —"

"Quiet." Barret silenced the boy with the single word, never taking his sharp, level gaze off Tom. "He can speak for himself."

Would Roper look away? "He shoved me — and looked to do it again, so I shoved back," Tom muttered, trying to look sullen.

"Hunt?" asked Barret.

Dozens of gazes glittered in the flickering light as they turned on the young priest.

"Catesby was spoiling for a fight, Doctor — and Roper … he defended himself."

Barret sighed. "Pray for a milder heart, Roper. A less prideful soul. We all should pray for that." And then he raised his voice for the benefit of the discomposed assembly. "Go back to your places, and listen well to Dr. Worthington."

Worthington didn't like it, by the way he stepped forward. "Should I not —"

As though he hadn't spoken, Barret went on: "And consider the evils of unbrotherly discord."

And with that, he turned and was gone, leaving Worthington with no choice but to take to the pulpit. Before he did, he stopped to shake his head at Tom in the saddest manner. "So now we know your mind, when it comes to turning the other cheek, don't we, Roper?"

At Tom's elbow, Kit Marley blew out his cheeks. "I doubt Worthington likes you much," he murmured.

No — nor did Catesby, nor the sour Gifford, nor Dickon Baines out there, nor Remi Thibaud — and surely, on his way back to London, neither did Watson. As for Marley, Tom didn't care to guess. A good few days, these had been!

"Had Dr. Allen been here..." someone murmured as they all sat back, the hall quietening down — with Bagshaw, Hodgson and Immes pacing along the tables like shepherd's dogs. Colson went to relight their rush, and Marley sat where Elliot had been.

Why didn't you say Downes had been friends with the cousins? Or that you travelled with Yates?

But there was no asking questions now — not with Worthington going on and on again about how all should be miserable and mourn and weep. He spoke with such vindictive sweetness, as though each word, each warm-voiced phrase were to wash Barret's slight from the memory of his hearers. All the time, Gifford's dark stare scoured the faces around the table. The Cyclops's watchdog — a foolish, aimless dog, only hungering for a fault to reprimand.

The college went to bed early, and in no great comfort. Nor in great cheer — though that could very well be from the mischief at supper. Tom was ushered into a narrow, bare room — one of several that lay above the hall, just under the roof's sloop, where pallets were lined up in a row against each long wall, and nails were driven into the whitewash for hanging clothes and satchels.

Ah, well. Wherever the Church of Rome lavished her riches, it hardly was on the Collège Anglais — and surely not on the comfort of the students, who undressed in scant light, and lay two or three to a pallet.

Sharing with Marley would have been convenient, but too much to hope — and in fact, Tom's bed-mates proved to be the righteous fellow from Worthington's lesson, who made a point of curling so to turn his back, and a more genial young man, who introduced himself as John Talbot, and their scoffing companion as Woodward.

And see how, three of four pallets away, Marley lay propped on an elbow, striving to catch Tom's eye. Ah, but Madame Jory had been right: no sense at all. Unless... Had any yellow roses bloomed at the Virgin's feet? Or had Marley anything to tell, for a wonder? Oh, he'd had much to say on the matter of murder and of Baines — but by what sieve the brat sifted what was of import and what was not, Tom would have liked to know.

Well, it would have to wait for morning. When the last of the rush-lights was snuffed, Marley was still there, propped on both elbows, head cocked and eyebrows raised at Tom for anyone to see.

Eager young fool.

The pallet was no less hard than that of the previous night — and at least the cupboard-like room had been quiet. This cursed dormitory was crowded, the air less than sweet, and the noise ceaseless — for these aspiring martyrs snored, and muttered in their sleep, and belched, and turned and tossed, and all the dampness of the season had taken residence under the roof, and grown heavy with a lack of air, and Woodward's choleric humours rumbled in his belly without cease, and when he happened to fall quiet for a blink, there went someone else, coughing, or breaking wind, or sighing.

Tom much regretted his solitary cupboard. For all the good it did him to sleep with all the others … and, in truth, for all the good of a full day in the college!

But now this was a piece of peevishness, come of being on constant guard, and of an empty stomach. There *were* things that he'd learnt, weren't there?

Lying on his back in the close, restless blackness, Tom rifled through the coloured pieces in the purse of his mind, and put them in a line:

Item: If a man slipped inside the stable-yard next door, with any luck, he could enter the college unseen — although that didn't mean he also could go about and poison a man, or perhaps two.

Item: Hunt's illness seemed to have little to do with Downes's fever or with Allen's stone. As for Fettiplace…

Quæstio: How had Fettiplace died? Nobody seemed to know or care.

Item: Catesby had found the body…

Only now Catesby was wherever the Collège Anglais kept its malcontents and brawlers — and even if he wasn't, he would bear a grudge, and be loath to answer Tom's questions. And, quite likely, so would the very nervous Elliot, for his cousin's sake. A shame, really, because…

Item: The cousins had been friends with the dead man, and known him well enough.

Item: On the other hand, Kit Marley had perhaps known Fettiplace — and was to be questioned, whether he liked it or not.

Item: Worthington and Barret were in disagreement, and the students divided in supporting one or the other.

It was, on consideration, a longer line than Tom would have expected, which could have been a slight comfort — but wasn't. Much as he tried, he failed to find meaning in what he knew. *Too soon*, his mind whispered. *Too little yet.*

With a sigh, he turned on his side and waited for sleep, hoping that he could uncover more before they sent him on his way — or found out who and what he was. When he fell asleep, it was to dreams of Sir Francis and the dead Fettiplace in his coarse shroud, looking down on him from the pulpit in the dining hall, both frowning very hard.

CHAPTER 10

25th of May

Wood creaking, clothes rustling, whispering in the dark … and had there been a bell?

Tom blinked awake — or half awake, at least — not knowing where he was. He sat up blindly, groping for the dagger that was not there, and a hand on his shoulder made him stiffen.

"Go back to sleep, Roper," a voice murmured.

"What's this…?"

"Matins, but you don't have to keep the Hours."

Someone opened the door, letting in enough light to thin the darkness into a procession of shuffling shadows, and the voice and the hand on Tom's shoulder became John Talbot.

Over Talbot's shoulder a round face hovered, greenish in the gloom.

"Though the Lord doesn't love sloth," this other fellow muttered, at which Talbot sighed.

"Nor a lack of kindness, Woodward. Let him rest."

They joined the shadows, Woodward huffing and stumbling into a pallet, by the sound of it.

A few lumps here and there showed a handful of others who didn't keep the Hours. Tom fell back on the pallet, rubbing his eyes and wondering. Should he follow? Would Roper do it? Did Marley? Would there be anything to uncover in the chapel in the middle of the night…?

The next thing Tom knew was the Marie again — more imperious now — and men talking aloud, and blue-grey daylight pushing at the one square window.

"Now for this you must rise," Talbot said, smiling from where he sat on the pallet's corner, lacing his shoes.

Tom bolted up. Oh Lord! Oh Lord — he'd slept! The frowning Sir Francis from his dreams was very vivid in his mind as he dressed in a rush. Oh Lord!

As though this haste at dawn could make up for the night's failing! Still, in a trice he was ready and out of the door, and at the head of the stairs.

The stairs...

For the first time since arriving, he stopped to consider. Was this where Downes had fallen to his death? Both hands on the sturdy rail, Tom leant to frown down the dark well. A goodly fall, likely to break a man's neck. How was it, though, that nobody had heard? Staggering out of the infirmary, swaying in his fever, catching himself against a wall at first, and then nothing to catch at, the scream, the long terror of hurtling down, the pain — all the worse for not being in his right mind — and then...

"Are you thinking of your friend?"

Tom startled, hands gripping the rail. How had Father Immes come to his side unnoticed? A darker shadow in the grey gloom, dark eyes forbidding in the craggy face...

"Father," Tom murmured, "is this where he fell?"

Immes pointed across the well, towards the front of the house.

"There's another staircase down there. When Downes took ill, we didn't know what it was, if it was catching, so he was put in the infirmary."

"Alone?"

155

"There was always someone watching over him, after he began to rant. But…" Father Immes turned a stern eye on Tom. "But what is Man's caution when God disposes otherwise? You'd do well to bow to His will, Roper, rather than question it."

"I don't question it, Father —"

"But you seek to lay blame." Something shifted in the dark, hard face. In another man, it would have been a softening. "You grieve for your friend, and I won't fault you for it. Our Lord did grieve for Lazarus — but you must learn to accept God's will in all things, meekly and gratefully. Go to Lauds, child, and pray for a humble heart."

A humble heart, ay — but that Our Lord hadn't meekly taken Lazarus's death, and brought him back to life instead… Which was no doubt a very sinful thought, both in the books of Papists and Protestants. Ah well.

Tom took the stairs, wondering as he went. Something nagged at his mind. He stopped to put a hand on the rail, and found it above hip-height. He tried to lean against it, and a little over it. It seemed sturdy enough to keep a grown man's weight. Would it truly be that easy to fall over it? How tall had Hugh Downes been?

When he looked up, he found Father Immes still at the head of the stairs, frowning down at the man who must have looked as though he questioned God's will — but who, in truth, was wondering if it hadn't been the will of someone else.

After cleansing their souls at Mass, it turned out, once a fortnight, Allen's flock also cleansed their bodies more thoroughly than the well allowed.

"'Tis Fridays, as a rule — but what with one thing and another..." Will Colson explained — one thing and another being a man's death.

There was a low little door by the well, and past it a flight of steps led down to a huge vaulted room. It was dark, but for what light streamed in through the door and two small grated windows right under the ceiling. It was light enough to see walls of raw stone and several huge vats, surrounded by a wooden constellation of smaller vessels.

Carter, Rudd and the students were put to work, carrying buckets of water from the well to fill these communal baths, and bringing piles of rough linen squares. Only a small amount of water arrived from the kitchen, warmed in large cauldrons.

Once the vats were half-full, all began to undress and wash, some even entering the frigid baths.

"The way the Romans did, eh?"

And there was Marley, stripped to the waist and grinning.

"They warmed their water, though," Tom groused, as he unfastened his doublet.

This earned him a laugh. "Not so keen on mortifying the flesh, the Romans were!" The boy pitched his voice above the noise of voices, splashing, and laughter that commingled in one roaring reverberation under the vaulted ceiling.

So it was that they managed to have a word, Mr. Secretary's two men, while sharing a smaller tub to wash, right next to the stairs that led to the courtyard. Tom hissed between his teeth when the wet linen rubbed his bruised cheekbone, and, between shivers, he told of his findings.

"And you didn't say you'd travelled with Fettiplace," he concluded.

Of course, Marley made nothing of it. "With Fettiplace's master, I travelled. With the servant, I doubt I had a dozen words."

For servants were beneath the notice of such as Christopher Marley, Bachelor of the Arts — especially when there were other matters to occupy his one-idead attention... Will Colson's tree beyond the wall, for instance.

"So Baines *can* enter the college at will!" The brat beamed in triumph — as though that alone rounded the matter of two deaths.

"It still doesn't follow that he can go about unnoticed, and poison a man, and then slip out again."

Marley made an impatient gesture. "There's a door in the garden wall. All the way down to the back —"

"What of the windows that look onto the garden?"

A narrowing of eyes... "Dormitories — our own, among the others."

Tom called to mind the low square casement. "Would anyone be up there during the day?"

Marley sluiced a pailful of cold water over his head and shuddered noisily, shaking off the water like a hound. A bid for time, if Tom had ever seen one.

"*Would anyone be up there...?*" he repeated, in exaggerated patience.

The scowl was not unexpected — nor was the answer. "Some go up there to read or pray — but not to gaze out of the window. Most of the time, Baines could just go and let himself out, and none would be the wiser."

"He could never know for certain —"

And that was where Marley lost his patience. "You've seen him: he's horn-mad!" he snarled, and then started so guiltily, you'd think he'd poisoned the whole College himself.

Tom sighed, affecting to shrug and rub at his wet hair with a cloth as heads turned their way. Now let no one come to his rescue — for there were things he needed to discuss with this ill-tempered dolt... But it was not to be hoped, of course. There was Hodgson approaching, shoes in hand.

It would have to be quick, then. "Was Downes a tall man?"

"A tall man — why —?"

"Was he?"

And trust Marley not to have noticed! "Like yourself or thereabout, I'd reckon." He gestured vaguely. "An inch shorter, maybe? But why?"

Why, why, why? Lord give strength! "I've been thinking..." *that you might be both right and wrong* — but this Tom swallowed, for at that moment Hodgson joined them and sat on the lowest step to put on his shoes.

"Don't let this one talk you witless, Roper," he said, looking up to throw an admonitory look at Marley. "He's got a wicked silver tongue, our Sherbourn. Disputes *in utroque.*"

But Roper would not know of Aristotle and Plato, would he? Tom frowned, and Hodgson waved a hand.

"But I forget, you're not one of my students." And he smiled so pleasantly, so kindly.

Was this another little trap, like Barret's questioning in French? They couldn't think a Queen's man would fall for it, surely? Had they ever caught one with such tricks? Had they tried them on Marley? But then, Marley was playing very much himself, a discontent out of Cambridge, not an uneducated barleycorn. And, come to that, did Hodgson, the farmer's son, teach philosophy to these aspiring martyrs?

Thoughts for another time, for right then several shadows crossed the doorway above them. Hodgson twisted to look up, and Tom, in his breeches and shirt, climbed high enough to observe. It was the old servant from the pantry, leading two men in drab-coloured jerkins.

"Early for visitors, isn't it?" asked Marley from downstairs.

The strangers crossed to the gallery and the pantry, just as Hodgson joined Tom.

"Beadles from Saint-Étienne," the priest explained. "Come for poor Fettiplace. They wouldn't have him yesterday, Lord knows why…"

And sure enough, a moment later, the two men reappeared carrying between them the corpse on the plank, tightly shrouded now, as for a pauper's funeral. Behind them came Dr. Worthington and a young flaxen-haired priest — and there went any chance to observe the body.

Several students who were done with their washing were loitering in the yard: they murmured their prayers as Worthington blessed the dead Zachariah Fettiplace.

"*Requiescat in pace*, poor fellow," sighed Hodgson, shaking his head as he made his way downstairs again.

And if Fettiplace truly was to rest in peace, it was time to dig deeper.

"Amen," Tom said, following the priest. "To die like this, among strangers…"

Hodgson hummed. "One moment he was there, waiting to see Dr. Allen… Then he told Elliot he was unwell, and not an hour later Catesby found him dead."

"Poor old fellow!" And it would be natural for Roper to be sad, wouldn't it? "To fall ill, and home so far away…"

"Not that he was old, was he, Sherbourn?" Hodgson asked. "Thirty years, no more. And he seemed hale enough when he was here at Easter."

Which had been a month earlier, and meant little enough — but surely he hadn't been throwing up like Hunt — or someone would have marked it. Oh, for a way now to ask about blue faces and tongues!

"I've no envy for Catesby," Tom ventured. "It must be a fright to find a man dead like that."

"Catesby knows no fear," Marley mocked, which Hodgson didn't like.

"A little charity, lad. And besides, Oliver thought the poor man was still alive. He was trying to revive him, when Gifford arrived…"

And he stopped, eyes running to something behind Tom's back: Dr. Worthington, beckoning from the head of the staircase. And, being thus summoned, Hodgson took his leave and climbed up to the courtyard.

This left Tom with Marley again, who smiled a slow, tight-lipped smile.

"You're good at this," he murmured. "You draw it out without asking… You believe Fettiplace was poisoned, then."

And so perhaps the boy wasn't a complete dunce. "I believe no such thing — but still I'd like to not ask Catesby a question or two."

A half grin, a shake of the head. "Cloistered away. Grinding at his *pater ave gloria*s for having a mind of his own — and very much *in secundis*, for trying to maul yourself."

And surely it would be bad to laugh at this, and to encourage such levity.

"Whoever thought you'd make a good Seminary man! What of Elliot, then? Perhaps Fettiplace told him just what ailed him."

Marley looked around the dark cavern in a manner that, no doubt, he thought subtle. "Punished too — for all they say they use no punishments here."

"What for? If anything, he tried to stop the ado."

"He'll have pled Noll's case once too many — or else begged to share in the penitence. You'll have to wait."

Wait — ay. But did Tom have to? Must he? Whatever the fate of Fettiplace and Downes, it seemed less and less likely that Baines had had a hand in it. Ergo, this being no Service matter, there was no earthly reason why Sir Francis's man should meddle.

It was a good thing that right then the Marie went a-peal — for Roper and Sherbourn had spent far too long a time in conversing of Kent.

Not that Marley saw it. "Oh, damn and blast it! I must go to Terce," he grumbled — though, for a mercy, he kept it to a whisper, if an angry one, as he dressed in a rush.

"Would Sherbourn curse like this?" Tom scolded with a half-smile, and the reproof earned nothing more than a shrug.

"Dick Sherbourn's a very bad subject."

"And yet he keeps the Hours."

"They wouldn't send me to the Université otherwise. I want to go to the Université."

Of course he did. A cobbler's son, a penniless bursar with little hope to travel and to study abroad, unless it was on Sir Francis's purse.

Tom climbed up to the cool air of the courtyard — and it was the strangest thing how the thick walls ate all the din from the vault. Even with the door open, it was like going deaf, as the freshly bathed students hastened to the chapel like a murder of large crows.

A good time to study the body — but that the body was gone. Devil seize the Parish of Saint-Étienne! Couldn't they have waited another hour? Tom stopped under the gallery, hoping that it would look like Roper wondering what to do with himself.

He didn't have to wonder long. As the courtyard emptied of all but a handful of men, Thurstan Hunt approached with a manner of unhurried purpose.

"You don't have to keep the Hours," he said, just as young Talbot had in the middle of the night. "Unless you wish it?"

And why such a simple question should wrong-foot him, was more than Tom could tell. "I…" he stammered.

Hunt nodded. "'Tis a great change in a man's life — and the Lord doesn't always send a thunderbolt to mark it. Will you sit with me?"

Among the benches against the wall, he pointed to the one by the well, and there they sat together on the cool stone.

So there it went again. Barret first — twice — then Worthington in a manner, then Hodgson, and now the saintly Hunt. But then, last evening in the dining hall, it was Hunt's word that Barret had wanted.

"Don't *you* keep the Hours, Father?" Which was ill-judged — Tom Walsingham breaking through again, for Roper surely had no irony.

Hunt's smile grew wider. "I told Dr. Barret that you seem no fool to me. So a fool's one thing that you are not — but we must see what it is that you are, what manner of man. You understand that?" Such frank earnestness … and it struck Tom that Thurstan Hunt truly wanted him to understand, to see and not be offended.

Tom nodded and looked down at his hands, and the priest leant back against the wall with a small sigh. For a while they just sat there, side by side, Tom brushing the crumbs of black moss from his palms. The yard was not quiet, with the praying voices wafting from the chapel now and then, and the servants at work in the kitchen, the swallows keening in the blue sky above, and the bustle and clatter of morning from outside —

but it was peaceful, with the blooms of the roses overhead and the air touched with soot. Hardly the sort of place where one expected treason to be plotted day after day, and murder done.

"It's not two years since I arrived in Rheims," Hunt said after a while. "One day Dr. Barret sat me on this bench, and asked me what I ask of you now: what are you seeking with us, Roper?"

A murderer, perhaps. And I'd be curious, too, of how you do treason with the Queen of Scots — although, when it comes to that, I don't know that I can find out... "I don't know."

Hunt hummed, as though for a well-reasoned answer. "I didn't know what I sought, either. Refuge, perhaps. For one thing, I was running from the ugliness that I'd seen back at home."

Not unlike Tom Roper's story of loss and betrayal — but that Hunt carried himself like a gentleman, and his was no Canterbury tale. "And what did Dr. Barret say?"

The squaring of shoulders Tom did not see, for he kept his head bowed — but it sounded in Hunt's words. "He said there's no refuge here, no peace. For a few days, perhaps, but then... The Lord won't give England back to the True Faith for prayers alone — and here is where men are prepared for the battle. For going joyously back where every step, every true word, every soul saved, the heretics call a crime, and punish with death. Think on this, and think well: can you consecrate yourself to do the Lord's own work? Each day of your life, each breath, each drop of blood to the very last?"

And to hear him, one would never tell that he was preaching treason, and the Queen's assassination! How he could have thought Thurstan Hunt of the same ilk as Worthington, Tom didn't know. Such quiet passion in each word, such a ring of truth. There was no studied sweetness in this man, nor the stony harshness of Immes, nor Bagshaw's ever-ready wrath — and this made him all the more dangerous, once he was back in England to do what he called the Lord's work. Even the compassion was frank and true, when he misread Tom's continued silence.

"Fear is no sin in itself," he said, a smile in his voice. "Or we'd all be damned. But we must pray to the Lord to give us heart to do what's good and right — in spite of our fear."

Which was all very well, and even better the lack of suspicion in it — and yet it was time to do a little sounding in turn. "Dr. Barret asked, have I a weak soul." Tom leant forward, elbows on his knees. "I think that I do. I counted on finding Hugh here. I thought he'd tell me what to do..." A shake of the bent head, a disheartened sigh. "It never came into my mind that he could be a priest already, ready to go back, maybe..."

This had Hunt frowning. "Who told you this? Downes never received even the minor orders."

"Nobody told me — I thought..."

The smile returned, if somewhat sad. "Oh, no. Not Hugh Downes. He was doing his studies here — but, you see, not all are made for priesthood. Some have the heart for it, but not the wit. Some have more head than heart... Your friend was the sort of man we have good use for. Some of us are not what you'd call worldly. They need guides, messengers, companions — men with a level head, rather than a learned one — and Downes was that..."

And here lay danger, in the little silence, in the half questioning curl of the words. Had Downes truly been that, or just a lack-wit, as his boyhood friend should well know? Were this Worthington or Barret, or even Hodgson, another trap would be likely. Hunt, on the other hand... Hunt was no fool — but was he devious?

Tom reckoned that he wasn't — and took a gamble. "A cunning lad, he used to be. He never liked school, but he was smart in many things."

Hunt chuckled — and unless he was a most accomplished liar, the gamble had paid off. "He had not changed, then. He picked up French marvellously, and there was no one Dr. Allen would rather have run his errands in the town. And always cheerful about it, poor Downes…"

Running errands in the town, coming and going — more or less at his pleasure…

Tom's sudden abstraction Hunt must have taken for sadness. He braced himself upright with a hand on Tom's shoulder, and kept it there in a warm clasp as he gazed down with all the earnestness in this world.

"Don't be sad, Roper. Or, if you must, be sad that your friend wasn't allowed to do more — but remember: he died a soldier in the Lord's own battle. Another boon we all should pray for."

And in truth Tom rather hoped to live a long life, and to avoid martyrdom — but for a heartbeat these hopes felt puny, and a little shallow, and a good deal more human than the fire that burnt in Thurstan Hunt's eyes.

CHAPTER 11

Dinner was perfunctory, and simmering with some expectant quality. Even the explanation of the day's chapter was cut short, and Father Hodgson had barely descended from the pulpit before servants and students all set to clearing the trestle tables, dismounting them and turning the hall into a chapel again.

"'Tis the sermon," Will Colson explained, as Tom helped him carry two piled benches. When the boy took a bouncing step, and the uppermost bench began to slide, young Talbot stepped in to stop the fall, exchanging huge grins with Colson. Even Woodward seemed a shade cheerier — although, what joy was to be found in yet more preaching?

"What sermon?" asked Tom who, as a boy, had never known how to sit still through one.

"In English," Talbot said. "We all practise and prepare."

"To show off to the heretics." And this, from Colson, was a little too much for Woodward who, red-faced and pursemouthed, felt it his duty to correct his younger fellows.

"Dr. Allen says the heretics do their studies in English, and preach all the better to the rabble for it — while we, who know our Scriptures and our Authors in Latin, must practise it…"

And on he went, and Tom soon lost interest in who preached what. Not that Woodward took notice, perhaps practising a sermon of his own. Instead, Tom watched the students and marked two things: for one, John Savage had reappeared; for another, neither Catesby nor Elliot had.

Which was no matter, was it? Not if Tom was to leave — which he'd better do before he betrayed himself to whatever doubts these people had of him. And since there was nothing here to concern the Service…

"Here they come!" Colson called of a sudden. He was at the yard door, hugging the jamb in his eagerness. "Go hurry Pitts, Talbot! They're here."

Judging from the way Talbot rushed away, and Woodward and a dozen others joined the boy at the door and window, one would think the Cardinal of Guise himself must be arriving. When Tom pushed his way to the mullioned window that looked out onto the yard, all he saw was a gaggle of men and women, and even a couple of older children — all dressed in their finery, all chattering among themselves and with the students. Bagshaw and Hodgson were there, too, offering welcomes, and Barret had a wizened lady on his arm who smiled up at him in a most motherly way.

"The English of Rheims," Colson said, with a breathless grin. "They come each Saturday to hear the sermon. And it's Pitts giving it today. He'll need the practice soon —"

"Colson!" a man scoffed in a harsh Northern voice — a tonsured student with pale eyes full of distrust. "Dr. Worthington said…"

Dr. Worthington said what? To keep things from all strangers, or this particular one?

For once young Will was not chastised. "Oh, drop it, Yaxley! He'll see soon enough."

But what he would soon see, Tom didn't learn, for the English of Rheims flocked into the chapel, and a bright-eyed Colson dragged him to see them, as though they were the greatest wonder. And perhaps they were, to the boy who missed his neighbourhood, his friends, his mother, and didn't know whether he'd see them again. It must be sweet to find himself amidst these good plain English people…

"See?" a voice whispered in Tom's ear, and there stood Kit Marley, bright-eyed in turn, though not with homesick yearning.

"People come in — and then they go away."

And so could Baines, hung unsaid, but it was as clear as day in the lad's triumphant little smile. As though this were a play, and Tom a groundling to exclaim and marvel as events were sprung on him. Oh, save and deliver — poets! Except...

"Each Saturday," Tom said. "Fettiplace didn't die on a Saturday. Did Downes?"

Look how the wind went all out of Kit Marley's sails.

"No ... no, but he could have —"

"What, stayed hidden for two days?"

"Why, no — but..."

And then, over the lad's shoulder, Tom caught Worthington, peering at them across the crowded chapel. When he found himself observed, the priest turned sharply away.

Tom nudged Marley into silence. "We talk too much," he murmured, and then turned to Colson.

All of it far too fussy, surely, and nothing that would assuage Worthington's misgivings. Devil take it, and them all, and Marley, who just stared, chewing his lip and itching to say more. And most of all, devil take Tom's own awkward doings. Had he at once betrayed himself to the Cyclops, and revealed the Queen's man within the lair?

To spare Marley even the temptation, he walked away through the crowd just as Pitts, a sour-faced, thick-necked young man, ascended to the pulpit, and began his sermon to the rapt attention of his friends, and the English of Rheims. And what must Pitts discuss, of all things, but the wickedness and malice, and ultimate fordoing of all deceivers?

169

A long, long piece of irony it was — and Pitts delivered it in the harshest manner, promising fire and brimstone, not just for the sinful but also for the weak. It had the stirring quality of a barbed whip; the English of Rheims drank it in most eagerly. Was this how Allen's men preached to recusants back in England? Then it was a wonder that there should be Papists at all ... but then, Puritans were no cheerier, and in truth the spirit of the visitors didn't seem quashed in the least as they took their leave, chattering as pleasantly as when they had arrived.

Tom counted not quite a score of them. If Rheims was truly a-swarm with the English, then few were Catholic exiles — or at least few attended the weekly sermons at the college. And, if these were the usual numbers, there was no chance that the wild-eyed, unkempt Baines could have entered or left among them unnoticed.

What air of holiday surrounded the English sermon left with the visitors. Teachers and students went their ways — some to the rooms upstairs, some out to the Université, some to read or pray on their own in the garden.

Tom waited to see who would be sent to sound him now, and was a little surprised that no one was. It would hardly be the servants, would it? And yet, when no one claimed him, it was Carter who beckoned to him from the hall's door.

"Have they left you alone, young master? Don't idle, then. Come and help an old man — there's a good lad."

Not that Carter was old, no more than forty by the look of him, and strong as an ox in spite of his limp — but then, why not? Back at Easter time, the servants must have seen more of Fettiplace than the students had. And they must have known Downes too, if he'd been Allen's messenger. All of it less than useless, since Tom would have to leave sooner rather than later … yet, while he stayed, he may as well try to uncover what he could.

So he soon found himself mounting trestles together with Joseph Carter.

"A deed of charity, that's what I call it, master!" the man cheerfully assured, as he limped sideways, holding one end of a trestle. "All ready enough to undo the hall for the sermon, they are, but once it's done, and the doctors are not about … eh!" He shook his head. "But no — that's not true. There are some as help. Take Mr. Hunt, him as is Father Hunt, now. A gentleman true, that one, and never too busy to lend a hand, until he took ill. Now he's weak as a kitten … no — the other way, there."

Tom obeyed, adding the moving of trestles to the list of things one did in the Service. "Father Hodgson's another to help, I'll wager," he said. "And Elliot, and young Will Colson. And poor Hugh Downes was another, surely?"

Carter had been smiling and nodding at the first three names. At that of Downes, he twisted his mouth. "Downes, ay," he hummed. "Rest his soul. Even too much he helped, that one. A bit of a Jack Stickler. Before he came, we used to go out, I or Rudd, if one of the doctors needed something. And none of them has money to waste, for they're all poor as church mice, here — nothing like the college in Rome. Dr. Bagshaw, as came back last month, he says they live on quails and raisins there. Well, we don't, and the doctors are as poor as the last of us, and yet they found a sol to vail us now and then. Then comes Hugh Downes, all smiles, with those crooked teeth, and never still — and before we know, 'tis him doing all the errands, and every chance he had to go out, he went, all eager, and wanting no vail. And I say, he must have had his own reasons to go, mustn't he, for he never let anyone else... Oh."

Discern men's hearts, Thomas, through their transparent faces.

Transparent indeed. It was writ large on Carter's creased forehead, the very moment when some scrap of gossip occurred to him — that Roper had been Hugh Downes's friend...

The servant went back to his trestles with new vigour — so much of it, in fact, that he all but upturned the next one. "And I'm not saying that he wasn't a good man, mind," he hastened to add. "And he's dead now, so the Lord knows him, and 'tis not for the likes of me... Now, you see to the benches, Master Roper, for they'll not see to themselves."

And after that, it was another Carter, tight-lipped and brisk, who busied himself with the benches, and nothing brought back the chattering one. Nor did Tom want to insist too much, although he did protest Downes's honesty — if more half-heartedly, perhaps, than Roper should. They fell to working in silence, and all the time he wondered at Hugh Downes. *He must have had his own reasons...*

Also Tom wondered at himself, never thinking to misdoubt Downes, just because he was dead. As though death — or murder — only befell the good. Marley had liked the man, and so had Hunt... But Marley hadn't known him long, and Lord knew how he formed his judgments; Hunt, on the other hand, was hardly one to disparage a dead man to his friend. Perhaps it had been foolish to tout such a friendship — for now there the pieces went, clicking into a new pattern, and into new questions worth asking, if only...

When he looked at Carter again, Tom found the servant chewing at his lip.

"'Tis out of turn that I spoke..."

If only he knew! Tom gave a heavy sigh. "It saddens me to hear what you said, but…" And see the relief on Carter's face at finding sadness instead of offence! So perhaps a whining Roper was less dangerous than a curious one. "I came at a bad time. I felt it in my bones the moment I saw that other poor fellow dead."

The servant shifted his weight. "Ay, Fettiplace — rest his soul."

"To come here, and to die within the day…" Was the shiver too much?

Carter gladly jumped at the turn in conversation. "Ay, but he was ill. Not that I saw him, mind. 'Twas old Bénoit as let him in." And, as he gathered his broom and made to leave, the servant even risked a half-smile in his relief. "'Tis not the bad air here, Master Roper. You can be of good cheer."

Which Tom was not, as he lingered on the threshold, an ear to the uneven clack of Carter's heels on the cobbles — for what he had now was a host of new doubts that were going to remain unanswered.

Supper came — and still no Catesby and no Elliot.

No one seemed to have a thought for their absence; they would at another time, perhaps — but tonight other business filled their minds.

No matter how Gifford and Woodward glared, scoffed, hissed and pursed their lips, the whispers ran around the tables like fire in the stubble. Whispers brought by those come for the sermon, and discussed already, and picked apart while Tom moved trestles with Carter. Whispers that the truce between the King and the Guise had come to an end, and war loomed large again.

Out of these walls, grim suppers must be shared in every house of Rheims. In here it was hope that quivered in each murmur, and gleamed in each pair of eyes. For the House of Guise were friends to the English Catholics, and surely a Guise on the French throne would be the answer to decades of prayers...?

The whole hall was a-simmer with it, devil take them all for fools and traitors! The Cyclops's sheep — and no mistake. And whether the Guise was the one-eyed monster, or Allen himself, it was hard to decide. But these men — even the best of them, the Hodgsons, the Hunts, the Barrets — could they not see? Had they no thought for England, at least, if they could have none for France? War, death, ruin, men burnt at the stake... Not that it was ever going to happen — not with the Queen on the throne, and Sir Francis to guard her — but still, what were these men dreaming of, in their whispers and their prayers?

And why he must find such angry surprise in it, Tom didn't know. All the more reason to go, in fact, to leave in the morning — and, unless he found orders at the Brebis-qui-File, he'd seize Baines somehow, and leave for England before the war broke out in earnest.

What to do with Marley was another matter. Marley who, from the table where he sat with Hunt and Talbot, kept glancing Tom's way — never mind how Tom ignored him.

Why, when supper was done, and all fell to dismantle the trestles for Compline, what must the lad do, but come to seek Tom and grab him by the arm!

Lord give patience and charity — for Tom was right out of both! "Do you want to be found out —"

"Catesby's gone. And Elliot with him," Kit Marley hissed right across the reproof.

"What the devil do you mean, gone?" Tom nudged the lad to the nearest table, and they began to move it between them.

"That they aren't here, I mean!" And with such breathless vigour did Marley push the trestle, he all but squashed Tom's already bruised hand against the wall with it. "Left the college. Went away. Old Allen himself tried to dissuade them … to dissuade *him*, for this is Catesby's doing, I'll stake my soul on that —"

"Will you be quiet!" Tom rubbed his mistreated hand, hissing between his teeth — and Marley decided this was a chance to catch.

"You're not hurt, are you?" he asked, loud enough to be heard. "It slipped… Come with me, comfrey salve is what you need." And, grabbing a rush-light, he dragged Tom towards the door.

The lie of the salve he repeated to Hodgson as they passed him, and Tom followed. In truth, as lies went, it wasn't too ill-thought, and it would serve.

Up the front stairs they climbed, and into one of the empty classrooms. As soon as they were inside, Marley blew on the rush-light, leaving them in the dark — just as the Marie sang Compline.

"They keep no salve here, I'll wager?" Tom asked, as he felt his way towards the nearest stool and sat.

"The infirmary's next door, but I don't want old Bénoit to walk in on us…" Marley's murmuring was taut. "What do we do now? Had I found out before, we could have gone after those two…"

"Marley —"

"No one knows where they're off to, so it will have to be Gifford. He saw Fettiplace's body, too. You must —"

"Christopher Marley, hear me!" The breathless whisper ceased. Tom began slowly, ordering his thoughts as he talked. "It can't have been Baines."

"Why —?"

"There's no way on earth that he could have come and gone — much less quickly enough to poison Fettiplace and then be around the Marché à la Laine to tussle with me. And even if he had —"

"You can't tell for certain! What of the garden door?"

"Wouldn't someone notice if it remained unbolted?"

"Perhaps…" The sound of pacing. "Perhaps a servant wouldn't tell for fear of being blamed… You can't know for certain!"

"Certain enough. But even if I'm wrong, even if Baines had found a way to get in and then out — why poison one man and then another a month later? And mind — the more I hear, the less I think it was poisoning."

"You don't know what killed Fettiplace."

"I'll lay you a wager: had it been a ranting fever like that of Downes, either the servant or Elliot would have said so."

"Ay, but…"

"Besides, Baines told you he'd poison the well. He knows where the well is: why not just throw a dead rat in it?"

"Even if he only poisoned one —"

"But why the devil would he? Neither Downes nor Fettiplace were here during his time. Had it been Allen, now…" Tom held up a hand when he heard Marley take a breath to speak, for all that the lad couldn't see him. "Allen wasn't poisoned. The stone is the stone, and there's no poison that will give you that."

There was a long, slow sigh, and the next thrust uncertain and childish. "It doesn't mean…"

"It means it cannot have been Baines."

This was met with silence. An unconvinced silence, but enough of it that voices could be heard from the hall downstairs, singing the psalms of Compline, and the Watch calling eight hours out in the street.

Time that they should go back, but as Tom rose to do so, Marley stirred.

"Well, then it was someone else. What are you going to do?"

Do! Was the lad blind? "What do you want me to do? If Baines has done no murder, and unless you have, this is no Service business."

There was no reaction to the mild joke, and Marley's voice went flat and cold. "So what?"

"So tomorrow I'll tell Barret that I've changed my mind. And I'm thinking that perhaps you —"

"Leave?" The contemptuous astonishment took Tom by surprise. "You leave, and turn your back on two murders!"

Tom swallowed an impatient groan. "You can't even be sure there was murder done at all! People die, hale young men take ill — and you've no proof that there was anything amiss."

"What if there was, though? What if someone killed not once, but twice? What if he lies in wait to do it again…?"

And that was when Tom lost all charity. Reaching blindly in the blackness, he found a sleeve and shook it. "What then? Are we to keep these people safe? You heard them at supper: they wait for the Guise to invade England — why, they pray for it! What do you think? Your Hunt, your Hodgson, even young Colson — what do you think they'd do if they knew what you are?"

Marley shook free. "Put me to the rack, ay — but then, what do we do, when we catch one of them in England?"

177

But we're in the right. They are the traitors — to their God and their Queen. But...

Ah, well. This was a decision made.

"I'm leaving tomorrow — and you're coming back with me."

"You can't —"

"You're coming back with me," Tom ordered, with the stone-like finality Sir Francis used, the sort no one dared to gainsay — not even Lord Treasurers or royal favourites. Coming from Mr. Secretary's kinsman, it was enough to silence Christopher. "Now, let's go back, before we're missed."

Once one's eyes were accustomed to the darkness, a ribbon of the faintest light showed around the door they'd left ajar. Tom was on the threshold before the lad spoke again.

"I expected better of you, Thomas Walsingham."

"Don't!" Tom scolded — more out of habit than necessity.

"Watson says you have wits, courage, and fairness."

Ay — try and ask him now, most specially of the fairness... "Does he!"

"But perhaps he's wrong. What have you done with him, I'd like to know? Summoned back to London ... fiddle-faddle!"

If I were you, I'd be wary of his friendship — but then, you bear no name he'd ever use for his own gain. "That you'll have to ask of him."

And this time Marley's silence had a different quality to it.

Tom sighed. "Come, now. We didn't find the salve."

"Didn't we?"

"Comfrey smells."

Marley followed without a word as Tom made his way to the courtyard.

In the hall, they were still praying. Praying most devoutly for the confusion of the Queen — and, no doubt, all the Queen's men.

CHAPTER 12

On Sunday morning they left early to hear Mass in the church of Saint-Étienne.

When he stepped in the street, it seemed to Tom a long time since he'd seen the outside of the Collège Anglais — for all that it had been only two days. He took a deep breath. It had rained in the night, and a little after dawn Rheims had a fresh-washed scent that wasn't going to last, and the air quivered with the bells of a dozen churches calling their flocks to early prayer. Tom's eye fell on the little tabernacle at the corner... Oh Lord! Two days and three nights — and not once had it occurred to him to check for Madame Jory's yellow roses.

"Not since you arrived."

The murmured words startled Tom — but it was Kit Marley, of course, passing by without halting his step, without turning. A sign of displeasure, no doubt — but then welcomed be displeasure, if it made the lad discreet.

Tom fell in step with the others, as Dr. Barret took the head, and they moved in a thick, soldier-like clutch.

The students and the teachers from the Collège Anglais walked in proud, black-garbed silence. In his travelling clothes and flat hat, drab-coloured as they were, Tom felt nothing less than garish, and woefully out of place — and while it stood to reason that the college wouldn't dress in their black such a bird of passage, it was hard not to see Roper's welcome wearing thin.

They passed church-goers — families in their Sunday best, a few ladies carried in chairs, a small gaggle of bourgeois wives. Most of these turned to peer at the English exiles: some with curiosity, none with the least warmth. There was a wariness instead, a look of counting heads. Whatever their Guise Archbishop said, the good citizens of Rheims were French enough to mistrust the English for being English, no matter their faith.

Nor did the *Rémois* grow friendlier when, at the crossing with the Rue de Saint-Étienne, more black-clad men joined the march. Among them, a dozen or so, Tom recognised John Savage — the soldierly fellow who had gainsaid Worthington on turning the other cheek. The others he didn't know by name, but he'd seen most of them at the college. So some of the students lodged elsewhere — another fact that Marley had neglected to mention.

Before Tom could work through the meaning of this new piece of knowledge, he found he had acquired a walking companion — John Savage, shortening his long-shanked step to cross the street apace with Tom Roper.

He hadn't forgotten Worthington's lecture, either.

"The one who'd lay down his life for a friend," he said under his breath. "Roper, are you?"

Before Tom could answer, they turned into the tree-dotted Place de Saint-Pierre, and a young boy ran up to them, threw a handful of filth, and shrilled a little rhyme about spitting the English pigs. A few other urchins took it up, the pigeons took to the air in a clucking flurry, and the church-goers stopped to have a look at what mayhem may arise. It was too much for young Colson, who whirled around on the cackling child.

"Don't, you churl!"

Without thinking, Tom caught the boy by the arm and held him back, and Savage stepped between, and in a trice Dr. Barret was on young Will's other side.

"We bear in silence, Colson," the priest said, holding up a hand when Will would have protested. "We're strangers here, and there are those who don't understand — but we forgive, and pray for them, and keep to our work."

And, with a nod to Tom and Savage, the Superintendent resumed his way, taking a flustered Will with him — but there was no mistaking the worried gaze he turned around the square. The crowd lost interest, and the children ran away under Savage's stern glare. In the shadow of the trees, three city archers stood idly in their white and red sashes and plumed hats.

When the college men all moved with Barret, just as the unmusical bells of Saint-Étienne started to clang again, Savage caught Tom considering the soldiers, and snorted.

"You mark me, Roper," he said. "The day the good folk here decide to tear us all to shreds, those fellows won't make haste to help us."

Barret and Worthington must have thought the same, hurrying their flock as much as it was seemly towards a lesser door on the church's side — and Tom found himself glad that Hunt had stayed behind at the college, or he would never have kept the pace.

Oh, what a lack-wit — Mr. Secretary's man, fussing about these traitors! A fine one he was, to have upbraided Marley for a trusting fool.

The sooner they both left, the better — and meanwhile… Meanwhile, Baines.

He begs in the street, or by the Church of Saint-Étienne.

But no yellow-haired beggar showed. Tom slowed his step, straining his neck under the pretence of admiring the belfry — until an older man he didn't know by name called to him.

"Don't tarry, lad. You've seen what happens."

So there was nothing for it but go inside with the others, and ignore Marley's pointed glances — all the more because, once the college formed into loose ranks in the frigid grey aisle, Savage was still there, at Roper's side, looming so tall, and straight, and stiff that he could have been one of the stone pillars of Saint-Étienne.

There was much singing, much Latin, much frankincense, and much praying for deliverance from the ills of war — though on this subject the priest was so circumspect that one could not tell whether the King or the Guise enjoyed his sympathies.

So much of it all, in fact, that the jewelled sunlight had moved well down the pillars by the time the last benediction was imparted, and the assembly sent on its way.

The English students formed up again, ready for as hasty a retreat as dignity allowed, because the square was far more crowded now, for the next, more fashionable Mass. There was enough of a crowd that Baines would have been able to lose himself in it, but there was no tarrying to observe — unless...

Beadles from Saint-Étienne had come to collect Fettiplace's body, hadn't they?

Tom sought Hodgson — one of the doctors, and one who would look kindly on his request — but Hodgson was deep in conversation with John Savage, he of the dogged, searching manner. Who of the others, then? Never Worthington, nor Bagshaw... Barret it had to be, who had just seen Tom save young Colson from a brawl.

And there Barret stood, brow knotted, shoulders bunched as he counted his students, very much itching to depart — and it struck Tom that, for all his forceful ways, Richard Barret was afraid.

He drew himself straighter when a hesitant Roper approached him.

"Is it here, Doctor, that Hugh Downes is buried?"

"No, he…" Barret looked around, half flustered and half watchful — and never be it said that Kit Marley wasn't quick-witted. He'd ambled by on catching sight of the conversation, right in time to hear the gist of it, and step in.

"I'll show him to the graveyard, Doctor," he offered.

And if Barret had any doubts about the boy's promptness, it was lost in his anxiety to be gone. "Be quick, though, and see that you catch up." He shook his head. "'Tis a bad day, Roper. I'm sorry."

A pity that the graveyard wasn't close by the church, but farther along the Rue de Saint-Étienne.

"Not that it will help," Marley said, as they trotted side by side. "If you still seek Baines."

"Of course I do!" Tom snapped. "I thought the graveyard would be a good place… Couldn't you have told me?"

"Couldn't you have asked?"

They came to a stop at a walled square of land by an ancient gate's arch, beyond which, at some distance, more spires and slate roofs huddled together. The old burying ground had a jumble of moss-covered gravestones and shallow mounds, with statelier tombs and small chapels lining the wall. One stunted apple tree grew in a corner, and by that was a square of soft earth.

"But then it doesn't matter." Marley led the way to the common grave. "Not if Baines isn't the murderer…"

"I still must bring him back to London."

Baines had greatly occupied Marley's mind in the guise of a poisoner; now that suspicion was dropped, a shrug was all the boy had for the innocent madman. "And you still must find who did the murders," he said. "I've been thinking: that other man you said, that Lyggon. Here after Easter, was he?"

"And in Antwerp by the end of April — we know that for certain."

Antwerp Marley dismissed with nothing less than contempt. "His sort, they travel post-haste. For all you know, he might have come and gone a dozen times!"

And wouldn't one think, to hear him, that he knew all about Lyggon's sort?

"Still, he wasn't here when Downes died," said Tom.

"Ay, well, there are poisons that are slow in killing."

Were there really? Poisons that killed over days? There may well be — but still...

"Why would Lyggon murder those two? If he did, he must have had a reason —"

And then a step sounded on the wet gravel, and it was too late to make shows of low-headed prayer. The approaching figure wore the college black, and it was tall and broad-shouldered.

"Savage," Tom whispered, and then, in irritation — as though their conversation had been an argument of sorts, "Well, he was my friend!"

Once more, Marley proved quick-witted. "Ay, ay — don't take it in snuff," he grumbled — and turned to meet the newcomer.

Savage stopped a few steps away. "Father Hodgson sent me to hasten you," he said. "Come, Roper. You'll pray for your friend's soul at the college."

They followed him, Tom affecting a half saddened, half sullen manner. He never looked up — but felt Savage's considering eyes on him.

"Had you known him long?" the man asked, after a while.

Roper would not be talkative — not with this curt fellow. "We were friends as boys."

There were no more words as they trotted at a brisk pace, until a certain house's door, where Hodgson stood waiting for them. What had happened in the past to make them all so fidgety?

"Don't fret, I've fetched them." Savage patted the priest's arm with a curl of the mouth that, in another man, could have been called a smile, and Hodgson grinned in answer. So they were friends, the priest and the soldier — for there was no mistaking what John Savage was. And Savage had more to tell on the subject of Hugh Downes. "Boys grow," he said, the square face hard. "It may be that your friend had changed from the lad you remember. Or if he hadn't…"

"John," warned Hodgson softly — or perhaps it was not so much a warning as a plea.

How well it worked was doubtful, for Savage only shook his head most mulishly. "All I say is, there are some things the Lord won't take kindly to. Nor we, in truth."

And then, with a nod at Hodgson, Savage stepped inside the house.

Father Hodgson hastened them on, down the Rue des Anglais, and soon they could see the black-clad group ahead.

Tom followed in silence.

Savage's words had set all the coloured pieces a-whirl inside his mind. Here, then, was someone else who had no liking for the dead Downes — and even thought him a traitor to the cause. For what else could it be to displease the Lord himself?

Did he think that Downes had met his just deserts? Had he had a hand in the dispensing of justice as he saw it? But surely he would never speak it aloud to a stranger, would he? Unless it was a warning... A warning to Roper, devil take it! Roper, who would be stunned and angry on his friend's behalf! Ulysses's assumed fleece was slipping, slipping badly — and sure enough, while Marley walked in unwonted silence, Hodgson wore an unhappy frown.

"You must not..." the priest sighed at length. "John never liked poor Downes."

Which was where Marley's spell of silence broke into a noise of disbelief. "Never liked him? He all but called Hugh a traitor!"

And see the unease in Father Hodgson's face and manner, all the good-natured cheer gone. "Savage will tell you, if you ask, that Downes was too bustling and cheerful, too often outside. Too worldly."

Much what Hunt had said — but with a very different colour to it. One that would leave Roper dismayed.

"And you, Father? Do you believe this too?"

Hodgson struggled a little. "What I believe, is that Downes was seeing a woman." And he fell silent, ill-humoured of a sudden. "Come now, let's make haste."

And off they went, without another word, to join the rest of the students and bury themselves in the Collège again, where perhaps someone was quietly poisoning traitors.

Things, Tom told himself, had a different complexion now.

Or had they, truly?

What if Hodgson was right, and Downes's blackest sin was a break of celibacy with a pretty wench? But then, what if there was substance instead to Savage's suspicions? The fellow seemed wary enough of Tom himself — for which his sense couldn't be faulted. Or was John Savage just one of those morose characters who looked on everyone slant-eyed? Or it could be that Savage was thoughtlessly truthful, and Hodgson lying to disguise his friend's ill-considered words... Not that Hodgson struck Tom as the sort to lie, but then, weren't Papists renowned for having all manner of subtle justifications for lying and every sin?

Hear all reports, Thomas — but judge well where to trust.

So, the complexion of things being uncertain, it seemed wise to seek all reports that could be had.

For one thing, what of Fettiplace? If he'd arrived ill at the college, perhaps his death mattered little? Carter said so, but on hearsay — and so did a few others, who hadn't seen Fettiplace on his return — not until he was dead.

'Twas old Bénoit as let him in, Carter had also said — which was easy enough to settle.

There was no talking to the old man as he served dinner (which comprised the luxury of ill-cooked tripe) — but afterwards, when the tables had been cleared and the day's chapter ferociously explained by Dr. Bagshaw, it became apparent that the college's notion of Sunday recreation offered a choice of solitary reading or solitary praying. Most students chose to do so in the sunlight of the garden and yard — and was it very unchristian to suspect that all their thoughts were not on the Scriptures?

Little wonder that there was a certain laziness to the quiet, warm afternoon, with the swallows overhead, and the bees humming in the garden — and it suited Tom very well, as he wandered around like one much taken with his thoughts, all the time seeking old Bénoit.

It wasn't long before he found him in the pantry, muttering to himself as he tried, on his toes, to reach a jar on the tallest shelf.

"Wait, let me," Tom called, and fetched the jar. Salt and herbs of some sort, by the look of it.

Bénoit was most grateful. "Eh, I grow old," he said, in halting English. "I become small. Taller than you are, I was — but ... eh!"

And with a shrug, he tottered away to the next room, where he had a mound of gutted fish and a pan, side by side on a bench. This was the room — why, the very bench where Fettiplace's body had lain... Wasn't this as perfect as it was gruesome!

Bénoit struggled to open the jar so much that Tom had to do it for him, freeing a scent of dried rosemary and garlic. The old man began to sprinkle this into the pan.

"Fish we eat on Friday," he grumbled in French. "But no — people must bring fish for Dr. Allen on Sunday! Not that he can eat it now, mind — no matter the day. But still, on Sunday they bring it! So what must one do?" He began to lay the fish jowls one by one on the layer of salt, patting them into place, and as he did, he smiled at Tom and shifted to bad English again. "But these are good like so. Good with the salt, eh?"

Which, reckoning by the day's dinner, was rather to be doubted.

It was easy to affect Roper's shudder, as he realised that... "This is ... 'tis here that you had that poor fellow, the servant."

"Eh?" Bénoit, it seemed, was also a little deaf, but nodded sadly when Tom repeated his question a little louder.

"Ah, Zacharie, *pauvre garçon* — poor lad." The old man crossed himself with fish-wet fingers. "We never know when the *Bon Dieu* calls us, eh?"

Now to stir a little the servant's placidity. "Poor fellow. Perhaps when he took ill, he thought to come to a place he knew."

"Ill? Oh, *malade*? But no, it is *le Docteur* Allen that was ill. And I told the lad, and told him — but he must see *le Docteur*..." Another shrug — such as Bénoit must have given to the insisting Fettiplace.

"Perhaps he wanted confession."

"And must he bother *le Docteur* Allen, who was *malade*! Do we lack priests, here?"

"Well, Fettiplace was *malade*, too. Perhaps he wasn't thinking straight."

"Zacharie? *Malade*? But no!" The old man dismissed the idea with a wave of one gnarled hand.

This now... "But he must have been, Bénoit. He was dead by Vespers..."

This had the man rubbing his chin, leaving a smear of salt there. "*Un coup, alors*. A calenture. It happens: one moment, they laugh and drink; the next..." Bénoit blew out his cheeks. "Dead!"

And he gave Tom the jar to hold while he laid more fish in the pan.

A sudden death. A calenture — or a poisoning.

"And he wanted to see Dr. Allen."

"Eh?"

Tom repeated the question, and Bénoit nodded.

"Oh, that he did. *Très inquiet*, he was. Agitated. And angry, that he could not see *le Docteur* Allen. But I told him, he could *mettre en garde* the *Docteur* Barret instead..." And here the old man stopped and sniffed, and perhaps the herbs had gone up his nose, for he sneezed one, two, and three times, all over the salted fish.

Ay, well.

But here was something far, far more interesting than Bénoit's slatternly ways.

"*Mettre en garde* Dr. Allen? Warn him against what? Did Fettiplace say?"

And if he caught the sudden eagerness in Tom's manner, the old man didn't show it. He rubbed at his nose with the back of his hand instead, and frowned.

"Fettiplace had a warning," Tom repeated, striving to keep his voice low. "What warning? Against someone? Something that —" Oh, devil take Bénoit's threadbare English! Devil take caution, too! Tom shifted to French to ask again: "What warning did he have for Dr. Allen? Was he sent from his master?"

The change of tongue worked wonders. See how the old servant beamed in a half-toothed smile … but, it appeared, of Fettiplace's warning he had little to tell.

"He didn't say, and I didn't ask. I told him: wait — because the doctors, they were all giving lectures."

"And how did he like it?"

"Ah, he wasn't happy — but he sat to wait for Dr. Barret. So I put him in the room across the passage — they do lectures there, sometimes, but it was empty that day — and I sent Rudd to tell Dr. Barret." And suddenly he glanced over Tom's shoulder, and called, "Eh, Rudd?"

Soft and fair, now. Tom made himself keep still, except to look around and find young Rudd standing on the threshold, listening as Bénoit reverted to his halting English. Listening calmly, as though there were nothing strange or suspicious in Roper speaking fluent French…

190

He had a stolid countenance, this Rudd. It held no wariness, no alarm as he said that yes, he'd been sent to tell — but Dr. Barret had his students, and must not be disturbed.

"But *le Docteur* Hodgson, eh?" Bénoit prodded. "You told him."

"Ay, and Dr. Worthington, too." Rudd walked to the row of sacks under the window. "I told them as Mr. Yates's man was back, and wanting to see Dr. Barret. Dr. Allen, truly, but…" A shrug — then Rudd hauled a sack over his shoulder, and off he went.

Off to tell Barret that Roper, of a sudden, was speaking tongues and asking questions? It was hard to imagine much conversation between the Superintendent of the Studies and the kitchen lad — unless, of course, Barret had sent the servant to watch Roper.

Oh Jupiter above…

One more reason to go, and go in haste… Only now perhaps the death of Zachariah Fettiplace was not of little account. Not if he'd come back hale and then died. Not if he'd come back to warn Dr. Allen — and been killed for it.

"Bénoit, how long did Fettiplace wait?" Tom asked in English — only to meet a blank gaze. Oh, curse it all, hadn't he given himself away enough? He shifted to French again. "You sent for Dr. Barret. How long did Fettiplace wait?"

"*Ah, ça!* But it must have been…" The old face knotted. "I'd just rung Nones when he arrived — yes, that I had, so it was three or thereabout. And it was a good two hours before Monsieur Catesby found him dead."

And was it too fanciful to think that, during that couple of hours, someone who'd heard of Fettiplace's return had killed the man, to make sure that the warning he brought should die with him?

191

It was at that point that young Colson skidded to a halt on the threshold. "There you are!" the boy exclaimed, and then shouted his findings to someone unseen in the yard: "Here he is!"

And behind Colson came Gilbert Gifford. Dr. Barret wanted Roper, he said, and all the college had been searching high and low for him. The grimace Colson made behind Gifford's back told a rather different tale — but Tom gave back the jar of salt and followed Gifford, affecting a manner of chastised meekness to hide his eagerness.

Catesby was trying to revive Fettiplace, when Gilbert Gifford arrived... With Catesby gone, here was the other man who'd found the body. The Fates must be smiling.

Gilbert Gifford, on the other hand, was not. He was a slight man about Tom's age, with one of those faces that Tom's old nurse called elfin: a pointed chin, a large, sallow brow, and large eyes, so black that the pupils were lost in the dark iris. An attractive enough face, but for the shifty eyes, and the ever pursed lips.

The reedy voice didn't help, either — nor the horse-holy manner. When Gifford said, "You ought to seek counsel, Roper — not waste your time with the servants," it was with such petty condescension to make a man's blood boil.

Tom Walsingham felt an itch to box the man's ears, but he needed to question Gifford, so Tom Roper just tilted his head. "The old man asked if I'd help, and then he was all a-chatter..."

"Bénoit always is," Gifford conceded. "Not a bad man, but rather foolish. Come now, you've wasted enough time."

He led the way to the front staircase — the one where Hugh Downes had fallen to his death. It boasted a carved newel-post and a finer railing, but was just as narrow as its fellow in the back. An ugly place to fall.

"Have you never seen a staircase?" Gifford groused. "Idling is as bad as gossiping."

He was thrown out of the Seminary in Rome, Catesby had said … so on probation here, most likely, and desperate to show zeal. Also, perhaps, the sort who wouldn't resist a scrap of importance?

"Bénoit, he's full of that poor man they buried. Why, he says 'tis you who found him dead."

Gifford scoffed. "One should never indulge in idle talk."

"Making it up, was he? Thought so." Tom shook his head.

"In truth…" And there it was. See how Gifford struggled, see the battle of Virtue and Importance — and Importance winning the day, yet lacking the heart to triumph. "Catesby did — and then I, yes. In the big classroom. And why they'd put him in there…"

So it was just natural that Roper should throw a glance down the stairs, and begin to cross himself, and stop halfway.

Equally natural it was when Gifford scoffed again — and walked into this smallest of traps. "You can cross yourself, here. And it's a foolish superstition to be afraid of the dead. Come!"

Follow upstairs, then, with a lowered head, and prod some more… "I found a fellow 'prentice dead, once. Dead in his bed, all stiff and wide-eyed, and all blue in the face." Another shudder. "I still have dreams of it at night."

"Childish fancies." And there was, in Gifford's flustered briskness, that lack of compassion that to some comes of seeing their own faults in another. "Besides, this fellow was neither stiff nor blue. He looked asleep — why, Catesby was trying to wake him when I arrived — and that's all there is to it."

The last flight of steps they ascended in silence, to the gallery upstairs. There, leaning side by side against the parapet and gazing down at the yard, stood Barret and Hodgson. They were speaking low and earnest, but fell quiet and turned at the noise of approaching steps.

"I found him, Doctor," Gifford called — as though Barret could have missed the presence of Roper.

Neither priest spoke. They just watched — Barret with his clear, level gaze, Hodgson with a frown on his freckled face — and it occurred to Tom to worry. He'd been too busy questioning Gifford to wonder at the sudden summons. Had Rudd made his report already? Would they throw him into the vaults? Did they have their own rack down there? Ulysses caught — and no sharp point to blind the Cyclops... Who would get to tell Sir Francis of his cousin's immeasurable stupidity?

But perhaps not — for Barret had a half-smile for his zealous underling. "Thank you, Gifford. You may go back to your reading, now. I'm sorry I distracted you."

It was the politest of dismissals — but it was writ large on Gifford's sallow triangle of a face that he wished for no dismissal at all. And did the fool think Barret might miss the glance he aimed at Hodgson? *See*, that glance said. *See the way it is?*

Whatever Gifford's grudge, Hodgson just tilted his head a little — half comfort, half exhortation. *Gib*, he'd called this ill-humoured elf at supper. A friend's name — though how could a man be friends with Gifford and John Savage at once?

If Barret observed it all — as anyone must who was not blind — he gave no sign of it, and waited until Gifford dipped his head in obedience and strode away, his only protest a clacking of heels down the stairs.

Only then did Barret allow himself a little sigh — and then he turned the full weight of his searching, hooded gaze on Tom. "So, Roper. Have you thought on what you'll do?"

And if there was a clearer manner of saying, *either become a priest or go your way*, Tom didn't know it. Not that it came as a surprise — but Roper would be flustered and uneasy, surely. He would blink and stammer.

"I ... I don't know, Doctor. I hadn't thought past coming here…"

He would be lost and frightened of being thrown out, left to fend for himself in foreign parts.

Hodgson shifted his weight.

Barret, either unsurprised or well-schooled in hiding his irritation, just nodded, although it wasn't an especially benign nod. "A few more days, then. But you must think, Roper. Make up your mind. Much as I — much as Dr. Allen would like to keep all who —"

Tom looked up with all of Roper's gratitude, and some relief of his own. "I want to be no burden, Doctor. I'm ready to work for my keeping."

This eagerness seemed to please the two priests. They pitied Roper a little, each in his way — which was a very good thing in view of all the unanswered questions that were breeding in Tom's mind, and yet rather irksome. Foolishly so, perhaps, for building Roper's pitifulness had taken some pains — but being pitied, even under a poor sheep's fleece, was no pleasant exercise.

There was consolation in the lack of suspicion in Hodgson's eyes, and in Barret's half-smile. A strange smile it was — a slanting curl of the lip, and a small muscle jumping at the corner of the man's eye, barely seen as the Superintendent of the Studies turned to put a hand to Hodgson's elbow.

"While he's here, we may as well see to his instruction."

Hodgson looked Tom up and down, for all the world like a tailor sizing him for a doublet. "Catechism, I'd say. Take no offence, Roper — but you don't seem ready for philosophy to me."

And that was when Barret narrowed his blue gaze at Tom. "Or are you?" he softly wondered, in the manner that wants no answer. It was a heartbeat — and then he shook his head. "But yes, let it be the catechism for now."

After which, Richard Barret took his leave.

Shoulders stiff, breath curdled in his throat, Tom watched him walk down the gallery, towards the back stairs — a stooping, dark figure in the dimming light of the afternoon. He watched, and wondered what had been hidden behind that cold nod and the half-smile: irritation at the dull-witted, beggarly fellow from Kent, or suspicion that both the dull wits and the beggarliness may be feigned?

"So — catechism will do for now, eh?" Hodgson's cheerful voice and a pat on the shoulder drew Tom out of his wool-gathering, just as the bells of Vespers began to swell the evening sky. "Come, lad — don't begin by missing Vespers. Our Superintendent has no patience for idlebys."

Side by side they followed Barret's steps, and as they went...

"Roper," Hodgson began slowly, "you've made friends with Sherbourn, haven't you?"

Tom's shoulders knotted anew. "He's from Kent…" *And he was friendly with Hugh Downes* — but on this it wasn't wise to insist, not if Savage was right about Downes. "And he's a heartly lad…"

Hodgson's face wrinkled in dislike — either of Sherbourn or of what he was about to say. "He's something of a fire-brand, too. Oh, he's clever, but has more fancies than faith, if you ask me…" Again, he narrowed his eyes at Tom in a sideways, measuring look. "In your place, lad, I'd choose someone less troublesome as a friend."

It was no great pretence to look troubled. This was the second warning Hodgson had issued against Sherbourn. The first had been more jocular, but taken together with this second… What did the priest know? What did he suspect?

With some unease Tom reached the conclusion that Roper would nod, and take the words to heart, and steer well clear of the troublesome Sherbourn.

Now Marley must hear of this, and leave the Collège as soon as he could. But at Vespers, supper and Compline, up the stairs, and in the dormitory, all evening Tom felt eyes watching him, spying and observing. Phantasies, perhaps, and foolish fears — but Barret's doubts were not thin air, nor Hodgson's words — and, as Tom would rather avoid discovery for both himself and Marley, wariness seemed the best policy.

Tell that to Marley, though! For here was another finding for the day: nothing made the lad fret as a sudden coldness. Another would take the hint, and stay away in turn — but no, never Kit Marley! Marley must be all questioning looks and little frowns — and no doubt he thought himself cunning, as he crossed half the dormitory to pass by Tom's pallet and drop a stocking, so he had to stoop just there... Oh, save and deliver! Surely Ulysses's companions never were this clumsy?

Without looking up, Tom gave the minutest nod, never pausing as he unlaced his boots. "Careful. They doubt," he murmured — and didn't look again when Marley straightened and walked away. Fates send the warning had been taken. More than this, he didn't dare to risk.

CHAPTER 13

27th of May

Because of the way the house lay, the chapel filled with light over Lauds and Mass, and it turned from rose to gold as the old Latin words were sung.

When Barret bid them all to pray for the brothers who were leaving for England, Father Henry Immes stepped forward together with the fiery-tempered Dr. Bagshaw. Dressed in doublet and breeches, and sturdy shoes, Immes looked as though he'd donned the clothes of another.

They walked up to the altar, soldier-straight, to receive their benediction, and after all there was nothing awkward in Immes's travelling clothes, as he stood tall against the golden glory that blazed in the windows.

At Tom's side, Hunt watched with hungry, shining eyes, and tears ran down young Colson's face. Even Marley's small smile held a colour of yearning. Putting it all in verse inside his head, as likely as not…

And why shouldn't he? Poets were mad, and it must appeal to a poet that these men would be in England in a week, disguised and falsely named, breaking every law of the realm, spreading sedition, hiding and preaching and saying Mass, and risking their necks day after day, until they were caught and hung, drawn and quartered. And here they went, under the eyes of not one, but two of the Queen's men. Had they no care? There were the false names, but…

A shiver ran down Tom's back. Would the day come when he himself would be called upon to recognise some man he'd known in the college? Summoned to some dark chamber? The rack, the stench of fear, and no room for doubt… And little as Tom liked men of Bagshaw and Immes's ilk, what of a Hodgson, a Will Colson or a Hunt?

Oh Lord — poets were mad, and their madness was catching!

When all was done, Immes and Bagshaw strode along the chapel like men going into battle, amidst the reaching hands, and the blessings, and many pairs of brimming eyes. It would go to a man's head, surely? All drunk on it, they must be, the young fools — and the less young, like Immes, who forgot country, family and duty, who turned traitors, who faced the worst of deaths, and thought nothing of facing Hell.

But then they believed they were going to Heaven didn't they? As martyrs and saints, no less.

In the press at the chapel's door, Marley found his way to Tom's side, and leant to whisper in his ear: "They have a knack for a certain heroic beauty, haven't they?"

Ut demonstrandum erat — as was to be proved — leaving it to be wondered: was Marley the heartless poet who liked to see tragedy unfurl, as long as it was beautiful, or was he the sort to forget duty, when weighed against enough beauty?

"See that you don't like it too well," Tom murmured back, and they followed with the others into the damp, cool azure shadows of the yard.

Next came the catechism, as Hodgson had promised. A whole morning of it, in the same room where Tom and Marley had held their Compline argument. And little as Tom had liked the argument, much worse were the countless virtues and profoundest meaning of the rogations that were just that day beginning. To explain it all in the dullest, most punctilious detail was none other than Gilbert Gifford, and either the bitter Gib or the rogations themselves garnered the most rapt attention. Why, a few of the students even had the heart to ask for still more intricate instruction! One might suspect Barret of hoping that Roper would tire enough to turn tail, rather than bearing more of it.

Let him hope, then. Tom sat through the morning with a look half eager and half lost, and an ear open for especially treasonous talk. In fair truth, he found none, or at least not in the letter.

Of course, when it came to the essence, it was treason to teach the Catechism of Rome and its superstitious trappings for use in England — but neither Gifford nor the students declared any interest in murdering the Queen.

What part of his mind wasn't occupied, Tom busied in sorting the pieces of his own riddle.

He had, he found, a good number of them — if only he could arrange them into a pattern...

Item: There was one way that Baines, or another, could have secretly entered the college.

But then...

Item: There seemed to be no way that the same man, having done his deed, could have left undetected — except perhaps through the garden, but only at great risk of being discovered.

Item: It seemed very doubtful that Baines possessed the wits to even attempt it.

Ergo: It was perhaps not impossible, but most unlikely that anyone — and Baines in particular — could have entered the college to poison anyone.

Ergo: It was a good deal likelier that someone inside the college had done whatever had been done.

Perhaps not by poison, though, because:

Item: Allen's illness was certainly not the result of poisoning.

Item: Hunt's could have been, but showed no similarity to the deaths of either Downes or Fettiplace — which were, in turn, very unlike each other.

Therefore…

Item: It seemed unlikely that anyone would dose two or three men with different poisons.

On the other hand, what of the two victims?

Concerning Hugh Downes:

Item: He'd been ill with a fever for several days before dying.

Item: He'd been watched over — but left alone for long enough to walk around in his delirium.

Item: He'd fallen to his death over a tallish banister.

Item: He'd been found right after his fall — blue in the face, according to Marley, but Marley's recounting could be coloured by his own fore-conceived suspicions.

Item: He'd been in the habit of going outside often, to run errands in the town.

Item: It was the servant Carter's opinion that he had his own reasons to do so.

Item: Savage thought him a traitor.

Item: Hodgson claimed he'd been seeing a woman.

Item: Of the three, Hodgson was the most likely to have lied.

Quæstio: Could Downes have died other than of his fever or a poison — for example, by being thrown over the banister?

Concerning Zachariah Fettiplace:

Item: He'd first come to the college in the company of his master and, more worryingly, of Kit Marley under his assumed name.

Item: He'd not been at the college at the time of Downes's death, but he had when Downes fell ill.

Item: He'd come back to warn Dr. Allen of some danger unknown — either on his own account or his master's behalf.

Item: He'd been in good health on arriving — as far as old Bénoit could judge.

Item: He'd agreed to wait for Dr. Barret — which excluded that Barret had been the object of his warning.

Item: He'd waited about two hours after announcing his intention, and then fallen deathly ill.

Item: He'd had the time to tell Elliot of his sickness, but at that time the sickness hadn't been such to alarm Elliot.

Item: Shortly after that, he'd been found dead by Catesby and Gifford.

Item: His body had shown no obvious sign of foul play — or at least, none that Gifford had observed.

Ergo: While his death could have been natural — still the time and circumstance of it gave food for suspicion.

Quæstio: Could Fettiplace have seen something on his Easter visit — something tied to the death of Downes — and therefore come afoul of the murderer who feared to be uncovered...?

It was at this particular point of his musings that the silence in the room struck Tom, and he drew back from inside his head to find all watching him — some amused, some mocking, young Will Colson wearing a grimace, and Gifford most vexed.

"Fasting, Roper! For the purification of ourselves and of England, we fast!" Gifford said, with the impatience of one repeating himself. And, when there was no answer... "Wool-gathering, were you, instead of paying heed? What you're doing here, I'll never understand!"

Tom could only stutter in apology, and a blush crept up his neck, because Tom Roper had to be eager, if not sharp — but also because Tom Walsingham loathed to cut a doltish figure.

The smirks and sneers helped little — and much less because Gifford found much relish in explaining how even a minor sin became less minor in proportion to the sacredness of its object. Rehearsing his next sermon, as likely as not — and looking forward to reporting the slip to Barret.

No show of bent-headed contrition was going to serve, so Tom made himself listen to the superstitious jabber, ready for the next question, should it come. This knack of unravelling murders while at the same time being someone else he had to perfect quickly — unless he wanted to have Roper thrown out for an unearnest dullard.

Which shouldn't have mattered — since he meant to go of his own accord — and yet...

And yet, his foolish mind kept circling back, gnawing at the knots, fretting to unravel this bloody tangle. Ah well, there was nothing for it but to make good use of whatever time Roper had left at the Collège Anglais.

For one thing, there was the infirmary where Downes had lain sick — sometimes attended, and sometimes not — until he'd walked out and fallen down the stairs. According to Marley, the infirmary lay just next door to Gifford's room — but of course, when the catechism was done for the day, young Colson had to attach himself to Tom, to offer comfort, and to guide him in the reading of the day's chapters. He was so sorry for his friend, poor boy, so solicitous, so eager, that there was no shaking free of him. Tom had to repair to a bench under the gallery, with a Bible and this young zealous lamprey, and listen to not only Saint Ambrose's endless homily, but also to the boy's wretched efforts at translating from Latin — and never once correct him.

Never had the summons to dinner sounded more welcome — although, this being a fasting day, only bread was provided, and not much of it, seasoned with endless prayers and readings. After the morning's stumble, Tom deemed it prudent to show the most pious eagerness all through the meal. He could have soothed his conscience, he supposed, by telling himself it was the heretical quality of it all that made it so wearisome — but in all truth, after less than four days he felt surfeited with religion. A sin, for sure — about which he'd worry later.

If nothing else, he was learning the ways of the college. After the dinnertime instruction, the students parted ways — some to the garden, some to more lectures or to read and pray on their own, some outside, through the unfriendly streets of Rheims, and to the Université. Marley who, over the night, had gone again from desperately trying to catch Tom's eye to ignoring him, was to join this last group.

It was a looser time, if a brief one, with the men lingering around the hall and yard as they were sorted to their various occupations. It was also a time when one could slip away for a little while, as long as he went quietly and swiftly.

Tom followed those headed upstairs, keeping last behind them. Some stopped at the classrooms, and others went on to the dormitories for their Bibles and books. Tom watched which doors they entered and, with his best air of purpose, walked to one nobody chose.

Now let no one come whistling in who had a right to be there... As soon as it was quiet, Tom slipped out. He hastened along the gallery to the front stairs. Across the landing he found a narrow, gloomy room, bare of all but a few old chairs, and three doors. The one on the right was the classroom, so next must be the infirmary, surely?

With no windows, this narrow place would be black as Tartarus at night. A man thinking straight could lose his bearings without a light — and all the more a feverish one.

And yet...

The infirmary's door opened right across from the stairs. Wouldn't this feverish man, once he left the room, stagger forward? Unless he felt his way along the wall on his right or left, and then away from the stairs... But if he'd stumbled forward, why had Downes fallen down the shaft, rather than down the flight of steps? Suddenly Tom felt very curious to know who had been watching over Downes that night.

And as he pondered this new question, a ruckus rose down in the yard, and a voice called from the stairs: "Dr. Barret! Master!"

Praying that it was empty, Tom dove into the classroom, just as a man came rushing up the stairs on one side, and on the other, the farthest door swung open.

There was another call for "Dr. Barret!" and then Barret's own voice, teetering out of its usual crispness.

"What is it, Rudd?"

"The *Milice*, Doctor!" the servant gasped, more breathless than the stairs would warrant, even at a run. "They've come to take us all!"

It was easy to imagine Barret agape — but arrest them all ... surely not? Not unless the Guise party had already suffered what Nick Skeres would call a trouncing?

It was a heartbeat before Barret recovered. "Soft now, lad. Have they said so? That they're arresting us?" he asked, and Rudd must have shaken his head, for the two men's steps moved to the stairs, but not at a run.

Rudd asked something as they went, to which Barret answered: "Yes — but none of your talk of arrests! Just tell him the archers are here."

Him surely being Allen in his sickroom...

The passage's wooden floor creaked under Rudd's steps, away to the far end. So that was where the Cyclops had his lair.

A knock, a door opening and closing — and Tom stole out of his hiding place and down the stairs, keeping a wary distance from Barret.

The yard was in upheaval. A strangely quiet upheaval — but still enough that nobody observed Roper joining the general commotion. A murder of crows disturbed, crowding and murmuring around these invaders who had so shaken Rudd.

And Rudd perhaps had taken too much alarm, for the invading force numbered a sole man — a very young officer who, head thrown back and hand on his sword's hilt, stood confronting Worthington, with an air of the greatest arrogance.

"*Mais je vous dis...!*" Worthington was protesting, having lost his serene manner, just as the students made way for the arriving Barret.

The officer turned to the newcomer. "*Le Docteur Alain?*" he demanded.

When, in his much-Englished French, Barret answered that Dr. Allen was ill, and he himself was the doctor's deputy, the archer gave him a prodigious frown under the brim of his plumed morion.

"I told this gentleman —" Worthington began, and found himself ignored, both by Barret and by the archer, who, coming to some sudden decision, drew taller still, and took a breath to say his piece. A more experienced man would have drawn Barret aside, spoken to him alone — but this fellow was barely old enough to grow a beard, and full of his own importance, and so proclaimed his tidings with a voice fit for the battlefield.

"A dead body was found, Monsieur. Lying in a garden in the Rue de Saint-Étienne that belongs..."

The rest was lost to a burst of cries and exclamations. A dead body! Even those who had not thought to tie Fettiplace's death to that of Downes, must now be counting to three. Tom caught Marley's eye, amidst the hatted and caped group bound for the Université — and shook his head. And trust the lad to look more than half tickled.

There must be no other poets among Allen's men: their louder and louder chattering had a colour of dismay, fear, and growing rage. Tom looked over the many heads, up to the window where, behind the leaded glass, a long, white face showed. Was that William Allen, risen from his sickbed to watch disaster descending on his flock?

Worthington's attempts to impose silence were lost in the mounting confusion, while Barret discussed with the archer.

"Another one!"

Tom turned to find Marley at his elbow, a little breathless to be sure. But there was no discussing murder, not as young Will Colson ran wide-eyed to join them, not as the men began to stream towards the passage, past the entreating Worthington, past Carter and Bénoit at the half-open gate, and out to the street. Bent on seeing for themselves…

Tartarus take it all…!

But perhaps this wasn't all bad? Tom followed the rush — not a great one, in truth, for only a dozen men dared to defy Worthington's anger — but enough. And as he went, he found he had a following of two. He paused to point a finger at young Colson.

"You stay here, Will!"

"But —"

"There may be danger yet." Which was mockery to a boy who had fled England to become a secret priest — but the last thing Tom needed was an eager pup dogging his steps. Thank the Fates for obedient hearts: young Will stood back and stopped.

Marley didn't, and went running with the others.

And what a sight they must make, a gaggle of black-garbed men, rushing in the street in grim silence, dodging a hand-cart, pushing their way past the good citizens — the English exiles out to do mischief! Small wonder it was that the good citizens gaped at them, that the populace pressed around and muttered, that there were shouts… Such a stupid, stupid thing to do in a town taut with distrust and the fear of war!

"If they take it amiss…" Marley gasped.

Indeed — and Marley wasn't the one who'd have to explain it to Sir Francis. *I plunged myself and another in the midst of a riot, Sir — and…*

But it was a short way to the lodging house, and that saved them all that day. In a breathless trice they were at the doorsteps, pushing past the wicket, down a dark, damp passage, and out again in the light of a garden.

There all urgency spent itself against a wall of two archers.

Marley stumbled in his sudden halt, catching himself on Tom's shoulder. "God's nightgown!" he breathed.

The garden was a largish place, and near the house it looked much like that at the college, with beds of plants and herbs, and badly gravelled paths. Beyond that, though, all order ceased, lost in a small wilderness of shrubs and coarse grass, with a few trees huddled in a corner. By those trees stood more of the archers, a plume-hatted officer among them, peering at something at their feet. A few Englishmen made up the numbers — one being John Savage.

On observing the newcomers, the officer pulled his hat lower on his brow and strode across to his young colleague, Barret, and Worthington. His blade-thin, swarthy face held little liking for the English — and perhaps no more of it for his underling.

"I told you to bring their Head," he barked. "Not the whole rabble of them!"

The youth reddened in blotches, and stuttered until Barret pushed past him, without the slightest trace of priestly humility.

"I am Dr. Richard Barret," he announced. "The Superintendent of the Collège Anglais."

They held each other's gaze, Barret's hard and level, the archer's half mocking.

"If you are, *Docteur*," he said, "then come and see what grows in your garden."

Barret followed him, with the students behind him like so many dark goslings — Tom and Marley among them. Worthington turned a burning scowl on them all, before hastening after Barret, and Tom was close enough to hear him hiss: "This is your fault, Richard! Dr. Allen would never allow…"

The rest he lost, as Worthington leant in closer to whisper. Barret took no heed. The archers moved aside as they approached, and Savage joined the Superintendent.

"I'm sorry, Doctor. The young fool who found this made such a din, there was no avoiding…" He threw a glance the officer's way. "I'd have sent word, but Maître Deboy here took it upon himself."

Barret nodded, without taking his eyes from the form under the trees.

It was a man, lying on his stomach, wearing a doublet and breeches of dark green, one hand outstretched — and that hand… Tom strained to look — and wished he hadn't, when one of the archers turned the body onto its back.

The hand was missing three fingers, bitten to stumps, and the face… Oh Lord, the face!

"Rats," Deboy said grimly, amidst the muted cries of horror.

Tom's gorge rose, and he spun away, knocking into Marley, who steadied him by the shoulder.

"God!" the lad muttered. He stared at the gruesome sight, green around the gills.

Savage stood stone-faced, while another man hastened away, retching — and look at Barret, white to the lips, rubbing together his long, thin hands, eyes fixed on the horrible ruin that had been a man's face.

"Do you know this man, *Docteur*?" asked Deboy. "Is he one of yours?"

A bitter sound choked its way out of Richard Barret. "How would I...?" He shook his head, lips stretched in a grimace — and small blame to him.

Whitish bone showed through the holes gnawed in flesh and scalp, and around the empty socket, and the teeth made a devil's grin between the ragged remnants of the lips, while the intact cheek was bruised black under the crusted mud.

The archer pitched his voice for the pale-faced students. "Does any one of you know this man?" he asked in slow French.

There were exchanged glances at first, and a whispered translation, and then a head shaken, and another, and a few murmurs of "No."

"He doesn't wear our black, poor soul." This was Worthington, and by the smooth, compassionable voice one would think him unaffected. Only the beads of sweat at his temples gave him away as he sketched a benediction over the corpse.

Deboy hummed, a pointed eyebrow raised at Tom, wearing no seminary black.

Worthington followed the glance. "What I mean is —" he began, and Barret cut through him, gaze level and steady again — to meet the archer's doubting eyes.

"Dr. Worthington is right. This man is not one of ours."

Deboy met this with a grunt and a question: "Then how came a stranger to die in your garden?"

To which Barret was bound to answer, as he did, that he didn't know, nor saw how he could tell.

But was the dead man truly a stranger? Barret hadn't known at first. What made him so certain of a sudden? So certain, or so anxious to deny? He hadn't recognised the mangled face, surely?

Tom made himself look again, swallowing hard and breathing through his nose, thinking of another time, another French archer sneering at his queasiness.

The dead man wore riding boots, and the breeches were muddied at the knee, or at least more muddied than the rest.

A deep breath.

The collar was unfastened, and the left sleeve hung a little, the lacing torn from the hooks. A fight, perhaps?

Another breath.

The left arm had lain under the body, and the hand was untouched, the back stained with mud, the palm clean…

The palm.

There was a gash in the left palm. An inch or so long, half scabbed but still raw. A jagged gash as one might suffer by falling against the rough edge of a table…

Tom's blood ran cold, and he forced his eyes up the arm and shoulder, up to the torn scalp, and the matted hair — the hair that, under the dirt, showed fair.

Golden-fair — for this poor dead thing was Robin Elliot.

Poor, gentle, fearful Elliot, murdered and left to the rats.

And Barret knew, didn't he? And had lied about it... Look at the Superintendent — pale as death, lines deeper around the mouth, shoulders hunched away from the body, still protesting his ignorance to the officer.

"Anyone could find their way in here," he was explaining, voice strained. "See for yourself, the wall is low, and there's a door..." He looked about, unsure. "There!" He pointed past the trees, on Tom's side.

"Not that we use it..." a flabby-cheeked student piped up — and quavered when Savage glared at him. "Not much — that is..." He cleared his throat. "We use it sometimes..."

No one was listening to him: all trooped after Deboy to the door — a rickety affair, half hidden behind a bush, and hanging on one hinge. Most remarkably, it had no bolt. There had been one, until recently, for two discoloured holes gaped where the hasps should have been. The archer bent to pick up something from the grass, and held the rusted bolt for all to see.

"No, Messieurs," he said. "You do not use it much." He tugged at the door. It had been jammed in place, but yielded easily. "So!" Deboy arched that eyebrow of his again at Barret. "If nothing else, we know how he entered, eh?"

And all the way Tom fidgeted, biting his cheek so he wouldn't snap at the Frenchman. *Observe the ground! There will be footprints in the mud — don't tread on them!*

Too late, of course. The dunce strode through the door without a look downward. Barret followed, and Savage, and two of the archers, and a few others — Tom among them, with Marley on his heels. By the time they were out in the street, any mark in the half-dried ground was trampled, as though a herd of oxen had danced a Morris across it.

213

There was no doubt, though: this was where poor Elliot and his murderer had entered the garden. And Catesby, perhaps… Where was Oliver Catesby? Had he escaped, or was he lying dead in some other dark corner of the town?

Apart from Catesby, of whom he could not know, Deboy must have been thinking much the same. "So here they come in," he proclaimed aloud — not a jot warier than his young underling. "That poor fellow and another."

"And this other poisoned him here?" Marley whispered in Tom's ear. "You can't say this one isn't blue…" He touched his own left cheek.

But no — not that. Another corpse in the yard of a French inn, the sickening purple blotches… "That's not the blueness of poison." Tom frowned at the little crowd that curdled in the street, greedy for the spectacle of an archer haranguing the Englishmen. "Blood thickens in the lower parts of a dead body, and looks like a bruise…" He stopped short, breath rushing out of him.

At the edge of the rabble, shuffling his feet and mumbling to himself, stood Baines.

"It's not to say it couldn't be poison," Marley insisted — a terrier with a bone.

Tom caught the lad's arm and murmured, "Baines is here… Don't turn!"

To his credit, Marley did no worse than stiffen. "See, I was right —"

Ay, well — surely that was one question that had just opened itself again. One that Tom had to answer once and for all. "I'm going after him."

"I'm with you —"

And have two going at once — twice as likely to be marked! "No, you're not. Try to find out how this one died."

"But —"

"Do as you're told, and be wary." Tom tilted his head towards the garden. "That's Robin Elliot in there."

Marley swore under his breath. "How do you know?"

Baines was gaping at Deboy, shifting his weight from foot to foot.

"The gash in his hand." Tom began to edge away towards the back of the crowd. "You never saw me go. Keep your eyes open, and your ears."

"But if Baines —"

"We don't know! And mind…" Because they *didn't* know… "If they misdoubt you, if they ask questions, steal away."

Tom stepped back, trying to melt into the murmuring rabble. A good thing that all eyes were on the *Maître des Archers*, busy declaring how the poor man must have been beaten — and hadn't they all seen the bruises? Just like Marley had thought — who was no officer of the law, though, and had no reason to know better. But there he went, the fool Deboy, herding the English back into the garden, leaving his men to disperse the curious.

And see how Baines scurried away, bent almost double in his haste, glancing over his shoulder as he rushed across the street.

Tom stole after him — and this time, he didn't mean for his quarry to turn hunter.

CHAPTER 14

Up along the Place de Saint-Pierre, Tom followed Baines with a manner of unhurried purpose that he dropped when his quarry plunged in the tangle of alleys around Saint-Symphorien.

Once in there he drew back to a chary distance, listening for the madman's steps splashing in the runnels, and keeping himself to the half-dried sides. On and on they trudged, and of course there was a chance that Baines knew himself hounded, and was leading his pursuer to some secluded corner where no one would observe another murder.

Oh, for the dagger that lay hidden in Blandine Jory's cupboard — or, in truth, anything sharper than Roper's eating knife!

They emerged in a larger thoroughfare at length, and Tom caught sight of Baines — hunched forward, arms crossed around himself, hands fisted under his armpits, barely looking up to dodge those he crossed. He never seemed to watch for pursuers as he swerved into an ill-smelling alleyway, and then another that seemed to double back. Whether the fellow kept a course or went by wandering chance, it was not long before Tom was lost. He'd catch sight of a tower-bell, now and then — little use in a place bristling with churches — and still Baines shuffled on, perhaps lost himself.

A murderer's trap would have snapped shut already, surely? Was Tom dogging a madman's aimless steps while the true danger lurked back at the Collège? Should he go back, abandon this pursuit? But Baines had been at the garden door. Why? What did he know?

They took a more densely populated street that ran along the side of a church — just as the bells began to chime in the needle-thin spire, right overhead. The madman stopped, rooted where he was. Rocking from foot to foot, hands on his ears, he gawped at the grey sky above, full of great iron chimes and gyrating birds as the hour of five was tolled all across the town. After a while, when the last echoes had died down, Baines shuddered and lowered his hands. He shuffled in place, jostled this way and that by the passers-by, until, all of a sudden, he shook his head and stumbled on, squeezing into a dark passage behind the church.

It was harder and harder to imagine this lost creature either luring or forcing Robin Elliot inside the garden — and then … what? Strangling him? Hitting him over the head? The more Tom followed, the more it felt like chasing wild geese. Had it not been that his orders were to bring Baines back to England, he would have left the man to his fate, and gone back. Back where, though? After this escapade, they'd hardly welcome Roper at the college again. The wisest thing would be to snatch Baines, retrieve Marley via the yellow roses, and leave Rheims — which was all very well, but how did one go about snatching Baines in this foul, crawling hive of passages and cramped yards, where witnesses abounded, should the fellow raise a havoc?

They'd come near the ramparts when Baines darted across a street. Tom hastened to follow, narrowly avoiding a cart heavy with casks — and…

And Baines wasn't there anymore.

Damn and curse it all — had he lost his quarry, now? Had he run from the college, lost his chance at unravelling the murders, and all for nothing? There was a long, thin isle of run-down houses, huddled against the ramparts. Tom hurried along it, peering into each doorway, straining his eyes, praying for a glimpse of the dirty yellow head, until he came to the mouth of an alley — and there he was, thanked be the Fates: Dickon Baines, head low between his shoulders, being staved off by a slip of girl with a broom.

"Come back when you've money, *pautonnier!*" she shrilled in coarse French, waving the broomstick in Baines's face. "We're a tavern, not the *Hôtel-Dieu!*"

And he would have gone, poor beggar, but that the alley was blind on one side, and up the other walked Tom.

"Then, Mademoiselle," Tom said, "if it is a tavern, we'll have a drink, my friend and I."

Baines whimpered low in his throat when Tom put a firm hand to his elbow.

The girl, no more than twelve or thirteen, gave the newcomer a hard look, shrewd enough for a woman thrice her age, gauging clothes and bearing. Tom knew himself promising enough as a customer, when this small dragoness lowered her broom.

"If you've money…" she sniffed, and stepped aside to let them in, grumbling all the while that Christian folks should use the street door.

Not that the place was the sort to require ceremony. Perhaps it had been once, for the whitewashed walls showed the shape of a great arch that had been filled up, but now the tavern was no more than a smallish room reeking of soured wine and sweat, with sand on a dirt floor that lay lower than the street, and a scatter of tables. At one of these, some men sat engaged in a boisterous game of dice. Tom dragged the bewildered Baines towards another, usefully placed in a corner, and ordered bread and cheese for both, along with wine and a bowl of stew. Stew, it turned out, was not to be had, but the rest arrived promptly enough, and Baines tore into it with famished eagerness.

And while the wine was watered-down piquette, and the cheese middling, Tom found himself glad of something that didn't came from Bénoit's kitchen, for a change.

He ate little enough, leaving the lion's share to his guest, watching for the moment when he could begin to ask questions. It was not long before the jug and trencher were empty. Baines then raised his head, half chagrined, and took a good look at his dubious benefactor. Only then did he observe that he'd been made to sit in a corner, and began to squirm on his stool, eyes darting aslant.

Before he could take fright, Tom held up both hands. "I mean no harm to you," he softly said in French, leaning across the table to be heard. "I've paid for your supper, haven't I?"

The man stank unwashed and ill — and yet the eyes scanning Tom from under the stringy hair were a surprise — very round but with no mad light in them. In fact, the knobby, scarred face looked at that moment like that of a sane man. Sane, and calculating.

"You're with them," he rasped. "You're at the college. You were…" He twitched a hand without raising it from the table. "You were *there*."

There at the garden? So much for being unobserved, then.

"I told you the other day: I'm sent from London, just as you were."

Now see how the scar jumped on the man's jaw, how the eyes shifted. He jerked one shoulder in a shrug.

"Baines, listen to me: why did you go to the lodging house this morning?"

Baines traced a black-nailed forefinger along the trencher's edge. He startled when the dice-players shouted at some lucky throw, and went back to his contemplation.

Ah well… Tom beckoned to the one tapster for more watered wine. He poured a good measure into Baines's pot, and he drained it at once.

"What brought you there, Baines?"

There was an intake of breath. "I keep watch. I wait…" A tilt of the head, a knowing look.

"You wait for what?"

"One of them shot out of the door, like the devil chased him. Came back with the *Milice*. And then the others came." A twist of the thin lips. "Allen's lapdog, Barret."

Precious few friends he had, poor Dr. Barret!

"And?"

A shrug. "'Twas all a-stir in the alley, and the archers, and you all, and —" Baines sat up, eyes narrowed at Tom. "And the one from London. 'Tis not you, the one from London. There's a boy, goes to Thibaud…" Baines half rose, voice rising — and Tom leant across the table to grab him by the arm.

"A boy, ay — and then I was sent, too," he hissed. "Be quiet. What do you think they'd do to us — us both — if they knew what we are?"

There was another outburst of cheerful profanity from the dicing men, and again Baines's shoulders went up to his ears. "I'm nothing," he muttered.

As he reached for the jug, Tom clamped a hand on his wrist. "A Queen's man, that's what you are. They had you imprisoned for it."

Baines tugged free. "Ay — and the Lord's vengeance is on them for it." He picked up the empty pot, turning it round and round. "*Dominus pugnabit pro vobis, and vos tacebitis.*"

Keep still, and the Lord will fight for you. The madness again, though it was a good deal quieter this time.

"But the man they found dead isn't from the college," Tom lied.

Baines never looked up, never ceased to turn the pot. "It will make trouble for them all the same. The Lord's own work."

Not even a hint of surprise, of disappointment, of suspicion … and those would show, wouldn't they, in one who had meant to kill a sheep of Allen's flock? And such a lack of pity…

"You care nothing that an innocent died, as long as you're revenged?"

A shrug. "He died by the Lord's hand…"

"And you helped the Lord?" Tom snapped. "Took it upon yourself to play God's instrument?"

Baines looked up, mouth slack, eyes blank. The wine catching up with him, no doubt — but also a blinking lack of understanding.

Tom leant closer. "You swore that you'd kill them all," he growled under his breath. "Poison the well."

There was a tiny nod, a knotting of the scabbed forehead. "Poison the well, ay — but I didn't know how to go about it. And then…" The words slurred. "Then they began to die. That fellow with the crooked teeth who came and went…"

"Downes."

It was no question — but Baines shook his head all the same. "Never knew him by name. Always about, he was, and idling. You don't serve the Lord by fiddling at the baker's… Then Thibaud, and now Allen's sick himself, and then this

221

other man…" And Dickon Baines smiled. A yellow, jagged smile full of beatitude, and the mad eyes filled with tears. "The Lord spared my hand and my soul: he smites them for me, one by one…" The smile wavered and fell, and the voice died into a whimper, as Baines hunched on himself, grasping his hair in fistfuls. "*Faciens misericordias Dominus et iudicium omnibus iniuriam patientibus,*" he sobbed.

Back to the Psalms — not a good sign. And that Baines thought himself the one suffering wrongs, and poor Elliot's death the justice of the Lord, should come as no marvel, perhaps. See how the man wept, and rocked himself, and muttered in Latin. Broken, and hardly knowing himself — but a murderer? With a sigh, Tom turned on the stool to call for more of the execrable piquette, and turned further, for the tapster was not in sight, and…

And there it was, past the gaggle of laughing dice-players — a flash of movement, a dark sleeve, and a face.

A face Tom knew. Oh, but he was a very, very great fool!

When the tapster arrived, he ordered more wine and another pot, and then beckoned for the solicitous red-bearded Samaritan to join them.

Redbeard took it in good nature. Not the sort to scurry and run, this one. On the contrary, he unfolded himself from the bench in the corner and strolled close with a courteous nod, and — devil pinch him! — a hint of a thin-lipped smile.

"My young friend from the alley," he said, giving Tom a searching glance. "Still rather bruised, but less bedraggled. And not as well-armed." He sat and observed the hunched Baines. "Found him, have you?"

And Tom took a small gamble, nudging Baines. The moment he blinked his teary eyes at Redbeard, the drunk drew up, taut as a bowstring, ready to bolt. Tom caught him by the sleeve.

"Soft and fair now, Baines. I won't let Allen's man touch you."

Redbeard's eyebrows rose. "*Allen's man.*"

"Baines thinks you are — and he's right, isn't he?"

A soft laugh, the grey eyes crinkling at the corner. "A hit." All of it full of the most amicable warmth.

Smiling back the way he would come on guard, Tom poured some wine for this well-mannered foe. "You'd already found him well before me," he said, in that even manner Sir Francis had when stating rather than questioning. From this old fox, it earned no better than a tilt of the head.

"Found and lost him, then sighted and lost him again... A slippery fellow, and a tight-lipped one — though I'll say it never occurred to me to pickle him." Redbeard raised his pot in toast and sipped, wrinkling his nose at the piquette.

Tom returned the gesture. "I caught him in a milder mood, I reckon."

"And he told you that Allen's man was after him?"

"That I learnt the other day, while we traded blows. I wasn't sure that I believed him — but then you appeared..."

Another of those small salutes. "I worried when you vanished so thoroughly after your little affray. You had to be either hurt worse than I thought, or an especially keen-witted Queen's man."

That he'd been neither, that it had taken him this long to put two and two together, Tom wasn't going to tell. Keen-witted — when all the careful subterfuge had only given him away! Could he hope that, at least, he hadn't led this fellow to the Brebis-qui-File?

Redbeard sat back, idly watching the ceiling. "What I can't quite fathom, though," he murmured, "is what a Queen's man would want with Baines here."

"Just to bring him back home."

"Even if he's murdered a man? They found a body in the Rue de Saint-Denis this morning — and your friend was there. And so were you."

So Redbeard had been there too. Had he also seen Tom among the men from the Collège?

"But in truth, I don't think Baines killed anyone."

"Ay, well — he's one of yours."

Never once had Tom regarded Baines as that — not truly. It was with some effort that he managed a contemptuous nod towards the now sleeping man. "Does he look like a savage murderer to you?"

"I hear he made plenty of wild threats, back when he was caught."

"That was … what? Two years ago?"

"And now he comes back — and Dr. Allen worries."

And small blame to him, in truth — but… "I'll tell you this one thing: Baines is amazed that the Lord smote that man dead on his behalf. Grateful but amazed."

Small wonder it was that Redbeard raised both eyebrows. "And why would the Lord smite him a stranger in that particular garden?"

"To make trouble for Allen and his."

"And that he did — whoever killed that fellow." Redbeard sat up, leaning forward, palm splayed flat on the table. "The city of Rheims has little fondness for the college. Entangling them with a murder might have them cast out. It strikes me as just the sort of thing a Queen's man would do."

A fair doubt — until one counted that, thrown out of Rheims, these zealots would just begin again elsewhere, in some place with no Thibauds — which this fellow must know only too well. And yet … *a murder*? Just the one? Could it be that Redbeard knew nothing of Downes and Fettiplace?

Pick it out of them piecemeal, Thomas, so they'll discover themselves.

Tom looked at Baines, asleep with his head on his bent arm, the other hand curled around the empty pot.

"'Tis a long time since he was a Queen's man."

"He still was, right after Easter. Prowling around the college, like a mangy wolf — the sort to kill if he had reason." A curl of the mouth, a glint in the grey eyes. "Unless you did it, that is."

This startled Tom into a laugh. "And if I had, would I loiter around the place? I haven't had my wits strained on the rack."

"For which you can thank the Lord." The smile widened in the reddish beard. "But let us say that you didn't kill this man, and our Baines didn't: the question remains of who did."

And a very good question it was — one of many that Tom asked himself. And another: who was this shrewd fellow, who called himself a man of Allen's and yet seemed to ignore so much? Time to dangle a morsel of bait.

"*If* he was killed, that is. Men do die —"

"In a garden belonging to the college?"

"Ay, well, there's that. And that archer spoke of murder — and I'll say Worthington looked much dismayed."

And there it was: the frown, the heartbeat of blankness.

"Allen's own right-hand," Tom explained, as lightly as he could. "He was there with the archer."

Redbeard hummed and nodded, as though for a matter of course.

But Worthington had not been there with the archer — nor was he Allen's right-hand. Barret was, and this man didn't know one from the other. He'd visited the college secretly enough, to meet Allen alone, who'd told him of his worries about Baines. And he had seen Baines for himself right after

225

Easter ... and then he'd done nothing about Baines — not until now. Nor did he know of the two dead men under Allen's roof.

The pieces fell into place inside Tom's head — with the well-known, well-loved sense of coloured panes of glass shifting to make a picture of startling certainty. And this time the picture was a name: Antwerp. This was why Redbeard knew nothing of what had passed after Easter: he'd been in Antwerp, courting Spanish generals, and he'd come back to Rheims only to find Dr. Allen too sick for visitors.

For this pleasant, sharp-witted stranger who sat across the table, sharing bad piquette and trading careful words, was no man of Allen's. This was Mary Stuart's man, Rafe Lyggon!

The Thomases could always tell when Tom had his epiphanies — Watson and little Phelippes both. But he was no longer that guileless lad, was he? Watson had weaned him out of it. All the same he was thankful that, just then, some throw of the dice had the players a-roar, and Baines stirred.

"Do you play dice?" asked Lyggon, eyes half sharp and half amused.

Cards, when I can afford it. But no, for cards were a gentleman's game, and Roper wouldn't... Not that he was Roper to Rafe Lyggon... *Oh, devil take it all!* Tom shook his head. *'Tis asses as shake their head no, Master Tom. Proper little gentlemen, the Lord gave them a tongue...* God — but this wretched piquette must be stronger than it seemed!

And see if the hesitation didn't make Lyggon's eyes crinkle at the corners. "Most wise of you," he said. "A foolish way to part ways with one's money — to stake it on naked Fortune and the rolling of a bit of bone. Still, I'm throwing my dice that you'll do as you say. That you'll take our March hare back to

England…" A cold look at Baines. "Or do what you will with him, as long as he's out of Dr. Allen's hair."

"And you won't kill us both?"

Lyggon smiled. "And make more trouble for the college? God alone can tell how many here would know you for Englishmen. If you force me, of course…" A shrug. "But I'd do without the trouble of two bodies."

And what it would take to force Lyggon into murdering two men Tom didn't ask, smiling back instead, and making no promises. Also, that he'd rather not kill them was not to say he wouldn't denounce them for English spies … another matter that was best left unvoiced.

"So, 'tis decided." Mary Stuart's man rose to his feet, looming over Tom. "You gallop off to England."

The gall of him! Tom let his smile widen. "And what of you?"

"What of me, ay." Lyggon ran a hand down his beard. "I may linger in Rheims a day or two. I find I'm itching to know more about this murder…" A shrug, and that curl of the mouth again. "Ah, well. If we ever meet again, I hope it will be over better wine."

And with that, he was gone.

Leaning sideways to peer, Tom saw him check his step just outside the door, and flick a small coin to a beggar before he turned away and disappeared.

So Tom now had Baines on his hands, and Lyggon's eyes on his back.

He couldn't hope to follow Lyggon — not with Baines, who had drunk himself into tottering meekness; neither could he bring Baines to the Brebis-qui-File — not with the danger of Lyggon following. Nor could he let Baines out of his sight again, now that he'd caught him.

If nothing else, Baines let himself be led out of the tavern and into the street. The sky was darkening, swollen with rain again. A thought came to Tom, of poor, fiery Noll Catesby's body, thrown somewhere for the rain to soak — and he squelched it, bringing his mind back to his own troubles.

"What am I going to do with you?" he asked the madman, not expecting an answer.

Nor that Baines should roll on him a fearful gaze, and mumble: "*Non secundum peccata nostra fecit nobis.*"

Oh, Jove… "Then I must be a very great sinner, if the Lord thinks you're better than I deserve."

And, because Baines's knees were beginning to buckle, Tom caught a grubby wrist, bent under the fellow's arm to support him — and did he stench! — and began to steer them both towards the unsavoury neighbourhood of the Rue du Tire-Vit. For there was one place in all of Rheims where they were both known, where the ill-looking Baines would be suffered to spend the night — and, most importantly, where Lyggon was welcome to follow, if he cared, and little harm done.

Half dragging the madman, soothing and scolding in equal parts, Tom picked their unsteady and winding way in as much haste as he could, before rain and darkness fell on them. No one bothered to light lanterns at street corners in this part of Rheims, and unwholesome characters lurked in the gloom. Devil seize the archers! Where were they when one needed them?

Had anyone told Thomas Walsingham the day would come when the sight of La Belle aux Pommes would gladden his heart…

It would have been a great deal better to know a back door — but still it was a relief to stumble into the dim, filthy court, just as the bells of Rheims began to chime Vespers.

Fricque's dingy room was more crowded than Tom liked at this time of the day, with Barbe playing hostess to a dozen rowdy men, sitting in one's lap and then another's, pouring wine and smiling her too-bright siren's smile.

Having dropped Baines on a bench, Tom was studying how to catch the woman's eye, when old Fricque appeared from the door under the stairs, and at once made his way to them.

"You can't stay here, Monsieur," he said, back turned on the laughing company, shrewd eyes going from Tom's dagger-less side to the drooping Baines. "I've two men of the *Milice* upstairs."

Which answered the question of where the archers were, instead of keeping order in the streets. And while Tom had no particular wish to encounter them in the chancy company of Baines...

"Good for them," he said, with all the unconcern he knew.

Fricque clicked his tongue at the madman. "But, Monsieur, this one — with all his talk of murder! They say there was a man killed — an Englishman —"

He went no further, for at that moment la Néné appeared atop the stairs, an archer's coat slung over her chemise. She nodded to Fricque — which sent the old man a-fretting.

"Away, Monsieur — away!" he half begged, half ordered, as he caught hold of Baines and dragged him to his feet.

And of course Baines must squirm, and try to tug free, and...

"Enough!" Tom snapped. "Just put us out of sight. We're not running from the *Milice*."

Fricque shushed him and turned to squint over his shoulder. Néné walked down the stairs alone, yawning and rolling her shoulders under the coat. The company downstairs caroused, boisterously oblivious.

"I don't want to know!" The old man went back to his pushing. "I don't care. Just bring away this loon: the archers promised trouble, if they caught him brawling again."

Which Baines was on the verge of doing, batting at Fricque's hands, rolling his eyes… Oh, devil seize it all!

"Stop it, Fricque!" Tom ordered. "You'll madden him."

And right then Néné joined them, with a hiss of "Papa, there's —" She caught her breath, eyes going round at the sight of Baines. "Dickon!" she exclaimed — and then turned to the room's one grimy window, which glowed red with torch-light. "The soldiers!"

Soldiers! Tom wanted to laugh in bitterness. Outside the court rang with laughter, and the strains of some campfire song or other.

Fricque turned on Tom a glare of the deepest reproach. "The Archbishop's men!" he grumbled, as though the two Englishmen were to blame for it.

And now, of course, the drinkers at the table were peering as well, alarmed at the arrival of the soldiers, or perhaps at Baines, who muttered in Latin, arm quivering in Tom's grip.

"*Dominus docet manus meas ad proelium —*"

"The Lord will teach you battle another day," Tom said — and there was nothing for it but to steer the madman to the door under the stairs and past the faded red curtain, without waiting for Fricque's permission.

The room was uninhabited — a narrow place in which three barrels and a cupboard were crammed around a battered two-poster.

On this bed, Tom dropped Baines, just as Néné followed them, drawing the curtain tight. Past the thin cloth, they could hear Papa Fricque welcoming his guests with great cheer. Now just let him not decide to present the soldiers with a brace of Englishmen...

Néné, looking younger than ever with loose hair and bare feet, cooed at Dickon — and see how the madman smiled up at her... He kept smiling when the woman turned to Tom and clicked her tongue, reaching to touch his still sore cheekbone. "What happened to you?"

That her Dickon had happened, Tom had no time to say, for Fricque stole through the curtain, looking thunderously displeased.

He shooed away Néné. "Before they think to come looking for you," he groused, and she disappeared.

As soon as she was gone, the old ruffian got down to business. "I don't want to know, Monsieur," he said. "But if this turns out badly..."

Of course. Ah, well. With a sigh, Tom sat on the bed and tugged off his boot. There wasn't much left in his purse, most of his money being at the Brebis-qui-File together with his dagger — which was just as well. He counted out three silver testons in his palm, then handed one to Fricque.

"The rest you'll have in the morning, when all has gone well, and we leave."

The old man didn't look pleased. "Monsieur..."

"A quiet night, Fricque, and you'll have your silver. Now, let's have some bread and cheese. And a jug of your wretched wine."

That the purse looked lean, that any soldier would filch the purse for himself, that even stabbing the Englishman in his sleep would yield little more than the promised three testons — it was a marvel, how it all passed in the old man's eyes. Tom held the calculating gaze until Fricque threw up his hands with a martyred sigh.

"Have it your way, Monsieur," he said. "I don't want to know."

He left and returned with a trencher, and then was gone again. By then, Baines lay across the bed, sleeping the sleep of the just.

Discovering a wooden door on their side of the curtain, Tom closed it. It had no bolt, but it was something. With half of the bread and cheese, and some of the foul piquette in his stomach, he reclined on the floor, back against the bed and legs stretched to brace his feet against the door. He listened to the merry-making in the next room, and the rain outside — knowing that he should consider Lyggon, and Marley, and the murders, but too tired to think.

At one point, a great burst of laughter startled him out of a doze. In the flicker of the guttering rush-light, he found Baines propped on an elbow, watching him with round, bird-like eyes.

"The Lord will smite old Fricque and tear down his den of iniquity," the madman announced in a portentous whisper.

"What, and la Néné, too?" Tom asked around a yawn.

There was a heartbeat of consideration, a scratching of the head, and a small, pained sigh. "She's a painted whore, poor chuckling."

Oh Jove… "Go to sleep, Baines," Tom ordered.

But Baines was warming to his argument. "The Lord will smite them all, as he did Allen, and Thibaud, and that one at the lodging house, and the servant, and the crook-toothed idler…"

And then came Downes, with those crooked teeth…
You don't serve the Lord by fiddling at the baker's.
Downes was seeing a woman.
He must have had his own reasons…

Tom found himself suddenly wide awake. "Baines, this crook-toothed fellow…"

A sour-mouthed nod. "Always about, he was —"

"And fiddling at the baker's?"

"The baker? No — the Pot o' Chance. Always there — always there. But he's dead, now. *Dabit Dominus inimicos tuos…*"

And with that he went back to his psalms first, and then to sleep, leaving Tom to consider that now, perhaps, he knew where to look for dead Hugh Downes's secrets.

CHAPTER 15

28th of May

Morning came, and with it la Néné, carrying old bread and ale so thick it must have been the last of the dregs. She asked three sols for it — which was rank thievery.

"You'd think we had featherbeds and roasted quails!" Tom groused, as he counted out the coins. "What are you, a fine *auberge* in Paris?"

Néné laughed — a sweet trill that had Baines smiling — but she still checked the money twice in her palm.

A chuckle came from the door. "Why, we save them, and he haggles!" Lison, of course, silver eyes a-sparkle.

"Why, you brat — we were in no need of —"

Tom's retort ended in a huff, when Baines shoved him aside, vaulted over the bed, and leapt for the young woman most lion-like.

"You painted whore!" he growled, catching Lison by the neck. "Give me back my cross!"

Lison screeched, and Néné wailed, and Tom jumped to restrain the madman, and in a trice Fricque and Barbe stormed through the red curtain.

"Baines, stop it!" Tom managed to throw the man back onto the bed, where he curled on his side, sobbing for his cross, his cross, his cross…

Lison was grousing bitterly — had they seen it? Had they? The lack-wit had tried to kill her!

There was little sympathy. Fricque cuffed her on the arm, and Néné said that this came of thieving, and Barbe was still more brisk in grabbing her fellow mermaid by the wrist.

"For God's sake, Lison, give it back!" she scoffed.

At which Lison cried to high Heaven that she no longer had the cross — given it to a soldier, a poor lad going to war … and all the time Baines whimpered on the bed.

"Oh, *Sainte Vièrge*, enough!" Barbe shook Lison, tore something small and glittering out of her skirts, and grasped Baines's hand to slap the small object into his palm. "There! That's for your cross, Dickon. Now hold your peace."

And Baines fell quiet, gaping at a tiny blade, curved at the end, a broken inch of ivory handle… The remains of a lady's penknife. It was likely not the best of notions to arm Dickon Baines, not even with so small a blade — but never mind now, seeing how Baines was made docile by his rapt contemplation of his new toy. Sparing a grateful look and his last sol for Barbe, Tom paid Fricque his two testons, drained the last of the ale in one gulp, and made haste to drag the madman away.

The air was damp and heavy in the streets. The sky overhead — what little of it showed between the roofs — looked gauzy with the promise of a warm day, for once. Tom took a circuitous route to the cathedral and then the Marché à la Laine. Not that he caught the slightest sign of Lyggon, but the man had more than proved his stealth and skill, and it was nothing but the simplest caution to take a few turns in the streets, and among the stalls of the busy market, before turning their steps to the Rue de la Bûchette. Alas, Baines's meekness of the past night had evaporated with the wine, enough that he spun this way and that, rolling his eyes, stiffening whenever he caught a louder voice. Perhaps some of Papa Fricque's piquette

235

would have made a better breakfast for him.

It felt like a long time before Tom knocked at the Thibauds' door. He pushed Baines with his back against the wall, pinning him there with a hand to the chest, before the peep-hole slid open — and whether Perrette knew to compose her face other than in a scowl, Tom didn't know.

"Perrette!" he called with his best smile. "Tell your mistress that her cousin Roland —"

The peep-hole slammed shut, and Fates send that Blandine Jory made haste, for Baines was eyeing the gate, bunching what muscles he had — a stray dog contemplating flight.

He jumped when the bolt was drawn, and the wicket thrown open, and Tom grasped him just as Blandine appeared on the threshold.

"Cousin … oh, Saints all!" she cried. Most women would have leapt out of the way, but not Blandine, who rushed into the street, grabbing a flailing arm and hauling.

"Look to it!" Tom hissed. "He's maddened —" His warning ended in a grunt as Baines's elbow caught him in the stomach.

"*Confundantur cogitantes mihi mala…*"

"Enough!" Tom caught the man by his front and manoeuvred them both through the wicket, which Blandine was quick to shut. When Baines stumbled in the sudden gloom, Tom pushed him into the nearest corner.

The madman never ceased squirming and babbling. "*Fiam tamquam pulvis ante faciem venti —*"

"Ay, ay — all dust in the wind, we'll be!" Tom leaned with all his weight against Baines. "'Tis not us who wish you harm, fool. Look at me!"

When he relinquished his hold on one shoulder, Blandine was there to take his place, scowling as she pushed with all her might.

"Baines!" Tom caught the man by the jaw, forcing him to meet his eyes. "Dickon Baines, we'll protect you from Allen's man. You hear? The Lord sent me to rescue you. To confound Allen's man."

Which must be a particularly wicked kind of lie — but it worked: see how Baines slackened into the corner, gaping in doubting wonder.

"The Lord sent you?"

"Ay —"

And then there was a shriek of "M'zelle!" and Tom looked over his shoulder to see Perrette armed with an iron poker. "M'zelle, stand back!"

Blandine stumbled in her skirt's hem as she rushed to stop the servant. "*Mais non, sotte!*" she scoffed, as she wrenched the poker from Perrette's hands. "This was a servant of my uncle from London. He was lost here in Rheims — oh, years ago. Now my cousin has found him, but…" She tapped her temple with a forefinger.

And wasn't she a marvellously quick-witted liar!

"Oh, *Anges saints!*" Perrette crossed herself, squinting to catch a glimpse of this spectacle — a man out of his mind — even as she was ordered away to fetch her master.

"My husband's back…" Blandine stopped, reddening when Tom grinned.

"Well, well, *ma cousine!* You have a good head on your shoulders."

A shrug, and a tiny answering smile. "It will do for a story, if we're to keep him here." She bent to peer at the crouching creature in the corner. "Is it true? That Allen's man —"

Baines tensed at the name, wriggling half free. As he did his best to press the fellow into the corner, Tom felt a sting in his forearm.

"Damn it to hell, you bedlamite!" Tom struggled, caught a flailing arm and twisted the wrist. Something clattered to the floor — then suddenly Baines was hauled away.

"Soft now," a man's voice rumbled in French. "Soft, I say!" And there stood a stout, big-boned man, shaking Baines like a rag. Perrette's master, no doubt — and Blandine's husband.

He was a large fellow of about thirty years, Jacques Jory, with a frank, ruddy face and a full beard, and a worried frown for his wife.

"Monsieur found Baines," she explained.

Jory gave Baines a good scrutiny. "'Tis him who came to see *Beau-Père* — and no mistake." And then he looked at Tom. "Are you hurt, Monsieur?"

Tom had pushed up his sleeve to uncover a small, ragged prick on his forearm. "A scratch," he said — and curse it! Why must he always come out bleeding against this particular madman?

"*Qui blasphemaverit, morte moriatur,*" Baines babbled, teeth rattling when Jory shook him again.

"'Tis your fault that I cursed, you hydra!" groused Tom. "Knifing me with…" With what, indeed? There it was, gleaming on the floor. Tom picked up Barbe's gift. "A penknife!" Of all things in this world!

Jory eyed the broken thing in Tom's palm. "That's never how he killed those men?"

Not one to mince matters, was Jacques Jory. Tom shook his head, with more firm certainty than he felt, and pocketed the bit of knife. "In truth, I misdoubt he killed anyone — but keep him well shut up all the same. Wine keeps him quiet."

Jory nodded. "We have a fine place for maddened old servants. Eh, fellow?" And, for a wonder, Baines suffered himself to be led away with no worse than some mutterings of how the Lord provides shelter.

Blandine ushered Tom to the little parlour, which looked as bleak as ever even in the sunlight. Even as she closed the door, she asked, "But if Baines didn't kill those two, who did?"

Ah this, now! "Those *three*," Tom said — and told her of Elliot.

"But why was he killed, this one?" she asked.

Which Tom would have liked to know. If he had to guess, though… "He was there when Fettiplace was murdered. He, or his cousin, or both must have seen something."

And, of course, just about every soul at the Collège might have had good reason to kill — not to mention the Scots Queen's man.

"Lyggon, Barret, Worthington, Hodgson, that Savage…" Names that perhaps meant little to his listener, but Tom was thinking aloud as he paced the length and breadth of the chequered floor. "All of them lied, all of them might have done it." Supposing that at least Downes had been a danger to them. "Madame Jory, think well: could Hugh Downes be one of ours? Did your father ever mention him?"

"Hugh Downes…" Blandine repeated, head tilted, brow knotted, eyes narrowed. After a while, she shook her head. "If *mon père* knew, he never told me. I never heard the name, not until your Sherbourn ran here crying murder."

Which might not mean all that it seemed. The Queen's favourite, Lord Leicester, sometimes thought himself clever enough to ape Sir Francis's work. And there was the Lord Treasurer Burghley, who very much wanted a Service of his own.

"But do you think that Dr. Allen had the murders done himself?"

239

Blandine's question drew Tom out of his consideration and into another: did he think so? This Allen, the Cyclops himself, who presided over the whole den of traitors, a constant presence even when unseen? And yet, tempting as it was…

"Why kill Fettiplace before he could talk to Allen, if Allen was behind it all the time?"

There was a knock at the door — and Blandine went to let in her husband. She asked him about Hugh Downes — and Jory shook his head.

"Still, he could have been thinking to sell them out," he said.

Yes, there was that. "It seems he was some sort of errand boy for Dr. Allen, coming to the town often enough. And it may be true or not that he met a woman. Do you know of a place called the Pot o' Chance?"

Husband and wife looked at each other.

"*Le Pot au Change*," Jory said. "It's a *rôtisserie* where the English go."

"Men from the Collège, too?"

"Sometimes." Blandine pursed her lips. "My father began to keep a man there, a couple of years ago. One of our old carriers who has some English, paid to sit there, and keep his ears open. He says that all they do is drink to England and speak English."

A resourceful family, the Thibauds. "But Downes never tried to talk to your man."

Jory shook his head. "Not that we know. Perhaps he just had a woman there."

Which was possible, of course, but did nothing to explain the man's death — much less those of Fettiplace and Elliot. Unless… A piece turned in Tom's head, a change of pattern — another picture entirely.

"Unless it is the other way around! Say that Downes saw something, or heard it — something that showed someone else a traitor."

"And this someone poisoned him?" asked Jory.

"I misdoubt it was poison. I think someone threw Downes down the stairs, and made it seem as though he'd blundered there in his fever."

Jory hummed doubtfully. "And the other two?"

"Elliot somehow knew, and kept the secret for a while, I reckon — and Catesby with him. Then they ran — but not fast enough, and the murderer caught them. Or it was about Fettiplace's death that they knew, and…" And that was where Tom's new picture came undone — for Fettiplace had left the Collège by the time of Downes's death. And if Downes had not been poisoned… "He may have marked something — something he didn't understand at the time…" True enough, and feeble enough that there was a short tilt-headed silence from the Jorys, before Jacques shuffled his feet.

"And…" He looked down, like one expecting little liking for what he had to say. "And what of Sherbourn, Monsieur?"

Ay — what of him?

There being no worse from Tom than a raised eyebrow, Jory forged on. "He was there when both men died — and if he's no danger to Allen and his, then I don't know who is."

Which was no doubt how it must look to the men in the college — but… "But if he'd murdered Downes, he'd hardly come here to make a noise about it, would he?"

"He tried to have this Baines blamed, though." Jory shook his head, stubborn and unconvinced. Marley had made no friends at the Brebis-qui-File.

But Blandine swatted her husband's arm. "And a right noise he made of it — when all he had to do was keep quiet, and

241

we'd never even know these two men had died. *Non,* Monsieur?"

"Yes, Madame. Yes indeed." And Tom was most surely going to recommend that this clever woman be left to continue her father's work. "But this won't serve, should anyone at the Collège suspect Sherbourn — or throw the blame on him."

Which seemed a great deal more likely, now that the Law of Rheims had been brought into the fray. The college must be in agony and uproar, now. No wonder that Barret had tried to keep matters quiet.

"Time to send some yellow roses to the Virgin, Madame Jory. Meanwhile, I'll have a look at this *Pot au Change.* Do only the English go there?"

"Monsieur..." There was another look between the Jorys — one of worry. "My husband just returned from Compiègne..."

"The roads aren't safe, Monsieur — worse by the day." Jacques stepped forward, all frowning earnestness. "And now the truce has ended, the soldiers are spoiling for a fight — King's men and Guisards — and even here... The City Council, they don't know which way to turn. In your place, I'd try to be out of France before they're all given their head."

The wise recourse, no doubt. Fetch Kit Marley, take Baines, and make for Calais. Sir Francis's bidding was done, after all: Baines was retrieved; Thibaud's death had been natural, and his daughter was more than able to fill her father's shoes; Lyggon was Allen's friend; Rheims was less agog for the Lords of Guise than the Lords of Guise may have hoped. All that Tom had been sent to do was done. And yet...

You leave, and turn your back on two murders, Marley had scoffed in the dark classroom. They hadn't even known for certain that murder had been done, back then — but now...

Now three men had died, now foul play was certain. Now Lyggon had taken an interest in the matter.

Across the bare table, Tom looked at Blandine and Jacques Jory. Good, solid people, who served Sir Francis well — and who must think they faced more and more danger with every hour the men from London lingered in Rheims. Which was true enough — and yet there was even more danger for them in a murderer roaming free, who may yet find his way to the Brebis-qui-File. A murderer who had thought nothing of killing Downes, and Fettiplace, and poor, young, timid Elliot…

Tom straightened into his best manner of firm command. "I must know how much of the trouble at the Collège is our trouble too. I'll begin with the *Pot au Change*. You summon Sherbourn, and keep Baines under lock and key."

Neither of the Jorys looked very glad — but neither said a word.

The *Pot au Change* was, it turned out, a *rôtisserie* near the Corn Market. It being early for dinner, there was no crowd, but much bustle of preparation. The *rôtissier* himself and several white-aproned youths hurried around with roasted hams, baskets of golden rolls, plates of pastries, and those airy sweetmeats, big as a woman's fist and filled with cream that the French called *beignets*. From the far wall, a huge fireplace gave light and warmth, and three young boys were busy turning spits above its flames. Rounds of cheese and strings of sausages were piled on a huge counter, while the middle of the room was taken by a huge table, where the good things were being piled. The air smelt of roast meat, rosemary, and sugar — and trust the English exiles to find themselves such a pleasant place!

There were also benches around the room and on one of those Tom sat himself, looking around with the huge-eyed curiosity of a country barleycorn. And, as he looked, he listened. A meeting-place for the English this may be, but the people of the house were French — the fat *rôtissier*, his fatter wife, an apple-faced daughter, and all their hands.

It was not long before the young woman made her way to the customer, to ask what he would have. She was a pretty little thing, with laughing eyes and dimples on her cheeks. It would be too good, surely, that this could be Hugh Downes's sweetheart? Making his accent heavier and his speech slower, Tom asked for a meat pie and a glass of wine.

The young woman clapped her hands. "Oh, but you're English!" she said. "Are you new-come to Rheims? Shame that you are so early. We always have some of your countrymen for dinner."

Tom smiled. "A friend told me of your shop, Mademoiselle. He said, if I ever happened to be in Rheims, it was like being at home."

"Then he's one of our Englishmen, maybe. My mother makes the pastries for them — the païses." By which, Tom gathered, she meant *pies*. "Did your friend tell you of the païses?"

"Why, yes!" Tom watched her very closely as he spoke. "Hugh turned all poet, when it came to your païses."

And there it was — but not the flinch of a bereaved lover. An intake of breath, rather, a faltering of the smile.

"Hugh?" she murmured. "Never Hugh Downes?"

"Ay, that's my friend. He still comes here, doesn't he?"

The young woman threw a glance over her shoulder. "Wait here," she said, and scurried away, to disappear behind the counter.

Now what if she'd gone to alert the wrong person? Some traitorous cut-throat, say, the murderer's accomplice — and Tom armed with no better than an eating knife and Baines's broken pen-trimmer? Would they cut him up and cook the shreds into païses — the Cyclops munching Ulysses?

Out of these gruesome thoughts he blinked to see a thinner, paler woman hastening towards him with a trencher.

"*Voilà*, Monsieur," she said — and then, so low it could be barely heard, "I'm Jeanne."

No dimples, here. No smiles. Here was the grieving sweetheart — and Tom found it irked his conscience to lie to her.

"Hugh's *mademoiselle*!"

A wan smile touched her lips, and wavered. "He told you of me?"

This was all to find the truth of Downes's death, wasn't it? Still, Tom felt like the worst of scoundrels when he assured her that Hugh had spoken of little else, and an even greater blackguard when her eyes filled.

"Don't you know, Monsieur?" she whispered, voice thick with tears. "Hugh is dead. It will be a month, tomorrow."

A show of surprise, then, and some grief, and a tale not unlike that of Roper — a boyhood friend of Hugh, a meeting back before Easter, a journey to Italy, and now…

Poor Jeanne twisted a kerchief between her fingers, and kept herself from crying. Hugh was to have married her, she said. He didn't want to be a priest. He'd meant to leave the Collège Anglais, to become a *rôtissier* himself. Jeanne's parents had opposed the notion of an English son-in-law at first, but had begun to mellow towards Hugh, and then…

"Jeanne!" the mother called from the counter. "Come and help, *enfant*…"

Jeanne rubbed at her eyes and made to go, but Tom caught her hand.

"How did he die?" he asked. "How did you come to know?"

"A man came from the Collège," she breathed in haste. "A friend of Hugh's. A fever, he said."

And then she ran to her mother, leaving Tom with his cooling pastry, and a new impression of Hugh Downes. So there *was* a woman — for this sad-eyed Jeanne was no liar. And while there was nothing to say that a man couldn't have both a sweetheart and a few secrets, still one who meant to betray Allen to the Queen's men would hardly set himself up for a life in Rheims, by courting not only a woman, but the woman's father, and the father's trade to boot.

In absent-minded haste Tom ate his pie — and it did have something of an English taste, of ginger, currants and cloves. Surely one of the English of Rheims had given the recipe to Jeanne's mother. One of the women who flocked to the college for the sermon, perhaps, or some sad inn-keeper who despaired of ever going back... Oh, foolish notions! What mattered was, nothing at the *Pot au Change* showed Downes as Savage's false-playing liar.

Yet, something he must have done— or seen, or heard— that sent him to his death. Treason to the cause? Some murderous excess of zeal? Something of a less Godly nature? For these were men, in spite of their black austerity and saintly speech — and even in a seminary men knew greed, passion, envy, and hate.

There seemed to be little for it, but to go back to Allen's door.

Meanwhile, the first customers were arriving in search of dinner. Was Thibaud's old carrier among them? Washing down the last bite of pie with the last of the wine, Tom left a coin with one of the scurrying youths and slipped away, before anyone came who might know him from the college.

Out in the street again, and now what?

If Tom's jaunt to the *Pot au Change* had served a purpose, it was to mark Hugh Downes as an unlikely spy — or at least to give weight to Hodgson's opinion of him, rather than to Savage's dark hints.

Why, had only Downes died, it would look of no importance, no matter what Marley said. But two more men had died, although, in the sunny morning — warm with the promise of summer, the sky full of swallows and the air thick with the scent of bread — Rheims hardly seemed a place for murder and mayhem. Nor for war, in truth, and yet…

Ah well. Best go to Saint-Symphorien, now, and wait for Marley, and make him see the virtues of retreat.

At the first crossroads Tom stopped to consider his way — a consideration that was cut short by a squawking cry of "Look! There!"

Two archers strode to bar his way in a clang of corselets and morions — and of course the whole street had to take an interest in it.

So Jeanne *was* a liar, after all…

Tom made himself unclench his shoulders and jaw, like one who had nothing to hide.

"What would your name be, Monsieur?" the larger archer asked, mouth drawn aslant.

He'd given no name at the *Pot au Change*. If he lied now…

"Roland! That's what he says. Thomas Roland — but it's a lie!" The squawking voice again, and from behind the archers who must appear, black-browed, and much pleased with himself, but Blandine's plaguey brother?

247

The cursed, witless whelp! Tom pinched the bridge of his nose. *Unus, duo, tres...* "Cousin Remi," he ground out. "This, now..."

"How cousin?" The archer scowled, turning from the boy to Tom and back again. "Monsieur Thibaud, is this man your cousin?"

"Yes," said Tom.

"No!" cried Remi, voice rising to a squeal. "He says he's my cousin from London — but he's not. He is an English spy!"

Damn it all to hell! Was there no limit to this snot-nosed lack-wit's jealous rage? Did he not see the danger he was bringing on his sister's head? But no, of course — he couldn't know. To his scantling greedy mind, Thomas Roland was out to rob him of his rights ... and in his rabid malice he'd stumbled on the truth!

Through a tight throat, Tom forced a laugh. "A spy! The boy is addled in his wits."

"I'm not!" Indignation painted Remi a blotchy scarlet, and he pointed at Tom, a jab of the forefinger for every other word. "He came to steal my father's inheritance. He says he has a contract for it, and keeps it hidden. He had a lawyer and a servant with him — and they're nowhere. He says he stays at the inn, and he doesn't!"

A dearth of wit, and some natural bent for rhetoric — what a charming combination!

"Messieurs, this is madness!" Tom spread his hands, palms up in an appeal for reason. "My cousin fears for his inheritance, and thinks to keep it whole by causing harm to me. If you'd only ask the boy's sister, Madame Blandine Jory at the Brebis-qui-File..."

To their credit, the *Milice* men showed a little doubt. The huge one smoothed his moustache as he contemplated the seething Remi. Had he been alone, faced with only a reasonable man and a spluttering boy, he might have shrugged and gone his way. But — Jove fulminate all market idlers! — a rabble was thickening all around, and murmurs of *spy* and *English* ran through it. No self-respecting French officer would disregard such a public incident — much less in these turmoiling days.

So it was no marvel that the archer fastened his sternest look on the foreigner. "Is it true that you have a contract, Monsieur?"

"Of course I have a contract." Weary patience, now — and a little irritation. "I have two of them, in fact: the old one between this boy's father and mine, and a proposal for a new one, since Monsieur Thibaud is dead. It's no secret —"

"Your servant nearly spitted me when I tried to see them!" Remi blurted.

A great sigh now, of patience wearing thin. "Yes, Remi — because he took you for a thief when you slunk into my room at the inn to pilfer my papers."

The lesser archer gave a guffaw at this, and swallowed it under his officer's glare. This glare was then transferred to Remi.

"Is it true, young man? You did this?"

"No — yes, I…" The boy swallowed hard. "I was not shown them, for all that I'm my father's heir — and that man who calls himself a lawyer…"

The populace murmured and sneered at the mention of lawyers.

"Ah, yes — the lawyer." The archer held up a hand for silence. "This lawyer, Monsieur. And this servant. Where are they?"

Tom explained how the servant had only come to summon the lawyer home, and how both would now hopefully be well on their way to London. A most reasonable, most sensible explanation, so why the onlookers must laugh, Heaven knew. There were even women leaning out of the windows above, adding their contemptuous opinions.

"And you've left the inn as well?"

"He wasn't there, last night!" Remi shouted, a notion the rabble greedily took in. "I went to seek him there, this morning, and —"

The officer waved Remi quiet. "You were not at your inn, Monsieur?"

"No, I was not." Tom raised an eyebrow. "I slept elsewhere."

Which was, after all, quite true — halfway to the implication the crowd's laughter suggested.

But young Remi was not amused. "He's lying!" he squawked, voice creaking in his anger. "And then spies go to brothels too!"

The ugly word again — and this time the crowd took it up. *Espion! Espion! Assassin anglais!*

"To the rack!" shouted a woman at the window, and a clot of something flew Tom's way. Oh Lord! To have lived through six years in the Service, and to be now undone by this stupid brat!

"Enough!" the officer roared, as he closed ranks with his man, hands on hilts, armours clanging. He gripped Tom's elbow. "We'll discuss this at the *Hôtel de Ville*, Monsieur."

It was a good thing that even the less respectable people of Rheims — and of many places in France — had learnt, through many years of strife and havoc, the wisdom of picking their battles with men carrying arms. This particular rabble gave place as the archers led Tom away, although with much hooting and whistling, and a few cries for the rack, and more throwing of unsavoury missiles, and a burst of ragged song wishing *la male fin* to all the English. Young Remi lagged behind in knuckle-biting uncertainty, until, at a nod from the officer, the soldier turned back to take hold of him too.

"But no!" the boy squeaked, dragging back like an unwilling mastiff at the bear-baiting. "I've done nothing, me!"

"No?" The officer looked down his nose. "You accuse a man of being a spy; I call it doing something!"

It was too much for young Remi, who gave his archer a great shove, and ran like a hare through the midday press, uselessly and briefly pursued by the armoured man.

A marvellously good thing, to Tom's way of thinking.

"You see, *mon* Maître?" he asked. "Is this how an honest man behaves?"

The officer sniffed. "Men and boys are not the same. Perhaps you're innocent as a lamb, Monsieur; perhaps you're not. They'll know how to find out at the *Hôtel,* eh?"

And with that, having retrieved his puffing and sheepish henchman, off he hied his prisoner.

CHAPTER 16

The *Lieutenant des Habitants*, much the same as a Lord Mayor, had his seat at the *Hôtel de Ville*, which sat by a square called Le Marché aux Chevaux — the Horse Market. That the French found nothing to amuse them in this — nor anything that should amuse an Englishman — was one thing. That throwing its grim shadow across this marketplace was the city's gallows was another. The horse trade must be a lark, in Rheims!

At first Tom thought that the *Hôtel* must be the stately, two-storeyed palace of clear-coloured stone, with a steep grey-blue slate roof and a row of dormer windows. Instead he found himself marched towards a row of old houses — some of stone, some half-timbered — that stood at right angles to the palace.

"That's the Siège Royal," the officer said, when he caught Tom looking at the much finer building — and by the way he said it, one wouldn't think there was much joy in being neighbours with the King's *Bailli* — or whatever it was they had in Rheims.

They entered a dark, damp hall with a dark wooden staircase and dark tapestries covering the walls. It all looked very old and glum, and a little cramped, with archers, clerks and citizens all brushing shoulders as they scurried about. Thinking of the palace across the square, it wasn't hard to imagine some King of France trying to browbeat the Guisard Rheims by sheer architectural magnificence.

Tom was hastily led around the staircase, and along a twisting dark corridor, to a small panelled room in the back of the house. There the officer left him with the archer, and disappeared without a word.

When he reappeared, it was to usher in the City of Rheims, in the person of a bloated character possessed of several chins, a red-lined short cape of black velvet, and a good deal of displeased dignity.

This personage gave Tom no more than a sideways glance.

"This would be the English spy?" he asked, pursing his small, fat lips.

That such a dismissive manner should sting went to prove, Tom supposed, the foolish vanity of human nature.

"No, Monsieur," he said, with a small bow. "I'm nothing of the sort. My name is Thomas Roland, and I'm a merchant of London, and…"

The man ignored him entirely and poured his annoyance on the officer instead. "To bring him here, like this!"

"But Monsieur le Conseiller, what was I to do — whistle for the sergeants from the Siège Royal?" the officer asked, with some irritation of his own.

But it was clear that his rank allowed him no irritation, for the *conseiller* gave a quelling look and jerked his head towards Tom, in the the sort of movement people seemed to suppose must go unobserved. But there was the crux of the matter: the city, the Archbishop and the King's man, each with their own power of law. And a foreign spy would be the *Bailli*'s business, surely — but to have seized such a dangerous felon, only to hand him over…

"Messieurs," Tom tried, "this is very easily solved, for I'm no spy at all. If you'd just send for my cousin, Madame Blandine Jory…"

Again, he could have talked to the door jamb, for all the good it did. The *conseiller* rubbed at his chins, with much portentous humming.

Having been caught between squabbling French jurisdictions before, Tom had a fair notion of the fellow's dilemma: to claim for the city the capture of such a dangerous creature was to displease the *Bailli*, the King through him — and perhaps also some other deity in the city's pantheon; to let the spy go across the Horse Market, was to spare himself much trouble — but also to humiliate the City Council. To decide that the spy was no spy at all would be the simplest course — but what if he was? And did it fall within the city's power to decide such things?

It was little marvel that the *conseiller* turned most viperously on the officer again. "Most ill-judged of you!" he spat, and stormed off with all his cape-ruffling dignity. The officer sighed and followed, with the soldier in tow.

"Monsieur!" called Tom. "If only you'd send…"

The only answer was the door's bolt sliding home.

Several hours passed, marked by the chiming of the bells, and, much less regularly, by steps and voices in the corridor outside. The sky changed colour past the one lead-paned window — and the one chair that, together with a bare table, made up the room's whole furnishing, grew more and more uncomfortable. So Tom paced back and forth, and busied himself with thinking.

He imagined messengers crossing the Marché aux Chevaux, to and fro, carrying notes between the *Hôtel de Ville* and the Siège Royal.

He tried to decide who would, in the end, do the pilgrimage in person: some frowning royal *procureur* in chain of office, or a *conseiller* — perhaps Tom's own many-chinned visitor?

Tom cursed Remi Thibaud in English, French, Italian and Latin, and wondered, between one curse and the next: had Blandine discovered what her miscreant brother had done?

He worried about Blandine: had he been rash to bring her into the matter? But no, the officer had addressed Remi by name, so it stood to reason that he must know who the boy was.

He worried about Marley at the college: had the young idiot obeyed the summons and gone to Saint-Symphorien and then to the Brebis-qui-File, or was he still under Allen's roof, at the murderer's mercy and under the exiles' suspicions?

He worried about himself, thinking of the gallows in the middle of the square — and, before that, the rack.

He called himself a fool, also, for not once in all his time in the Service had it occurred to him that he might have to sacrifice his name in the cause of England and the Queen. But, should the King's *Bailli* and the City of Rheims come to agree on him being a spy, he would have to give no other name than Thomas Roland through torture and to his death.

It was well past three, and Tom's thoughts were taking a grim turn when the door was thrown open to admit the officer, the *conseiller*, and a tall man with a long, fine-boned face and a flowing robe of black velvet. Was this then the *procureur* from the Siège Royal?

No explanation was offered, and it was the *conseiller* who asked: "Monsieur Roland, if that's your name you'll have the papers to prove it, surely?"

Yes. No. I lost them. I was robbed. I forgot... "Of course I have them, Messieurs — but not with me."

It was the tall man's turn to question, with a smooth haughtiness Dr. Worthington might have envied. "They will be at your inn, perhaps?"

They must have deemed him a very innocent sort of spy, to think he'd fall into such an obvious trap. "I left them with my cousin — for her and her husband to peruse. If only you would send for her, Messieurs…"

This, once more, the gentlemen ignored and, after exchanging dark glares, they left without a word. The officer remained just long enough to let in a man with a trencher of bread and cold meat, and a pot of ale.

Having forgone supper last night, and having hardly broken his fast since, Tom fell on it with a good appetite, although the ale was weak and savourless. Was a possible spy not worth the expense of even a sip of modest wine?

And after that, there was more uneasy waiting, more wondering, more worrying.

The light beyond the window had begun to grow golden when next he heard movement in the corridor. Steps and voices, and … could it be? Oh good Lord, did one of the voices belong to a woman?

The door was unbolted, and through it marched the officer of the *Milice*, two *conseillers* — the same one from before and an older, grey-bearded one — and, bless her, Blandine Jory in pattens and a green hood.

The moment she clacked over the threshold, Blandine threw down her hood, to show a most formidable pout. "Cousin Thomas!" she exclaimed. "They said you'd been arrested — but I would not believe…" She turned from man to man, as one seeking to have the inexplicable explained.

"So you know this man, Madame Jory?" the older *conseiller* asked, with the manner of an acquaintance.

"But yes, Monsieur, yes! This is my cousin from London, and how this could come to pass…"

She clucked, she disbelieved, she hit a small plump hand to her hip. In his mind, Tom bowed in admiration. Anyone would believe her a silly woman, beside herself with agitation, and something of a scold — never a liar, never a sharp-witted creature, certainly never an agent of the English Queen. For the first time since his arrest, Tom allowed himself to hope.

"Jory will be here at any moment — he will explain, he will vouch…" Blandine babbled. "Oh, Saints help — but truly!" She clutched the sleeve of the grey-bearded *conseiller*. "Truly, Monsieur Dumont, why would you arrest him, just because he's English?"

Monsieur Dumont hummed, his colleague said nothing, and the archer shuffled his feet. Were they perhaps beginning to feel foolish?

"But no, *ma fille*!" Dumont said — a fond but stern uncle. "Your brother went to the archers, and denounced this man as an English spy."

"My brother… Oh!" Blandine threw up her hands, before turning to Tom in a whirl of skirts. "What you must think of us, Cousin!" Another whirl, this time towards the City of Rheims. "My brother is a child! Ask Monsieur Dumont — he knows Remi from the cradle… Oh Saints! It's Remi's uncle — Monsieur Dumont knows him. He's making trouble; he whispers in the boy's ear because of the inheritance…"

Both Dumont and the archer looked a little shaken by Blandine's certainty — so much so that Tom was perfectly content to stand back and watch. Most interesting to see was the fat *conseiller*, who may not know whether he wanted a spy on his hands or not, but was most surely irked at being told off by a woman — respectable *bourgeoise* though she might be.

"Your brother thinks that you were taken in by this man, Madame," he said.

This earned him more of Blandine's scoffing. "My brother is not yet fifteen, jealous and spiteful, and has greedy people whispering in his ear! Of course I'm not taken in!"

"You wouldn't be the first woman to be taken in by a fine-talking cozener," was the *conseiller*'s haughty rejoinder. "So, unless you have good proof that this man is what he calls himself…?"

"Proof!" Blandine threw up her hands again. "What proof do you want me to have, Monsieur? We do business with my cousin's family; we've done so for many years — although if he wants nothing to do with us now, small blame to him! I wrote to say that my father had died, and he arrived… Oh!" She clapped her hands. "But I do have your proof! The papers for the contract — they were done by a notary in London!"

"And you have them here?"

"But no, Monsieur, why would I? If your archer had told me what the trouble was… But wait. I'll have them fetched." As though the *Hôtel de Ville* were her own home, Blandine tripped to the door and called, "Simonnet, come here!" And when her servant-lad appeared on the threshold, she began to instruct him on meeting his master halfway, and what he was to say.

It was greatly diverting, to see these three men of the law stand a-gazed before a little whirlwind of a woman. The elderly Dumont was eyeing Tom in the way of one rehearsing apologies in his mind.

And it was more than Tom could help. He shrugged and said, "Had you sent for my cousin when I first asked, Messieurs…"

Young Simonnet was in the act of leaving, when Jacques Jory appeared on the threshold.

"Master!" the lad cried, just as Blandine called, "Jacques!" and Dumont greeted, "Jory!" with much relief.

"You have the contracts?" Dumont asked, more than a little foolishly — but it was clear that, by then, the poor fellow wanted nothing better than to get rid of them all.

"What contracts, Monsieur?" Jory came forward to draw Blandine's hand under his arm. "I was told that my wife had been summoned here — and her cousin Roland."

"There!" exclaimed Blandine. "Tell them, husband. To me they wouldn't listen…"

Which wasn't quite true — as they'd all done a good deal of listening since the arrival of Blandine. Still now the two Council men were at great pains to regard the matter as beneath their attention, and the poor archer was left to tell the story of Remi's accusations.

When he was done, Jory exclaimed, "That little hellion! His father never caned him enough, if you ask me."

"It is something else that we ask you, Maître Jory." The fat *conseiller* pointed a stubby forefinger at Tom. "Will you tell us who this man is?"

"But I told you, Monsieur," Jory said. "This is my wife's cousin from London, Thomas Roland."

"Because your wife says so?" the *conseiller* sneered, chins wobbling.

Jacques Jory took his most stolid manner. "But no, Monsieur, because I've met him half a dozen times — in Calais and in London. We do business together, the Rolands and us. Ask Monsieur Dumont."

After that, the City of Rheims couldn't get rid of them all fast enough.

The better part of the afternoon had gone by the time Tom and the Jorys emerged in the Marché aux Chevaux, and they crossed it in grim silence, followed by young Simonnet. When he stepped into the long, thin shadow that the gallows threw across the cobbles, Tom had to keep himself from shivering. Curse Remi Thibaud and his unthinking jealousy. He would pay a fair price for this escapade, reckoning by his sister and his brother-in-law's scowls.

A taut wind was rising, shepherding banks of grey clouds.

Jory frowned at the sky. "And more rain to come," he sighed. "A very bad spring this is…"

He picked up the pace for the whole company, and not another word was exchanged until they were at the Brebis-qui-File, rid of Simonnet's company, and ensconced in the parlour.

Blandine lit the fat candles in the pewter branch — and, when she turned, her eyes were red. Poor little, brave, quick-witted, gruff Blandine.

Tom smiled at her. "Well, *ma cousine*, I can't thank you enough. You saved us all —"

She waved off his thanks. "Oh don't, Monsieur! I don't know what possessed Remi…" She clicked her tongue and turned away.

Jory put a hand on her shoulder. "'Tis his mother's folk. A bunch of leeches, that's what they are! They tell the boy he shouldn't share the profits with his sister's foreign kin…"

"Which is why we can't tell him!" Blandine twisted her hands, voice raw even though she whispered. "*When he's older*, my father used to say — but he was the first to doubt. And now…"

She swallowed a sob, and Jory shook his head — and Tom knew that they were all thinking the same thing. The Jorys were capable and discreet, and had their wits about them — but what of young Remi? Was the lad too much of a danger? How long before he did something to expose his sister and brother-in-law — and with them the man at the Collège, and all of Sir Francis's careful work? This day's near-escape — if they had truly escaped the trouble — boded ill for the future, and when Tom reported it all in Seething Lane…

Blandine ran a hand down her face. "Some supper now, eh, Monsieur?" she said, far too brightly. "And there's the matter of your man…"

Oh yes, good Lord — Marley, too.

For Marley, Jory said, hadn't been in Saint-Symphorien between eleven and noon. When Blandine returned, she brought an onion pastry cut into wedges, and the news that the lad had not turned up at all.

The fool must have ignored the yellow roses. Or had something happened to him? All they lacked now was for Kit Marley to be caught — or murdered.

Tom chewed on his pie and thought grim thoughts. Also, he watched the Jorys. Jacques devoured his supper like a wolf, while Blandine was not eating at all. They hadn't liked his visit to the *Pot au Change*. What he meant to do now, they'd like even less — not that he did relish it, either.

"Do you think the Siège Royal was made aware of the English spy at all?" he asked — and he recounted the fat *conseiller*'s distempers.

This had Jacques huff in amusement and Blandine raise her eyes to Heaven.

"That would be Monsieur Augier," she said. "My father always said he has the wits of a pheasant-cock. The wits and the pride. If he thought he could profit from catching you, he'd let the Vesle run dry, before giving you up. But…"

"But our *Lieutenant des Habitants* is not content with being head of the Council!" Jory squared his elbows on the table. "He's also an inquirer at the Siège — so if they don't know of you there now, they will soon enough. And he's all for the Guise, too."

Which meant one thing alone — and Blandine was the one to voice it. "You must leave, Monsieur. You must take Baines and leave."

"Baines and Sherbourn," Tom said, rising to his feet. "And much as I'd rather wait here for that young idiot, and enjoy your fine cookery, Madame Jory — I fear I'll have to fast some more at the Collège."

Jacques Jory scowled at the notion — and very nearly spoke his mind, but kept it to himself with no worse than a shake of his head and a sigh.

Blandine was less politic. "But it's madness, Monsieur! You ran away — what will they think if you go back?"

Ay — there was that, but then... Gilbert Gifford had been thrown out, and taken back, and even put to teach, hadn't he?

"That I'm a prodigal returned — and Allen has a fondness for those," said Tom, with a smiling confidence that, in fair truth, he didn't quite feel.

CHAPTER 17

29th of May

For all that he was awake well before cockcrow, Tom waited until the hour when Lauds would be finished. Then he went to the Rue des Anglais, in full — if timid — view of the college's door, and set himself to wait, looking as contrite and forlorn as he knew.

His stomach clenched when the bolts were drawn, and the wicket pushed cautiously open. What if Marley had been caught and forced into dangerous confessions? What if Lyggon had talked to Allen of crossing paths with a Queen's man far too interested in Baines? What if…

"Roper!" a voice rang.

Tom startled — which Roper would have done, too, wouldn't he? — and eyed doubtingly the men at the door.

There were three of them: the servant Rudd, who kept the door open for young Talbot, and a sour-faced fellow. Talbot crossed the street to meet Tom.

"You're back!" he greeted, too cheerful for suspicion. "We worried… Where have you been?"

Instead of answering, Tom made a show of gaping at the boy's travelling clothes, the sturdy shoes, the satchel. "You leave?"

Talbot had been grinning; now he beamed. "I'm for Douai, and William, here, goes —"

"Don't!" The other man, also clothed for the road, hastened to halt the conversation. "The less he knows, the better."

263

And he was right, of course, which made it all the worse when Talbot elbowed him good-naturedly, and smiled at Tom. "Never mind Pitts. Go ahead, they'll be happy to have you back."

Pitts, yes. The harsh preacher of sermons on the doom of deceivers. Little wonder that he should look askance at this less than half-Catholic who disappeared and then came back. Pitts's mouth was working, as though about to say something unpleasant — but Talbot called to him.

"Come now, Pitts. Off we go." He clasped Tom's hand. "Lord guard and guide you, Roper."

And they were gone. One to Douai and the other, no doubt, to England.

Lord guard and guide you… Tom felt like the blackest of scoundrels.

"You want to come in?"

Whether he shared Talbot's Evangelical welcome or Pitts's mistrust, no trace of either showed on Rudd's square face. The lad just waited on the threshold, letting the wicket slam closed the moment Tom stepped through.

"Wait here," he ordered, and disappeared towards the courtyard, leaving Tom in the half-gloom of the passage.

He'd been there barely long enough to worry when half a score of students came through from the courtyard, three-cornered hats on their heads and books under their arms — bound for the Université.

Tom stepped back into the shadows of the kitchen door, but not before a few of them caught sight of him. They nudged each other, exchanging doubtful glances.

Among the others was Marley, looking hale and well, and neither restrained nor closely observed. So this was one relief. He didn't try to speak, for a mercy — he just stared with the others, half blank, half curious. They all looked subdued. Admonished, perhaps, after their disobedience the other day. They filed out into the street, Marley lingering last to mouth, "I'll come back" — as useless as it was dangerous: what if someone marked it?

Hadn't Tom better slip out of the door, follow the students to some likely place where Marley could be detached from the others, and then run for the Brebis-qui-File, fetch Baines, and make for Calais…?

A sore temptation it was, and Tom was about to yield, when there were steps from the stairs, and Hodgson appeared.

"Roper," he saluted — a good deal less cheerfully than Talbot had. "I thought Rudd must be mistaken."

Tom said nothing. What did one say to such slow-voiced guardedness? All warmth gone from his manner, Hodgson seemed another man.

"Where have you been?"

"I…" Tom looked up and then away. "I don't know."

"Two days, and you don't know?"

"I ran. I was afraid…"

There was a sigh — half impatient, half sad, and Hodgson's freckled face knotted in a frown. He motioned to the stairs. "Come. Dr. Barret wants to see you."

Tom tensed for a heartbeat. If he ran now, if he shoved Hodgson, made for the door… Instead, he followed as he was bid. He'd wanted to come back, hadn't he? Now Ulysses had well and truly thrust himself into the Cyclops' maw.

In all fairness, Tom could not blame Barret and Worthington when they had him stand in the full morning light, asking why he had run, where he had been, why he had come back.

It was nothing Tom hadn't spent a whole night rehearsing in his mind.

The sight of that poor fellow at the garden had been too much, he said. He hardly knew what he'd expected to find in Rheims — but not…

"Not death," said Barret.

Tom felt the weight of the level blue gaze on him — but he didn't look up, and forged ahead. Hugh first, he said, then that servant, and then… Roper would shiver here, and fall silent at the memory of the mangled face — just as Tom Walsingham did. "'Twas too much, and I ran."

There was some silence. The two priests exchanging looks, no doubt. For all his outward warmth, Tom judged Worthington far less prone to pitying fear — so he was not surprised when the next cold question came from that quarter.

"And where did you run?"

Tom shook his head. He'd seen what men did, thought, and forgot under the scourge of fear — and surely so had these two.

"Truly I don't know, Father. I wanted to leave Rheims far behind, and the college…"

He waited to see whether they challenged him. When they did not, he told of how he'd entered some roadside tavern when he could walk no further, and sat there, and began to think where he was going. Back to England? Never! On to Rome? But to do what? A pilgrimage — and then? What could he expect of himself, what could the Lord expect of him if he took fright at the first hint of … not even of danger, because surely he'd never been in danger himself. But the danger of others, the suffering… Did it take so little to undo Tom Roper's heart? What would his mother think…?

"I never thought it would be easy — only that I'd be up to it!"

He stopped, a little short of breath, and looked up — amazed at himself, at how easily the lie tripped off his tongue. A particular manner of sin, surely — not just the lie itself, but the ease of it? Ah, well. If they wanted no liar for a son, his parents should never have sent him to be groomed for the Service.

"What then?" This from Barret.

Then they'd let him sleep in the stables, he said, and the next morning he'd worked for some bread and cheese. Good Christian folk — for all that they understood little of his speech, and he of theirs.

"And you came back." Barret again — without the slightest trace of question, or sympathy, or otherwise.

On the other hand, there was no doubting the colour of Worthington's scoff: "Because you were hungry, and penniless, and had nowhere else to go!"

And it was ludicrous, surely, to resent the contempt on Roper's behalf. "Ay, ay — but I could have gone to a church, couldn't I? To the *Hôtel-Dieu*. I came back here, Doctor, because I don't want to be a coward!"

Baines's madness must be catching — there was no other excuse: to bristle so for the sake of a man who didn't exist...!

"Come now, my son. No one wants to offend you."

Softly as they were spoken, the words had them all start. Worthington and Barret both leapt to the door at the room's corner.

Tom had doubted, during his second talk with Barret, that someone might be listening there. A reasonable doubt, after all, for now a man stood on the threshold, making it plain that he'd heard Tom's last outburst, and likely the whole interrogation.

"Doctor!" Barret hastened to offer his arm to this thin, sallow figure, and led him to the chair with a manner of great respect and affection.

"Thank you, Richard," the newcomer breathed, and lowered himself with the wariness of pain. Barret supported him by the elbow, and Worthington hovered close.

There was one person alone, Tom imagined, able to raise such filial solicitude in these two... And so this was Dr. William Allen, the president of the Collège Anglais, the traitor and maker of traitors, the intriguer, Polyphemus himself.

Not that he looked much like a Cyclops — thin as a rake, with hollow, wrinkled cheeks and a reddish beard. He was more lost than clothed in layers of warm robes that hung about him, and he smelt of illness — and yet the long hands were firm, and the deep-set black eyes alive as he observed Tom.

"You don't want to be a coward, Thomas Roper?" he croaked. "Men have come to us for worse reasons."

"I..."

William Allen looked weak enough that a breeze would throw him, as he sat painfully straight in the chair, eyebrows raised to line a domed forehead. "Some will seek us because they don't want to be *thought* cowards. Don't you think it worse?"

A much greater weakness, no doubt, to measure one's mettle by another's estimation — and yet so very human! Wasn't there something about this in Virgil? But Roper would know nothing of Virgil, and surely wouldn't discuss it with Dr. Allen.

"I don't know, Sir. Father," he would stammer, and correct himself. "Doctor."

Allen smiled a little, gently amused by the awkwardness — unless it was by the play-acting...

"Then we'll keep you here while you find out," he said between shallow breaths. "To begin, you may consider that there's a difference between cowardice and struggling through fear..."

"But Doctor!" Worthington had been squirming, and could help himself no longer. "This man... We don't know what he may..." He threw an angry look at his colleague, who stood silent and cross-armed. "Dr. Barret doubts too!"

A petty thing to do — and when Allen raised a hand and hummed, he looked for all the world like a schoolmaster settling some boyish squabble.

"He does, and he told me, and so did you, my dear Worthington, but..." The smile widened, showing square, yellow teeth. "I've heard you speak so movingly of the Lost Sheep, and the Prodigal Son. You don't forget your own fine words, do you?"

And no doubt Worthington had many well-turned, sugared arguments in favour of errant lambs and humbled scattergoods. Tom Roper, on the other hand, he'd be happy to see thrown into the street — or, even better, onto the rack. Small blame to him, in truth, though it was rather diverting to see the man fret and simmer, full of objection, and yet not daring to gainsay Allen. Or it would have been, but that the anger he could not vent to his superior would likely make him an unchancy enemy to the one who was the cause of it.

All the more because ... was it a gleam of smugness in Barret's vivid eyes? Barret, who — be it out of loyalty or policy — knew better than to argue before the lost sheep. Or perhaps Barret saw better than Worthington, just as Tom did, behind Allen's benign manner. For there was no doubting that, kindness and charity aside, William Allen wanted to keep an eye on this Roper, who perhaps was just a wavering soul seeking guidance — or perhaps was something else entirely.

It wasn't until dinner that Tom caught sight of Marley again — eager to talk, for all that there must be eyes a-plenty to watch what the lost sheep did or did not do.

Only for a heartbeat, amidst the press at the door, did Tom catch the chance to whisper that the lad make ready to leave. And leave it to Kit Marley to begin to protest! A good thing that right then young Colson came bouncing, eager as a pup.

"We worried that they'd done you in, too!" he said, round-eyed and breathless as he caught Tom's arm, and dragged him to the trestle near the pulpit.

Gifford sat there, and Hunt, and ruddy, righteous Woodward, and another, whose tonsure and pale eyes Tom struggled to tie to a name... Yaxley, was it? To be a priest in sixteen weeks.

Hunt nodded in welcome, Gifford didn't, and Woodward exclaimed: "Why, they didn't strangle you, then!"

"Woodward," scolded Hunt under his breath, and he gave Tom a small, grimacing smile.

Woodward huffed. "Well, we did think it — what with the doctors never saying a word... You thought it too, Hunt. We all did."

But had they truly? A number of them must have, reckoning by Colson's greeting; the others must have thought worse things — just as the doctors did. And if it was something of a marvel to see Woodward in the former camp, Tom found himself sorry that Hunt's guarded look placed him in the latter.

But then, what business had Tom liking Thurstan Hunt? Or Will Colson, or any of them? What did he care what these enemies and traitors thought of him? He'd be gone as quickly as he could. Better to ask questions instead. Not that he still hoped to unravel Elliot's death — but surely Roper would ask...

"Strangled? That poor fellow — is that what happened?"

"If you believe the *Milice*, ay." There was no saying, with Gifford's fussy sourness, whether he meant it *ad litteram* or in sarcasm — but, interestingly, neither he nor anyone else made mention of Elliot.

"Good Lord!" Tom shook his head. "But who —?"

"Who, says he!" Yaxley had North thick in his speech, and a harsh, thin-lipped mouth — and misread Tom's words thoroughly. "Some swine of the Queen's — that's who! Murdering some poor soul, foisting the body on us, to have us all kicked out of Rheims!"

Lyggon's very notion — although Barret or Allen must disabuse him the moment they told him of Elliot... But it was clear the students had no hint.

"Silence!" Gifford leant across the table to hiss. "Wherever you've been, Roper, it hasn't mended your manners. We don't talk at meals."

Which was remarkably unfair, for Woodward, and Gifford himself, and Yaxley had been talking just as much. Well, surely Gilbert Gifford had been wasting no anguish on the fate of the missing Roper!

After that, the day's reading began — done by a very young, very lisping boy, and later Hodgson gave the explanation, and then the students were loosed in the garden, to discard their worn doublets and work in the warm May sun. Old Bénoit had them lift and move a number of potted rosemary bushes, two stunted lemon trees, and other plants Tom had no name for, all needing better light and air. Tom manoeuvred himself into being paired with Marley for the work.

"We can't leave now!" was the lad's first fierce whisper as they lifted a rosemary bush between them. "Elliot was strangled —"

"Which is why we must go."

"Why —?"

"Softly!" Tom breathed in the rosemary's scent — smoke, and green evenings, and Scadbury — and strove for patience. *Why, why, why!* "Because if Downes was killed for knowing something — and the other two for knowing how Downes was killed — someone may well suspect you."

The pot tilted, making the bush sway in Tom's face. "Mind what you do!" he hissed.

"They suspect *me*?" came from across the scented boughs.

"And small blame to them. I'd suspect you too, in their place. Why, I'm not sure that I do not in mine!"

"Here, lads! This way!" called old Bénoit in his broken English, and led them to the corner where he wanted the pot, all the time muttering in French on the heedlessness of the young. Next would have been one of the lemon trees, but the old Frenchman raised his hands to the Heavens and waved them to another rosemary, lemons being too precious to be entrusted to such clumsy hands — and all the time Marley kept staring at Tom in betrayed outrage.

Couldn't the fool see a jest? Tom grunted as they lifted the heavy pot. "But think how it must look to them: you knew Fettiplace better than most here — and he you; if he came to warn Allen…"

The rosemary quivered in indignation. "Against *me*?"

"Of that we can't be sure — and much less can they. And I can hardly offer defence if they decide to make certain.

Besides, they also misdoubt *me* — and it may not be long before the King's *Bailli* does, too. Ergo, unless you fancy being put to the rack like Baines…"

There was a little silence across the bush. Then, very quietly, Marley murmured, "I wouldn't say a word."

Of course. Tom liked to think the same of himself — but … had Marley ever seen the rack at work?

"I'm sure that Baines thought just the same."

This time, it wasn't until the rosemary was set in its proper place that Marley found his voice again. All offended whining had drained out of it. "But, since I killed no one…"

"Since you killed no one, the murderer must be someone here. Someone who thinks that Downes, at least, was a Queen's man." *Which you and I are in truth…*

Marley was silent again, as he drew his own unpleasant conclusions. He was still quiet when Bénoit sent them to the well for water — and he raised no objection to Tom's further orders, other than looking thunderously grim as they made their way back across the courtyard, laden with full buckets.

"We go through the garden door, as soon as it gets dark —"

And then he stopped short — for a voice sounded from the passage to the kitchen, raised in impatience.

"Well, bless you, then I'm *another* John Harrison! The name's common enough…"

It was a voice that Tom knew well.

Hissing through his teeth, he pushed Marley under the gallery, both splashing water as they flattened themselves against the wall.

"Ay, ay, Harrisons to burn, we have." And this was Carter.

"Just go and tell Dr. Allen, for God's sake —"

"You just wait here." Carter's limping steps clacked up the stairs, and Tom, abandoning his buckets, peered into the pantry — just let no one come in the other way now…

"What the devil…?" Marley had just sense enough to protest under his breath.

"Wait!" Tom ordered. He slipped through the pantry and hurried to the door, to peek into the passage.

He could hear Rudd muttering, and then the known voice again: "Damn your face, you…!" And then tall, red-bearded John Harrison strode into view, bearing a ferocious scowl.

Only, of course, it wasn't Harrison at all.

Tom leapt back, retraced his steps — and, as he crossed the threshold, Marley met him, ready for mayhem and brandishing one of the heavy buckets high over his head.

"Oh, put that down!" Tom snapped. "We only lack that you break my head. That man who wants to talk to Allen is Rafe Lyggon — and he knows what I am."

"And who the devil … oh." Marley's eyes went round. "Mary Stuart's man? What's he doing here? You think…? Is he the murderer?"

Was he? Tom half thought not. Lyggon had seemed ignorant of Downes and Fettiplace's deaths — although he could have been lying.

"Even if he's not, he's come to tell Allen of Baines — and me."

Marley whistled low. "You've found Baines? And this fellow knows? God's nightgown!"

"Indeed. Now come, we must find a way to run before Lyggon sees me —"

"Oy, Roper! Sherbourn!"

Because, of course, young Colson was seeking them. Colson, sent to find the errant water-bearers. Colson who saw the buckets, and ran to help, grinning from ear to ear.

"Playing truant, are you?" He hauled up a bucket, slopping half of its contents on them all in his eagerness.

"Here they are, Father!" he called the moment they stepped into the garden, with all the cheer in this world. "They haven't fallen down the well!"

And the one who straightened and smiled, the one who had noticed Tom's absence, and now watched him thoughtfully, was Hodgson.

After that, there was no way to run. Hodgson had chore after chore for Tom, and always kept him under his eye. There was nothing for it but to pretend to find pleasure in the quiet work, and to keep his back to the house and the windows, hoping that Lyggon wouldn't look out on the garden.

CHAPTER 18

At Vespers Hodgson was there, and so he was at the fasting-time supper of bread and water. For a mercy, there was no sign of Lyggon. There were many others, though: the hall was crowded with the men from the lodging house, who'd come to share the Eve of Ascension, Savage among them.

Hodgson sat in Yaxley's place, ruddy with the afternoon's sun — and so cold-eyed it beggared belief that the others would not mark it.

Had Hodgson — with or without Lyggon's help — discovered Tom's true colours? Or did he think him the murderer? Or was *he* the murderer, contemplating more blood to be shed...?

One thing was certain: they had to run. After supper, if it grew dark enough, in the stir of dismounting the trestles. Or at Compline, perhaps, while all the men gathered for the long prayers of the solemn eve... Not by the garden, though: it would have to be Colson's way. If they helped each other, surely they'd manage what one man alone could not.

So busy was Tom considering these matters and munching his bread, that he nearly missed it when young Colson arrived late and breathless at the table. Gifford took it upon himself to dole out reproach — oh, but the fellow must like to play the scourge!

For once, the boy stood his ground. "What was I to do?" he protested. "Bénoit is old, and Carter and Rudd are busy here... They asked that I bring a bowl upstairs for Noll — 'twas Christian charity to go!"

Noll? That could never be…? Tom held his breath. Did he dare to ask right under Hodgson's eyes? He didn't have to, bless Woodward's curiosity.

"What Noll is that?"

Colson swelled with his news. "Why, Oliver Catesby!"

They were all left so speechless, even Gifford had no reproach.

Hodgson was taken aback — or perhaps didn't want the news known — for he frowned at the boy.

"Don't be foolish, Will," he said.

"But yes, Father!" Colson all but burst with his tidings. "He's upstairs in the infirmary. All grey in the face, he is, and weak as a kitten. Some fellow brought him back this afternoon… And I'm to go back and sit with him tonight."

And then the reading began — but Tom heard very little of it.

Catesby alive and back! And a stranger bringing him … Lyggon, most surely. Which then absolved Lyggon, for Elliot's murderer would seize the chance to get rid of Catesby too — never bring him back to the college. Except, Catesby himself was now in great peril, under the same roof as the murderer he had most surely seen.

Tom looked up to find Gifford's black eyes fixed on him, grim and stern in the rush-light's sallow glow. Did Gifford suspect, too — or must he be an object of suspicion? Could he have killed Downes and the others? Why had he been kicked out of the Seminary in Rome?

Whatever he was, whatever he'd done, the fellow nodded scowlingly at Tom's untouched chunk of bread.

We do not waste the Lord's gifts, here…

With a fleeting thought for Blandine Jory's onion pie, Tom applied himself — finding that each bite tasted of ash.

What was he going to do? Get himself and Sherbourn out of the Collège Anglais, and abandon Catesby — and Will Colson — to the murderer?

But if he warned Allen that one of his men had done three murders and could do more, he risked himself, Marley, and the Jorys — and he failed in his duty to Sir Francis and the Queen.

And yet, to let a man die — poor, blunt, fiery-humoured Catesby, who lay up there, grey in the face and weak as a kitten. And young Colson...

The supper and the readings done, students and servants fell to change the refectory into a chapel — and all the time Tom chewed at his dilemma.

He'd learnt, in his years of solving riddles for Sir Francis, that murderers did go unpunished for one reason or another — and that was one thing; but having the means to save two lives and not do it ... oh, that was very different. He could turn his back on three dead men, perhaps — but on two who were alive and in danger of death...?

Oh, curse it all!

What would Sir Francis do? Put the Service before every other consideration, no doubt...

Tom's heart sank. For the first time in his Service years, the answer his mind supplied was not unquestioning obedience. And perhaps this meant he wasn't cut out to do the Queen's work — but this was for later, for when he was back in London to confess this particular weakness to his great cousin. For now...

Tom squared his shoulders.

For now, as soon as they could slip away, he'd steal upstairs, warn Colson, and then run, before the boy raised the alarm. Hardly the most accomplished plan — but it would have to do. Now to impart it to Marley...

But Kit Marley was nowhere to be seen.

Swearing under his breath, Tom scoured the dim, busy hall in search of the brat.

Had he gone already? Had he been caught? Had he somehow betrayed himself — betrayed them both? How was Tom to find him —?

And then Compline rang. Never had the Marie sounded more shrill.

"Oy, Roper!"

A jab in the ribs startled Tom, and Woodward dragged him to join the assembly — not half as near its back as would have been prudent or useful. Then the first hymn started, and a small procession marched to the altar to receive Worthington's blessing. And there — there went Kit Marley. Alive and free — but somehow pressed into service among the readers for Compline.

Oh Lord — there went all hope of going.

Compline was endless on this eve of Ascension Day, stretching well past the wonted time. Tom spent it all chafing, and concealing under a pious manner — for surely someone was observing Roper. And while he chafed and pretended to pray, was the murderer at work upstairs? Had Tom's dithering conscience thrown away all chance of both running and saving Catesby?

It seemed a fitting mockery that, outside, a thunderstorm gathered, rumbling in the distance.

There was one blessing to it all, however: once Compline was done, the night was to be a long vigil, with the men free to pray as long as they wished in the chapel or to snatch some sleep in the dormitories before Matins.

This was not to say they wouldn't try to keep an eye on Roper — but it afforded some hope of stealing away, and all the more because the chapel would be open and dark but for the altar candles.

On the stairs, Tom managed to pass by Marley and whisper: "Go — by the garden door. Wait for me at the Brebis."

Wait for how long? If he was caught... Ah well, if he was caught, Tom trusted the Jorys to pack Marley and Baines off to London — but, even more, he trusted himself not to be caught.

First of all, he'd better count on having little time, so once upstairs he quietly melted into the shadows of the gallery. The storm had broken out in earnest, bolts of lightning painting everything in livid white and deepest black at intervals.

More breathless than he liked, Tom slid against the wall. No light showed under the closed doors, and the front staircase was just as dark and silent. He crossed the landing and peered out in the windowless passage where the infirmary and Allen's room were. He held his breath and listened.

Nothing.

In the gaping silence between thunderclaps, the faint echo of praying voices wafted up from the chapel. Praying for the conversion of England, at sword's point, if need be — for such were the rogations made here — and look at him, Sir Francis's own kinsman, risking his neck to save two of these traitorous rogues! With a small sigh, Tom pushed away from the wall and stepped into the passage toward the infirmary door, and...

And an arm snaked around his neck from behind, a hand catching his wrist.

Tom scrabbled, drove an elbow hard into his assailant's stomach, and tugged half-free, drawing his knife as he spun around. His eating knife — curse it! He wanted to laugh when he felt a dagger's point prick the skin of his throat. The dagger's owner, a long-limbed shadow, turned behind Tom to take the knife and push him through a door. Gifford's empty classroom.

Tom stumbled across a bench, the shadow looming over him in the gloom. Close enough that Tom kicked at one knee, shoved hard, and leapt for the other door, the one he knew must open on the gallery...

Closed!

The key was in its hole, but before he could turn it, Tom was pushed against it, the dagger at his kidney.

"Curse you!" he ground out.

"Curse *you*!" gasped the man, and roughly turned Tom around. "You broke my knee..." Right then, a flash of white-purple light filled the unshuttered window. There was an intake of breath and a quiet chuckle.

"Well, look at you!"

Tom blinked in the darkness — but he knew the voice. Knew it beyond doubt.

"Good evening to you, *John Harrison*," he greeted, putting in the words all the disbelief he knew.

Rafe Lyggon let go of his prisoner. There was a small rasp, and a beam of light from a blind lantern — by which Tom could see that his captor hadn't sheathed his dagger.

"I lay a trap for the murderer — and catch a Queen's man," Lyggon murmured. "I thought we said you'd gallop back home?"

"*You* said it." Tom gave a small shrug. "I had an itch to find this murderer myself..."

"And you seek him here?"

And wasn't this something, coming from this man! "Well, so do you."

Another chuckle. "So do I, indeed. And I wonder…" The words took a thoughtful colour. "I wonder if I haven't found him."

Oh Lord, again! "Had we not settled this the other day?"

"The other day I hadn't caught you prowling this place at night — however you let yourself in. For all I know, you could be here to finish what you started."

Tom's cousin Frances liked to play chess — and very good at it she was, quietly thinking ahead, laying her traps and letting Tom fall in them. This conversation put him in mind of one of those games — but this adversary was a foe of still unfathomed deadliness.

"But why would I?"

Lyggon hummed — much like a fencer acknowledging a hit. "Ay, there's that. I cannot think of a good reason why you'd want to kill young Catesby — want it enough to venture coming here, instead of running."

"Why, thank you."

"But…" Lyggon held up a forefinger. "There are those two other murders. You knew the other day — and told me nothing."

Ay, well, in fairness, none of this could look innocent. And it was hard to gainsay — for Tom, while innocent of murder, was guilty of other things. But then…

"You hardly needed my help, if you knew to seek out Catesby —"

"But I did not!" By Lyggon's manner you would think they were conversing in a London street, instead of whispering of murder in the dead hours of night. "Why, 'tis you that I was after. I don't like to be given the slip — and you'd done it twice…"

"And you ran into Catesby instead."

"In a very sorry place, in a faubourg outside the walls — half out of his wits."

"And you knew to bring him here, to use him as bait for your trap…"

"To bring him here — ay. That he'd make good bait I only learnt an hour ago from Dr. Barret."

Then Barret must be innocent of murder — or why would he give Lyggon the means to set such a trap? So taken was Tom with the pieces spinning in his mind, that he missed Lyggon's tensing stance at first.

"The question is, though, how do *you* know?" The dagger's blade glinted feebly when Lyggon shifted his grip on the hilt. "But then Dr. Allen thinks you have a man in here…"

Sudden and cat-like, he sprang to his feet, the dagger at Tom's chest.

"Who is it, lad? Sherbourn or Roper?"

The laugh that crawled up his throat, Tom blamed on too little sleep and too much fasting. Otherwise, it would have to be sheer stupidity. "*Sherbourn or Roper!*"

"Two most dubious young fellows, Dr. Allen says. And Gifford makes a third. Mostly Sherbourn, though — who'd also make a likely murderer, for he knew the dead servant. I myself like the sound of this Roper, for all Dr. Allen says he wasn't here when —"

This time Tom did laugh, and Lyggon stopped short — reckoning him as mad as Baines, most surely, and making ready to use that dagger of his.

Tom moved sideways towards the benches. "And not Gifford?" he asked, as lightly as he knew. "Unpleasant little man — and did you know he'd been kicked out of the Seminary in Rome? One wonders why. Also, in your place, I'd consider Father Hodgson and his friend Savage —"

"Qu'est-ce que vous faites là?"

Tom's heart jumped, and Lyggon froze. There was a third door at the room's far end, and on its threshold, holding a candle and blinking his rheumy eyes, stood old Bénoit.

Was this the end of it all? Would these two raise the alarm, and have Tom seized?

The candle's flame danced in the old man's shaking hand. "Young master Roper!" he said in French. "Rudd said you'd come back. Who's that?"

At some point Lyggon must have sheathed his dagger, and he stepped forward, unarmed, into the bilious light. He threw Tom a look of amused appraisal, before smiling down at Bénoit. "I'm sorry, *mon* Maître," he said, all charm and fine French. "I'm coming down with an ague, so I asked young Roper to show me to the infirmary." Fearing to roust the other Queen's man into flight, if Bénoit raised a noise — or reckoning the servant wouldn't take a stranger's word.

In fact, the old man studied Lyggon, eyes a-squint, still trusting him less than he did Tom. "The one who brought back poor Catesby, are you?" A sniff. "I won't have you inside to upset the boy. I'll have little Colson bring you a physick."

"No need to bother —" Lyggon protested.

Bénoit waved him silent. "The child needs his bed. Not one to keep a whole night's vigil, Colson is — never like young Elliot." Bénoit shook his head and rumbled on, shuffling towards the door. "Half a physician, was that one — if only he'd stayed! When poor Downes was ill, he tended to him so well that I hoped... Ah well, *le Bon Dieu* wanted different."

Elliot! Fidgety little Robin Elliot a half-physician — and yet... Tom stopped the old man. "Why didn't Elliot try to help Fettiplace when he took ill?"

"Eh?" The old face knotted in thought when Tom repeated the question. "He didn't know."

"But he did. He told his cousin that Fettiplace was unwell."

"Did he?" Bénoit rubbed at his bald head. "*Me* he told that the man was leaving."

"What's this about now?" Lyggon asked, voice tense of a sudden. "Wasn't Elliot...?"

Tom ignored him, for the coloured pieces were shifting inside his head, making a new pattern entirely. *It was Elliot that he told, wasn't it, Robin? He said he was unwell...*

"Are you sure, Bénoit? Didn't Elliot say that Fettiplace was ill?"

"But no!" Bénoit said, with the weak impatience of the old. "He said he'd met him going away. A fool, I thought — for he'd waited this long, he could wait some more — but then, the English..."

Tom wasn't listening anymore. Of course — of course, and he'd been blind!

"What are you playing at, Roper?" Lyggon frowned, hand on his hilt. He frowned more when Tom shook his head.

"Elliot lied. Catesby lied. Fettiplace had not been leaving — nor was he ill. I've no idea what his warning was — but... Elliot was with Downes the night he died — wasn't he, Bénoit?"

The old servant gaped from man to man. "Oh, but ... yes. And when he fell asleep, poor Downes slipped out..."

Lyggon's mouth stretched into a thin line. "Does that go to the infirmary?" he asked, pointing to the small door in the corner. Bénoit nodded.

"And there's another door to the passage," said Tom.

With a nod, Lyggon went for that. Tom grabbed a stool and made for the little door. So ill-armed, he opened it quietly, just in time to see a shirt-clad figure push its way out to the passage.

Curse it to hell — there went Catesby. As he leapt in pursuit, Tom caught sight of a heap lying by the hearth. A curly head in the red glow of the embers, an outstretched arm... Will!

"See to the boy, Bénoit!" Tom called over his shoulder, and rushed through the door after Catesby.

What he found was Lyggon, picking himself up from the floor in the faint light from the open door, scrabbling for his dagger.

"Are you hurt?" Tom asked, over a roll of thunder.

Lyggon pointed to the stairs. "Down!"

And down Tom ran, in the purple darkness, armed with nothing better than a stool, a corner of his mind wondering as he went: would Mary Stuart's man send him chasing wild geese — or worse? Down at the foot of the staircase, he half-saw a white figure hunched and heaving, trying to unbolt the door to the courtyard — and thanks be for rusted bars and lazy servants!

"Catesby, stop!" Tom called softly.

There was the pale blur of a face, a snarl, and then the man was gone, bare feet slapping on the steps down to the cellars.

And wouldn't anyone with a grain of sense about him and a stool in his hands, make for the courtyard, haul himself over the wall, and run, and leave Allen's people to sort their own mayhem?

Tom Walsingham instead, being a born fool, and having the still, crumpled form of young Colson in his mind, followed a murderer down into the dark belly of the Cyclops' lair.

It was dark indeed. As Tom descended, what little light from the storm had filtered through the windows upstairs was lost to the thickest blackness. He pressed his back against the wall, stool held high — cursing in his mind that he was armed like a tavern brawler.

"Catesby!" he called, letting his voice carry under the vaults, for the thick walls muffled all noise, didn't they? "Catesby!"

It sounded different at night, as though the darkness padded the curved ceiling, swallowing the words. Fanciful conceits, and distracting. In the silence Tom heard it well: a faint rustling, coming from his left.

The bath — and the door to the courtyard...

Tom slid along the wall, felt for the arched doorway, crossed it, stool at the ready — and stumbled into the first step. As he regained his balance, something heavy whooshed above his head.

Damn the man! Tom swung the stool, its legs glancing against something. There was a gasp, so close... Tom reached to grab, and a fistful of shirt was yanked out of his fingers.

A roll of thunder, muted as it sounded down there, swallowed the scuffle of bare feet. Where the devil was Lyggon when one needed him? Just as Tom scrambled up the steps to cut the way to the door, something caught him hard in the shin — the same heavy thing, no doubt, that had been aimed at his head before.

Tom jumped off the steps, catching himself against the wall.

"Damn your fool head, stop it! Do you want more sins on your soul?"

There was a laugh — a horrible, harsh, sobbing laugh. "I'm going to Hell already — whether I kill you or not!"

"The way you killed Downes?"

Catesby groaned in the darkness, and it was cut short. It was easy to picture the man biting his own fists for silence — but Tom wanted him to talk, wanted to hear the foe he couldn't see.

"Hugh Downes, who was your friend," he insisted.

"My friend, ay!" Catesby's voice choked to a raw whisper. "And he wanted to leave. To marry that French girl. To become a cook here... Lord God — a cook! You're free here, he said. You go to Mass when you please, you live in peace... When he took ill, and was out of his wits with fever, even then, all he did was call for that slut. *Jeanne, Jeanne, Jeanne...*"

Another groan, a few steps away from the door, and a wooden thud. The next bluish flash rained down the window high up under the ceiling, showing the white-shirted figure slumped against the largest tub.

"One night you went to sit with him and Robin, didn't you? And he kept calling for his sweetheart —"

"Robin was heeding him!" A muffled cry. "I could tell. I knew Robin like I know myself, and he was weakening. How long before he wanted a girl too, and peace, and..."

A chill ran down Tom's spine. Was this why...? So that Robin Elliot wouldn't eschew martyrdom?

"So you threw Downes down the stairs."

"No, no, I..." Catesby was barely visible, curled up in a ball, wedged between the tubs. "Robin had dozed off, and Hugh kept at it: *Jeanne, Jeanne, Jeanne...*" A shuddering moan. "I tried to make him stop, put a hand over his mouth... He struggled, he wouldn't lie still, and his neck broke, and Robin said they'd send me to the gallows, so we ... so I..."

"So you threw him down the stairs."

"They all thought he'd fallen..." Catesby broke into sobs. "But then that servant came back, with things for Allen's ears alone. Things he'd seen, he said... He was a small fellow, Fettiplace. *His* neck I didn't have to break."

In the faint greenish flicker of the storm, Oliver Catesby wept as he talked of killing, tears glimmering in runnels down the wax-white cheeks.

"And Robin lied for you again, although he knew: whatever Fettiplace had had to say, it wasn't about Downes's death. Why, he wasn't even here at the time. You killed him for nothing — and poor Colson, tonight —"

A sharp intake of breath, and Catesby's face changed into a mask, all black eyes and gaping mouth, awash in a feeble glow that shone from behind Tom's back.

Tom half turned, unthinkingly, to catch a glimpse of yellow light staining the darkness — and Catesby sprang.

Caught at the knees, legs going out from under him, Tom crashed to the floor, hit his head against wood, and the stool went flying and clattering. Before he knew it, he was sprawled on the wet bricks, with a knee burrowing in his chest, and hands squeezing his throat.

"Roper!" came Lyggon's voice — calling from too far away.

With sparks dancing before his eyes, Tom struggled against the large hands, the thick arms. He tried to roll, to push away from the floor — and something bit into his hand. Something small and hard-edged. This was never...? Breathless, he gripped the broken handle of Baines's penknife, and thrust blindly for Catesby.

Catesby yelped, throwing up an arm to protect his face. It was enough. Enough for Tom to shove, to unfoot the larger man, to drag himself to his knees, coughing and gasping, and feeling for the stool. He found it just as Catesby came in for another bout, with a mad-eyed snarl. Tom swung the stool, and Catesby stumbled out of harm's way, into the largest tub, and across it — curse the fellow — splashing in two inches of water, fully visible now in the glow of Lyggon's lantern.

"The other door!" Tom croaked, climbing to his feet. "The stairs!"

There was a shout, and booted steps as Lyggon gave chase — both half lost in the thunder from above. Tom had dropped the bit of knife again, but he didn't stop for it. He limped after the lantern's receding halo, through a doorway, and into a long, cluttered room that must lie beneath the pantry. Was there another door at the far end, to the back stairway? A rat scurried, hissing between Tom's feet as he made his way among the piles of broken casks, an old prie-dieu, and what looked like a sideboard under a sheet. On this, Lyggon had left his lantern. Tom picked it up.

This had been a wine cellar at some time: now it remained a dusty shambles, with half a dozen ruined racks of undone barrels. The air reeked of soured must and mouse droppings. Tom discarded the stool in favour of a sturdy-looking stave, and hastened into the long room's depths after the noise of brawling, the lantern making black shadows swell before him. A few strides ahead, Lyggon had cornered Catesby, and held him at dagger's point, pressed against the last of the racks, a rickety affair, tall as a man that somehow still stood upright.

In the lantern's glare, Catesby's eyes rolled white in a grimy, bruised face. He panted hard, and blood ran from a cut on his cheek — Tom's work, likely.

Lyggon didn't turn away from their cornered quarry as he asked, "Are you hale, young Roper?"

Tom gave a snort as he took stock. A bruised hand, a scraped cheekbone, a battered shin, a hit on the head, a tender throat where he'd nearly been choked to death...

"I don't think I've a great liking for Rheims," he rasped.

This earned a chuckle. "Well, you found the murderer. Of the two of us, you have the keener wits." And, again, that fencer's half nod.

Tom nodded back. "I knew more than you did."

Was it very bad that the praise of Mary Stuart's spy should please Mr. Secretary's man so much? And what must Catesby think of the two of them, trading civilities as they worked their way towards the point where civility must end?

Be it reluctance or genuine curiosity, Lyggon had another question. "You also know why he killed his cousin?"

And out of the whole ugly story, this was the ugliest, the saddest thing. "Robin wanted this weight off his heart. He wanted to confess, didn't he, Oliver?"

Catesby's mouth worked. "I said we'd go away, to Spain or somewhere, that I'd do penance for the two of us, for it was all my fault..."

"But he wanted to come back."

"Allen he couldn't face, nor Barret. So he ran to the lodging house to find a priest — and I followed. The garden door was rotten, we all knew..." Catesby's shoulders shook as he sobbed. "He said I should go, run, do my penance — but he could not. He'd pray for me, he said. Robin was betraying me, and he would *pray*..."

This time Lyggon turned to Tom, shaking his head, half in disgust, half in pity. But one should never turn away from the likes of Oliver Catesby.

Tom caught the movement with the corner of his eye. The hand tugging at the rack, the creak of rotten wood, the tumbling of the casks...

"Beware!" He grabbed Lyggon and dragged him out of harm's way. The lantern swung wildly, black shadows leaping

291

up the walls to dance on the vaulted ceiling. Outside the thunder rolled, so loud the noise seemed to fill the vaults.

Catesby lay unmoving amidst the ruin, his head half buried under a broken cask. Lyggon went down on one knee and reached under the pieces of wood.

"*His neck I didn't have to break,*" he breathed, crossing himself.

Tom dropped his stave and limped away. The prie-dieu creaked under his weight when he sat down.

"Roper?"

He looked up to see Lyggon, armed with the lantern like a dusty Diogenes.

"You've found the murderer."

"Ay — and he's dead."

Lyggon tilted his head. "He'll go to Hell for what he did."

Oh, so he would. Oliver Catesby, who'd lived in anger, thinking that all were out to hinder and betray him, and now would go to Hell, while the three men he'd killed — four if Colson was dead — would have no earthly justice. Tom rubbed a hand across tired eyes. "Is it such a bad sin that I'd rather have men face justice on this earth, and still have a hope for God's mercy?"

"Ah, Roper, lad…"

There was a hiss of steel and, when Tom lowered his hand, Lyggon had laid the lantern on the floor and drawn his dagger again.

"Will you believe that this pains me?" he asked, face knotted.

Damn justice, and damn compassion, and most of all damn fools who lowered their guard and dropped what little they had in the way of weapons — not that a wooden stave would serve against good steel. Tom twisted around and sprang to his feet. Where was that cursed stool now?

"I can't let a Queen's man go, you understand?" Lyggon asked. "Much less one who knows as much as you do of this place."

Where was a weapon, a bit of wood, anything that would…?

Backing a step towards the door, Lyggon motioned with his blade. "Come now, don't make me kill you. I will if I have to — but I'd greatly dislike it, and you unarmed!"

"Well, when compared to the rack…" And then Tom blinked at the shadows beyond the man's shoulder.

Rafe Lyggon smiled his charming smile. "You never think I'd fall for it, do you?"

There was a crash and, without a sound, Mary Stuart's man crumpled to the floor in a heap.

Behind him, round-eyed and brandishing a piece of wood, stood Kit Marley. So that's where the stool had gone…

"Well then!" the lad said, with an uncertain smile.

Tom found himself gaping. "I'd told you to go!" he blurted.

The smile on Marley's face grew wide and rather wild. "Aren't you glad that I disobeyed?"

When Tom limped up the stairs, the thunderstorm was raging, the rain hard enough that its hiss and the thunder swallowed all sounds. There were lights in the chapel, and on the stairs, and in the gallery upstairs. Bénoit must have raised the alarm — Heaven knew what he'd told … and what of poor Will Colson? But there was no time for it.

Tom and Marley let themselves out to the courtyard, crossed it at a splashing run, and pushed and dragged each other over the wall, and into the fig tree on the other side — to the Chevreau d'Or, and to safety: Ulysses fleeing the cavern while the Cyclops, though not blinded, was otherwise occupied.

EPILOGUE

30th of May 1585, Ascension Day

Tom mounted his horse in the stable-yard of a roadside inn — three good leagues out of Rheims. An enamel-coloured sky mirrored itself in the puddles, and the air smelt of horse manure, cooking meat, and honeysuckle. Church bells pealed from the nearby village.

Ascension Day, and summer standing on tiptoe just outside the fields of Champagne, the hem of her gown wet... Tom shook his head at his own fancies.

Marley, already in the saddle, observed with impatient contempt as Baines lingered on foot, lost in a wary study of his nag.

"Unless you think to walk home, Baines..." Tom called.

The madman glowered and obeyed, clambering awkwardly into the saddle. He'd been glowering and obeying all day, and muttering in Latin at times — which Tom counted as good enough. Jacques Jory's wine at breakfast was to thank for it — but perhaps the piquette at the inn hadn't been enough, for Baines, once on horseback, frowned at Tom, as though he recognised him from some distant and hostile past.

"You took my knife," he said, clear-voiced but not clear-eyed. "The painted whore took my cross, and you took my knife."

The broken penknife from the siren Barbe that now lay lost in Allen's vaults — and that had likely saved Tom's life...

"I'll buy you a new one in London. Now come along."

This pleased Baines enough that he let himself be moved, and Marley followed.

They were out of the yard and on the road when the lad drew abreast with Tom.

"Really?" he asked, one eyebrow raised. "A knife for this crack-brain?"

He didn't even try to be quiet — and Baines, hunched in the saddle, threw a growl over his shoulder, and a mutter that could have been ominous Latin.

And leave it to Marley to bristle. "What's that, you —"

"Must you goad him?" Tom snapped, all the more uneasy because Baines had been on his mind. "Have some charity. God knows what will become of him, once we're back home."

Could Dickon Baines ever be left to himself — to his wild fancies of priesthood and poisoning?

"The Bedlam, if you ask me," Marley said, all airy unconcern. "Before he does mischief that can't be mended."

"Supposing he hasn't done so already…"

Marley narrowed his eyes at Tom, then at Baines, and then back. "Oh," he said. "Your Madame Jory." He said it in a manner that Watson might have used, and that set Tom's teeth on edge.

"Hardly *mine*," he bristled. "But she and her husband are clever, and brave, and trustworthy… It would be a shame if Baines had brought them in harm's way with his ravings." Not to mention the little jealous, greedy fool, Remi.

Marley hummed. "I'm not so enamoured, myself — but ay, a shame: gulling Allen all these years, and now they must be lost because of a half-wit."

"Ay, well…" *There are times, Thomas, when the subtlest mind can do little against the strength of impregnable stupidity…* And stupidity was a great sin in Seething Lane. "Ay, well, 'tis for Mr. Secretary to decide."

Just as the fates of Baines, Thomas Watson — not to mention Tom's own. Entering the Collège Anglais to unravel three murders that had nothing to do with the Service, disrupting Marley's mission and learning little enough — unless one counted learning to like some of these traitors. Oh Lord, the story he'd have to tell Sir Francis!

And perhaps Kit Marley read minds, for he asked, "Won't he like the way things went, Mr. Secretary?"

In all cheer, he asked — as though it were his business, Sir Francis's reckoning of all the ado against the doubtful service to the cause of justice…

And curse all horses, ever sensing a rider's unease! It was Tom's notion that the less well-tempered took malicious pleasure in it — like this one, who stepped sideways and frisked. Tom tightened the reins, and slowed the huffing beast to a settled pace — and if there was no answer, perhaps Marley would drop the subject…?

But no, of course.

"He'll never grumble, will he?You've found the murderer—"

Found the murderer… Lyggon's very words! Tom laughed bitterly. "Ay — a murderer that had nothing to do with us, and I only found him because I put the claims of my conscience before the Service! What if I'd let them catch me, and you, and…" Fool, fool, fool! What was he doing, unburdening his heavy mind to this heedless brat?

The heedless brat had a frown for this outburst — a surprisingly earnest one. "But you weren't caught. And you got me out, and found that Thibaud wasn't murdered, and you saw what Lyggon does at the college, and you saw justice done for three men — and you rescued the bedlamite, and proved him innocent. Although…" He tilted his head in unfriendly contemplation of the sullen Baines. "Although that's something of a shame."

A shame! This startled Tom out of his black humour. "Would you rather have him a murderer?"

Marley tossed his head. "Just think what a story it would be! So much grander than poor, puny Catesby seeing betrayal everywhere…"

Poets were mad — and no mistake.

"He killed three men, your poor, puny Catesby." Three — for young Colson Tom wanted to think alive.

"Ay, but…" Marley turned in the saddle, eyes a-fire. "Think how bold: a man half-mad for revenge against a bunch of zealots who did him wrong. A whole convent, say. Killing them all — not caring whom he destroys. Now *that* I call a story. But…" He glanced Baines's way, mouth twisted. "Life never happens the way it should."

Baines glowered back — and small blame to him. "*Humiliabitur altitudo virorum,*" he spat, glowering darker when Marley laughed.

"And who will humiliate my haughtiness — you?"

Tom sighed. This was going to be a long ride home. "Oh, leave him alone! 'Tis the notion you need — not the fact. Are poets not on this earth to mould life into meaningful beauty?" Supposing that the poisoning of a whole convent could be regarded as beautiful…

Marley threw back his head, frowning into some golden poetic distance. "I might write it, at that. A tragedy… Now, just think if our friend's son were in that convent, for some reason? Or his daughter — a daughter running from her father…" He turned to Tom with a happy laugh. "Mould life

297

into meaningful beauty, eh? Why, Thomas Walsingham, underneath it all, you've the soul of a poet!"

"Save and deliver!" Tom laughed, and reined his horse in, for ahead was a village, and yet another knot of soldiers who'd want papers and bribes, while they waited for war to come.

The war they prayed for, those men back at the Collège Anglais. Traitors, plotters and murderers, working to undo the peace of England, unless the Queen's men — and Sir Francis's — stopped them, and sent them to the gallows.

Tom Walsingham was no poet, and never would be — but he would have given much for the means to mould the bleak ugliness of life, if not into beauty or meaning, at least into a semblance of fairness.

HISTORICAL NOTES

24 April — Yates has left with his servant, who is named Fettiplace.
29 April — Hugh Downes has died.

...And I could go on quoting from the Second Diary of the English College of Douai. This manuscript book, together with several others, contains the records, correspondence and documents (mostly in Latin) of the Catholic institution founded in 1575 by Dr. William Allen, who would go on to become a cardinal. The College of Douai was meant to shelter and instruct the English exiles who aspired to priesthood. Thanks to Allen's strong leadership, it quickly became a key centre of the exile community, providing cultural, spiritual, and political guidance to those who fled from Protestant England, where life for Catholics was made increasingly hard. One of its most famous and relevant outputs, in time, would be the Rheims-Douai Bible, a collaborative English translation of the Scriptures.

In its early days, the college prospered, growing from the six initial students to some 150 over the first few years — but the university town of Douai, then part of the Spanish Low Countries, had little sympathy for the English upstarts, and expelled them in 1578. Allen and his flock found then refuge in the French town of Rheims (as it was spelled at the time) where they would remain until 1593 under the patronage of the very powerful — and very quarrelsome — house of Guise. It was something of a mixed blessing, with the ultra-Catholic lords of Guise up to their ears in every political and religious turmoil that troubled France in those years. In 1585, when the events of this book take place, Henry III of France was a childless king, squeezed between a Protestant presumptive heir who refused to convert, and an ultra-Catholic Guise cousin who was busy stirring civil war with the aid of Spain. The Guise were old hands at the game — and this time their scheming resulted in the Eighth War of Religion. Ensconced in Rheims, Allen must have felt that he trod on very thin ice — and all the more because the locals couldn't help disliking and mistrusting the English, whatever their religion. In his correspondence, Allen laments that just about everyone in Rheims looked askance at the exiles, and suspected them of actually being Elizabeth's spies.

In this uncertain situation, the college kept instructing and ordaining scores of priests, who were sent back to England to clandestinely provide for the spiritual needs of crypto-Catholics and recusants — and to have a hand in a number of plots against Queen Elizabeth.

Many plotters, martyrs-to-be and would-be murderers studied in Rheims, and it comes as no surprise that, because of this, and because it had ties to Mary Stuart's adherents in France, the English College was an object of interest to Sir Francis Walsingham. Elizabeth's spymaster made a point of keeping an eye on Allen, his students, and their contacts by planting spies in what he, rather understandably, viewed as a nest of traitors.

Richard Baines was one such man, a Cambridge graduate, from the very Catholic Caius College, sent to Rheims as a plausible plant. He doesn't seem to have been overly effective. He blended in well enough, and even took holy orders — but it's likely that he fancied himself more of an agent provocateur than a gatherer of intelligence, and his lack of discretion ended in disaster. He was found out, arrested, and perhaps tortured.

After a longish stint in prison, he wrote a very detailed, very flowery, somewhat dubious confession, and then was sent on his way. Afterwards he disappeared for several years, and there is nothing to indicate that he remained in Rheims, unhinged and vengeful... But there is no proof to the contrary, either — so I've felt free to keep him there to make trouble for Tom.

Also, there is no written proof that Christopher Marlowe was ever in Rheims — or, in fact, that he was ever one of Sir Francis's agents — unless one counts the letter from the Privy Council to the authorities in Cambridge, commending young Kit's "faithful dealings and good service ... in matters touching the benefit of [England]..." and officially frowning upon the university's foot-dragging about the lad's master's degree. In his book *The Reckoning*, Charles Nicholl argues rather convincingly that this letter points to some sort of intelligence work — likely for Sir Francis, and likely in Rheims as a fake Catholic. There is much scholarly debate on the matter, but frankly, from a novelist's point of view, Kit Marlowe as an intelligencer is pretty much irresistible.

We — and Tom — will see more of both Baines and Marlowe in the next few adventures.

These two are far from the only real-life characters in *Death in Rheims*: Dr. Allen, Richard Barret, Thomas Worthington, Christopher Hodgson, Gilbert Gifford, Christopher Bagshaw, Henry Immes, Thurstan Hunt, and John Savage are all well-known and well documented figures of the time. So are Thomas Watson, a poet and intelligencer with a definitely devious streak, and Rafe (or Ralph) Lyggon, an agent of Mary Stuart's who visited the college in late April 1585 to retrieve a letter. Equally historical are the servant Fettiplace, Elliot and Catesby, William Colson, and Hugh Downes. I've found no other trace of them except in the Douai Diaries, and therefore

I've made free use of their names to populate my story; the dates of their arrivals, departures and deaths, though, are faithful to the Diaries themselves.

In this respect, the Muse of History was kind to me: while checking the times of Marlowe's longer absences from Cambridge against the Douai Diaries, I very happily landed on the weeks between the middle of April and the end of May 1585, whose timeline of arrivals, departures, deaths, and events provided me with a perfect scaffold for Tom's adventure. And if Tom's journey to Rheims is entirely fictional, as are the Jorys-Thibauds, the context in which they move is as close to history as I could make it.

I only took one liberty with the Second Diary, by having "John Harrison" arrive on the 29th of May instead of the 30th… What can I say? The plot required it — and after all, if the havoc I imagined had truly happened, a little slip in the records would be understandable, wouldn't it?

A NOTE TO THE READER

Dear Reader,

Thank you for reading *Death in Rheims*. I hope you enjoyed it.

So Tom Walsingham has reached (and survived!) his third adventure! To tell the truth, until a couple of years ago I didn't plan on writing a mystery series. Well, I've always loved the genre, ever since I first picked up *Sparkling Cyanide* from my father's huge stack of Agatha Christie novels when I was thirteen, and spent a good part of my summer vacation devouring mystery after mystery. Then, over the years, came Dorothy L. Sayers, Ngaio Marsh, Margery Allingham, Josephine Tey, and then Mary Rinehart, Edgar Wallace, and Ellis Peters.

Back in my school days, you see, historical mystery was not much of a thing in Italy — unless you count Umberto Eco's *The Name of the Rose*, and I don't. And since I spoke very little English at the time, I didn't meet Brother Cadfael until his stories were translated into Italian in the early 1990s. Discovering how well history and mystery mixed together was a happy revelation, and historical mysteries became a favourite genre as my proficiency in English grew.

Still, I never thought of writing in it — not really, not beyond toying, now and then, with ideas for two possible sleuth-characters. One of them was Thomas Walsingham — the great spymaster's cousin and Marlowe's patron. But they were all very, very nebulous ideas, of that lackadaisical wouldn't-it-be-fun-if kind, and perhaps nothing would ever have come of them if I hadn't crossed paths with Amy Durant and Sapere Books a few years ago.

And now look: three Tom Walsingham books already — and more to come! It's certainly nothing that young girl and her mystery-loving father would have imagined, during that long-ago summer.

I've grown very fond of Tom, and hope to go on writing his adventures for readers like you. Meanwhile, if you enjoyed *Death in Rheims*, I would be very thankful to you for posting a review on **Amazon**, **Goodreads**, or the other e-places where word-of-mouth nowadays lives and works. Could we call it word-of-mouse, perhaps? And, of course, I'd love to hear from you through my **website** or via Twitter — where I tweet under the handle **@laClarina**.

Thank you — and we'll meet again in the next Tom Walsingham book!

C. P. Giuliani

Sapere Books is an exciting new publisher of brilliant fiction and popular history.

To find out more about our latest releases and our monthly bargain books visit our website:
saperebooks.com

Printed in Great Britain
by Amazon

37612923R00169